SONG QUEST

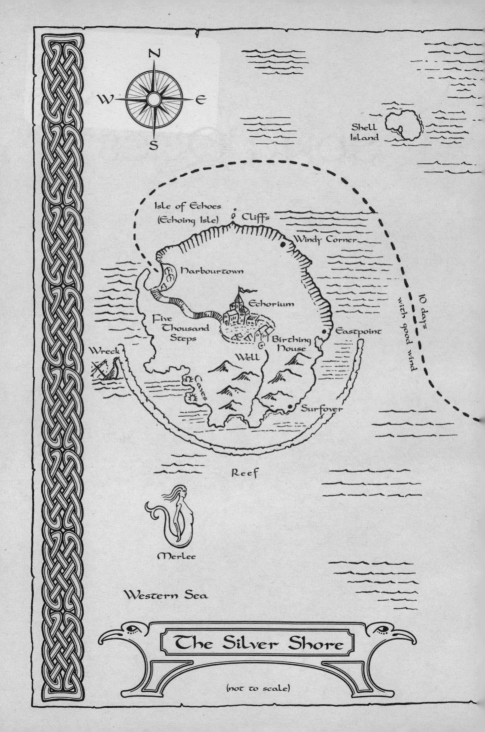

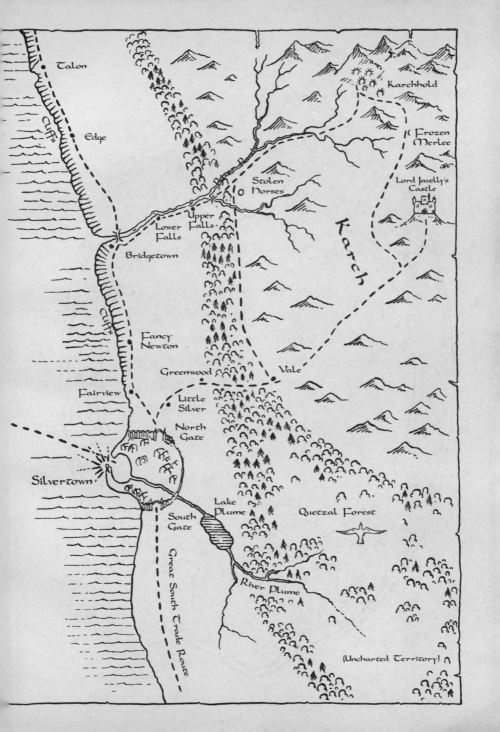

SONG QUEST

Echorium Anthem

For healing sleep of lavender dreams,
For laughter golden and gay,
For tears shed in turquoise streams,
For fear, blood, and scarlet screams,
For death of deepest midnight shade.
For these the Songs,
Five in one.
Challa, Kashe, Shi,
Aushan, Yehn.

THE
— Echorium Sequence —

SONG QUEST

katherine Roberts

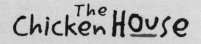
The Chicken House

Scholastic Inc. / New York

For my brother Walter,
sailor of many seas.

© The Chicken House
Text copyright © 1999 by Katherine Roberts
Illustrations copyright © 1999 by Chris Down

First published in the United Kingdom in 1999 by
Element Children's Books, Shaftesbury, Dorset SP78BP.

Published in the USA in 1999 by Element Books, Inc.,
160 North Washington Street, Boston, MA 02114.

Published in the United Kingdom in 2002 by The Chicken House,
2 Palmer Street, Frome, Somerset, BA11 1DS.

Library of Congress Cataloging-in-Publication Data available.

ISBN 0-439-33892-1

10 9 8 7 6 5 4 3 2   02 03 04 05 06

Printed in the United States of America   37

First American edition, February 2002

CONTENTS

*Imagine being taught to hear a voice on the other side
of the world without using a telephone.
Imagine learning to heal without medicine, or discovering
the dreadful power to kill without a weapon. All this and
more is possible in the world you are about to enter.*

*It is a world from another time where legendary
Half Creatures still exist and live alongside their human
neighbors. A world where the wind, the waves,
and the land itself can be controlled by an unearthly
music. A world where the forces of good and evil are
held in harmony by those who have mastered the
secret Songs of Power. A world very different from
our own, yet inhabited by people who laugh and
cry just like everyone else.*

Welcome to the world of the Singers!

1

SHIPWRECK

The day everything changed, Singer Graia took Rialle's class down the Five Thousand Steps to the west beach. They followed her eagerly enough. A Mainlander ship had broken up on the reef in the recent storms, and the Final Years were being allowed out of the Echorium to search for pieces of the wreck.

This was such a rare treat, the very air thrummed with snatches of the laughter-song *Kashe* as the class gathered around the rock that Singer Graia had adopted as a lecture podium. Graia's formal robe of gray Singer silk billowed in the wind, but she'd braided her thick blue hair into a rope that hung over one shoulder, softening the effect. When she called for silence and led them all in the Echorium anthem, thes Final Years sang with more enthusiasm than usual — most of them, anyway. Rialle had a nagging headache, which even the *Kashe* failed to shift. Frenn and Chissar, forever doing silly things to try to impress her, were mouthing the less reverent pallet-ditty under their breath. While at the very back of the group, jaw set in typical Kherron fashion and eyes burning a hole in Rialle's back, the most unpopular boy in the class wasn't singing at all.

"For healing sleep of lavender dreams . . ." Graia sang.

"Challa makes you dream. . . ." muttered Frenn, his blue eyes full of mischief.

A few people giggled and joined in, slightly off-key, making Rialle long to push through all the white-clad bodies and find a space where she could breathe. She'd already had her toes trodden on twice this morning and Gilli, clumsy as ever, had even managed to step on the ends of her hair coming down the Steps. That was the trouble with being small. When people got excited, they tended to forget you were there. Frenn had once joked she should cut her hair before she fell over it herself. But Rialle wouldn't let the orderlies near it with their blades, no matter how often they complained she used twice as much dye as any other Singer. The blue tangles helped hide her boring gray eyes and freckles.

". . . For laughter golden and gay . . ." Graia.

". . . *Kashe makes you laugh. . . .*" Chissar.

". . . For tears shed in turquoise streams . . ." Graia.

". . . *Shi makes you cry. . . .*" Frenn again.

Rialle stood on tiptoe to check that their teacher wasn't looking, then slid her hands under her hair and covered her ears. Even so, the final part of the anthem trickled through. For some reason she'd never understand, people always sang louder at the end.

". . . For fear, blood, and scarlet screams . . ."

". . . *Aushan makes you scream. . . .*"

". . . For death of deepest midnight shade."

". . . *Yehn makes you DIE.*" Frenn's voice squeaked on the last note, and Graia glanced their way with a frown. Both boys assumed innocent expressions until her gaze moved on.

At this point, someone prodded Rialle in the back. "Pay attention, teacher's pet," sneered a boy's unbroken voice. "Or you won't be top of the class today."

She looked around, and her heart sank. Kherron trouble was the last thing she needed today.

Frenn scowled and Chissar stiffened. Kherron's eyes flashed green. He raised his chin, challenging them to make a fight of it. But Frenn, whose fists were large enough to knock most of the boys in their class halfway to Shell Island, pulled Chissar away and winked at Rialle. "Ignore him," he whispered. "He's only jealous."

She gave him a grateful smile, pressed a hand to her forehead, and tried to concentrate on what Singer Graia was saying.

"Don't just use your eyes, use all your senses," she told them. "For example, you might step on something strange before you see it. Even if it's covered by sand or seaweed, you should feel it beneath your sandals and this'll give you a clue where to start digging. Stay alert for alien smells. But most of all, use your ears." She gave them a meaningful look.

Frenn and Chissar cast impatient glances at the long stretch of glistening sand, but Rialle's gaze was drawn to the sea. Storm clouds, solid as another island, blotted out the western horizon. She shivered as the wind lifted her skirt. It was at times like these she envied the boys, who wore calf-length leggings under their white tunics.

"Don't waste time," Singer Graia went on, almost as if she knew what she was thinking. "We haven't long before this weather turns. And don't forget that when you get back, the

First Singer will be interviewing each of you to find out what you've learned."

There were several groans. Rialle's stomach gave an uneasy flutter.

"What's the matter?" Kherron whispered in her ear. "Afraid you'll find a dead body?"

She jumped. She hadn't realized he was still there. A few paces away, Frenn and Chissar were plotting something, their blue heads close together.

"You'll never make a Singer if you're afraid of death," he went on softly. "Never could sing *Aushan* or *Yehn* properly, could you? I'd say it's obvious why Eliya sent us down here. She's weeding out the weaklings." He smirked at the group. "I'm surprised she bothered. I can tell you right now who's going to fail. You for a start, fat old Gilli, that lump Frenn —"

"Shh!" Rialle hissed back, seeing Graia's eyes flick their way. It was true she felt uncomfortable singing the last two Songs, and this made her voice weak when they practiced them. But she'd never heard *Yehn* sung on the Pentangle, and was in no hurry to — unlike some of the boys, who thought it great fun to trap First Years in the corridors and hum a few bars until the poor things fainted in terror.

Kherron chuckled. "See? Now you're afraid you'll get into trouble. You're much too soft to be a Singer."

"Leave me alone, Kherron. I've got a headache."

"That's your fault. You should have asked for *Challa*." Unexpectedly, he seized her wrist. His nails might have been clean and neatly clipped, but they still hurt where they dug into her skin. "Come with me, and we'll search the coves around the headland, just the two of us."

Rialle snatched her hand away, skin prickling. "Stop it, you idiot!"

Up to now, they'd been speaking in the near silent pallet-whisper novices used when they didn't want to be overheard by their teachers. But the shock of Kherron grabbing her like that destroyed her control, and her voice squeaked louder than Frenn's had earlier.

"Rialle?" Graia frowned over the blue heads, some of which twisted around to see what was the matter. "Is there something wrong?"

Kherron edged away, his glare daring her to tell. Rialle pushed windblown hair out of her eyes and shook her head. "Nothing, Singer. I'm sorry I interrupted. I don't feel very well, that's all."

Graia frowned at her a moment or two longer, then pursed her lips and continued to lecture them all on how to behave, reminding them they were almost Singers now. Even if some of them would later become orderlies or serve in the Birthing House, today they were all equal and should behave accordingly. They weren't the only ones on the beach, remember, and the villagers expected a certain amount of decorum from those who would one day be responsible for curing their sick.

Rialle watched Kherron edge his way around the back of the class until he was out of Graia's sight, then jump down onto the sand and duck into the shadow of the cliff. If anyone else noticed he'd gone, they pretended not to.

"Let the idiot look," Frenn whispered. "He won't find a thing. If there were any bodies down here, the villagers would've have dealt with them already. They stink something awful if you leave them lying around too long."

"Oh? And how would you know?" Chissar said, giving Rialle a sideways look. "Have you seen one?"

"No, but I heard the orderlies talking about them."

"Ha! Means nothing. Everyone knows orderlies tell more lies than Mainlanders."

"And how would you know?" Frenn said, winking at Rialle. "Ever heard a Mainlander?"

"I've heard people shouting in the cells."

"Those aren't real Mainlanders, stupid. Those are Crazies. They talk garbage, everyone knows that."

Rialle closed her eyes. Their voices, especially Frenn's with its tendency to shoot high and low in the same breath, were hurting her head.

"Stop it, you two," she hissed, casting a worried glance at Singer Graia. "Or we'll all get Songs tonight."

Chissar gave her a playful push. "*You* won't! You're going to be a Singer, and everyone knows Singers aren't given too many Songs themselves." He grinned at Frenn. "We'll all be Singers! I hope we get chambers on the same corridor — do you think Eliya will arrange it for us, if we ask early enough?"

Frenn frowned, and Rialle's stomach performed another uneasy turn. It was true they were all nearing the time of change, when they'd learn if the promise in their voices would survive into adulthood. This happened to girls a couple of years earlier than boys, but classes were arranged so everyone approached the change together. If there was going to be a final test as Kherron claimed, then it would be their voices that mattered, not whether they screamed if they found a dead body on the beach.

"All right!" Singer Graia said at last, spreading her arms and treating them all to a rare smile. "I know you don't want to spend the whole day listening to me, so we'll go onto the beach now. Spread out and keep your eyes and ears *open*." Again, that meaningful look. "Anything you find, bring it to me first. The villagers have been instructed to bring carry-baskets to collect the most interesting items, but we won't be taking everything back up the Steps with us." As she spoke, she'd been running her gaze over them, counting. She looked around with a frown. "Where's Kherron?"

Heads shook innocently. Then someone pointed to a white dot halfway down the sand.

"The sneak!" Chissar exclaimed. "Now he'll find all the best treasure."

Rialle watched Kherron's dwindling figure with mixed emotions. Even though he acted so stupid, she couldn't help feeling sorry for him. He was the best of the boys in their year, and quite often he'd come close to doing as well as her. But instead of being content with second place, he'd get into trouble for disrupting the class, and be sent to the Pentangle stool in disgrace. "He's such an idiot," she whispered. "He'll get a Song if he's not careful."

"Serves him right," Frenn said.

"Maybe Graia will let him off, since we're going that way anyway."

But Singer Graia was already filling her lungs for a shout down the beach. Only just in time, Rialle slammed her hands over her ears, fingers snagging in her hair. From the corners of her eyes, she saw the others doing the same.

"KHERRON!"

The tiny figure flinched. Rialle thought she saw his head turn, his blue curls blow briefly in the wind. Then he began to run — in the opposite direction.

Singer Graia's brows came down. She hummed low in her

throat, a snatch of pure *Aushan* that made Rialle's bare arms break out in goose bumps. Even though the fear-song wasn't directed at them, the other Final Years edged out of Graia's way.

"He's in trouble now, all right," Frenn said.

Chissar shrugged. "Oh, Kherron's always in trouble. Forget him. C'mon, Rialle. Let's find Mainlander treasure!"

*

It was a big beach, and the three friends soon left the rest of the class behind. As they wandered along the tideline, Chissar and Frenn darted back and forth, digging up pieces of broken shell and popping the seaweed pods, teasing each other they'd found things when all they had were handfuls of silver sand containing tiny specks of bluestone. Rialle walked slowly, eyes half-closed. Her head was throbbing now, like one of the drums their teachers used to keep rhythm, yet she couldn't stop thinking about Singer Graia's words.

Use all your senses. Use your ears.

The boom of the surf, the screeching gulls, the others' laughter farther up the beach, all this only made the pain worse. She began to wish she didn't have ears. When Chissar crept up behind her, draped a long piece of slimy weed over her shoulder, and hummed a bar of *Yehn* in her ear, she whirled and threw the thing into the waves with a little scream.

"Fooled you!" Chissar said. "Thought it was an arm, didn't you?"

"That wasn't funny, Chissar."

"Hey, look at this!" Ahead of them, Frenn whistled and extracted something from a pile of weed. It glittered in the stormy sunlight, a ring of fire. "It's a bracelet, pretty heavy, too. Wonder what metal it's made of?" He held the bracelet out of reach as Chissar dashed across, but the boy leaped on his arm, using his whole weight to force it down, and soon the two of them were arguing over the find.

Rialle stayed where she was and gazed out to sea. The storm clouds were creeping closer, sliced now by green flashes. The distant thunder seemed to get right inside her head. She sank to her knees in the wet sand. Her hair dropped across her face in a tangled blue curtain, but she didn't have the strength to push it back.

"Better take it to Singer Graia," Chissar was saying.

"In a moment — Rialle, come look at this! It's got Mainland animals carved on it. . . ." Frenn's words trailed off when he saw her. "Hey, what's up?" He came back, lifted a strand of her hair, and peered under it. "Rialle? What are you doing under there? Echoes! You look awful!"

The concern in his eyes, and the way he tried to hide it with his lopsided grin, made her feel a bit better. She managed a weak smile. "I feel awful! I thought it was just outside sickness, like I got last year, except —" She glanced at the sea again. "Frenn, can you hear anything?"

He cocked his head. Even without Singer Graia's meaningful looks, they all took such a question seriously. Their teachers asked them the same thing, again and again, every day of their lives.

"Um . . . Singer Graia humming to herself — she sounds really annoyed; Kherron's going to be in for it when she finds him. Gilli puffing and panting as usual. Echoes only know how she'll get back up the Steps; the villagers will probably have to carry her in one of their baskets. Surf, of course, over the reef. Chissar breathing down our necks — back off, you idiot, give her some air! A couple of gulls on top of the cliff, squabbling over a fish . . . or maybe sea-eagles, I never was much good at birds —"

"No, I mean out there. Out at sea."

"At sea?" Frenn scanned the empty waves. "Just wind and thunder. Anything out there's got a death wish with these storms around, if you ask me."

"I can't hear anything, either." Chissar frowned at the approaching storm. "That's coming in awful fast, though. Maybe we'd better get back to the others."

True enough, the darkness was creeping closer and closer, swallowing the water even as they watched. Rialle shivered.

"What do you think you heard?" Frenn said softly.

She shook her head. "Just my imagination, I expect. You're right — anyone out there must be a Crazy." She climbed to her feet, pushed her hair behind her ears, and forced another smile. "Come on, you have to show your bracelet to Singer Graia. It's pretty. Do you think she'll let you keep it?"

"Hope so!" Frenn said. "It's a bit big, though." He dangled it on his wrist to demonstrate. Chissar, seeing his chance, snatched it off and fled up the beach. Frenn gave chase, and soon the two friends were engaged in a mock wrestling match that involved fountains of sand and breathless snatches of *Aushan*. Rialle giggled. Most un-Singerlike behavior. She only hoped Graia was too busy looking for Kherron to notice.

She'd started to follow the boys when the sun plunged behind the cloud bank, embroidering its edges with gold. The beach darkened. The wind dropped, and her skin tightened as if she'd plunged into cold water. She turned to look at the sea. There *was* something.

The first wave, foaming so suddenly around her ankles, startled her. She looked down in surprise as it sucked out again. Was the tide coming in that fast? The wind picked up again, blowing spray into her eyes, tangling her hair into knots. She licked salt from her lips and frowned at the horizon. Far out beyond the reef, a song seemed to be coming from the black center of the storm, a song like none she'd ever heard before. As wild and uncontrolled as the sea.

"Who's there?" she whispered.

The pressure in her head grew. Then, as if someone had dropped a sheet of Isle glass, the pain shattered into words.

Danger! Strange ships sailing! Children dying, children eaten . . .

The message was so full of terror, Rialle forgot decorum and screamed. The next wave crashed over her head, knocking her flat. Her nose filled with bubbles, her mouth with sand. There was an unsettling jerk, as if someone had pulled her pallet from under her while she slept. Then feet splashed into the surf behind her, and strong arms closed around her waist, pulling her back.

"Rialle!" Frenn sounded nearly as frightened as she felt. "What are you *doing*? You could've drowned!"

She blinked at his dripping chin, aware of his warmth pressing through her wet tunic. "The others are coming," she whispered.

Frenn flushed and released her. He stepped back, trying to make a joke of it, which was lost in a sudden crack of thunder.

Her scream had attracted attention. Those villagers within earshot started toward them, carry-baskets bobbing on their backs like giant shells against the darkening sky. The Final Years abandoned their treasure hunt and came running, kicking up great crests of sand. "What's wrong?" they clamored. "What happened?" "Rialle's a salad-brain! She tried to go swimming with all her clothes on!" Giggles. "Take them off, Rialle!" one of the boys called — a Kherron-comment if ever there was one, except Kherron would have made it sound like an insult, not a joke. Then Singer Graia, humming *Challa* to calm everyone down, pushed through and wrapped a cloak around Rialle's shaking shoulders.

The weight and musty smell of the goat hair brought the beach back into focus. The giggles and comments fell silent as a sudden gust filled Singer Graia's robe and the first big drops splashed down. Within the space of a few heartbeats, the gray silk turned black, and the sand all around them dimpled like Gilli's flesh.

Graia tilted Rialle's chin and looked into her eyes. "So you heard them, did you?" she said. "Good. Maybe now we can all go back inside and get dry."

*

The rain came in slants, hissing into the sand. Kherron made a dash for the cliffs and ducked into the nearest cave. He rested his hands on his knees, panting and chuckling in the same breath. "Idiots," he whispered. "Out there, getting soaked."

He smiled as the echo came back, slightly distorted. The caves had been a stroke of luck, but he'd been right about the tide. It had been far enough out for him to splash around three headlands without getting much more than the hem of his tunic and the bottoms of his leggings wet. No one had come after him. Kherron smiled again. Ha, the others were pathetic. Follow meekly where Graia led, getting all excited over a few moldy old timbers and broken lanterns, when it was perfectly obvious the best treasure would be found where there weren't any people. And when he found it, even old misery-guts Eliya would have to recognize he was no longer a child and let him sing.

He ventured deeper into the cave, his sandals crunching shells. Soon the storm noise faded along with the light and a strange moaning took over. Probably the sea sucking through another channel, or the wind howling down a hidden shaft. The orderlies said some of these caves went right through the Isle and out the other side. The thought made him shiver, and he stopped to check the echoes again.

The moaning seemed closer. Kherron frowned, and closed his eyes a moment to get the direction. There — it was coming from behind that rock. Sounded a little like a wounded animal. He crept forward and tripped over something soft in the gloom.

He flattened himself against the wall, heart thudding, then looked closer, scarcely able to believe his luck. At his feet lay a human hand, half buried in sand.

Kherron held his breath, counted to ten, and let it out again very slowly. The hand lay palm up, its fingers curled. A red metal bracelet encircled the thick wrist, and a dark arm led behind the rock.

He crept farther in and peered over the rock. A man's body was folded into the small space. Maybe he'd crawled in here to die? Kherron reached out and tentatively poked one broad shoulder. The man didn't move.

Kherron shivered in delight, already planning how he'd trick the others into coming down here. He could almost hear Rialle's horrified gasp. Chissar would be furious Kherron had found the body first. Frenn would crack some joke and pretend he wasn't interested. Gilli would *faint*.

He eyed the long hair, woven into thin, straggly braids. The sailor had a messy beard, allowed to grow much longer than any orderly's. His skin was darker than any Kherron had ever seen, his clothes roughly woven and very dirty. Kherron returned his attention to the bracelet. Grinning, he began to tug it free.

The dead man snatched his hand back with a bellow of rage. "Khiz! Gerroff me, or I'll skewer you like a fish-man!"

Kherron leaped back a second time, and hit his head on the low roof of the tunnel. *Challa* came out automatically. Shh, calm, *Challa* makes you dream. . . . He eyed the glimmer at the cave mouth, ready to make a dash for it as soon as the man moved. But after that one bellow, the sailor collapsed behind his rock with a groan.

"Are you hurt? Do you need help?" Kherron risked a step forward.

"Gerraway from me!"

The accent was difficult, the voice rougher than those he was used to in the Echorium, but decipherable with a bit of concentration. "Don't worry," he said. "I'll help you." More *Challa*.

Meanwhile, Kherron thought fast. The sailor seemed to have some kind of weapon — a sword? He'd tried to whip it out of the scabbard when he woke up but it was jammed beneath his body.

Kherron eased himself farther forward. "What happened? How did you get here? Did your ship go down?"

"Lost the whole khiz-stinking lot," the sailor moaned. "Idiot lowlanders, goin' on 'bout magic this and magic that — killed us all, didn't they? Might as well have killed me, too. Me leg's broke, smashed it on them khiz-cursed rocks swimmin' ashore."

"Are you sure?"

"Course I'm sure! It's my leg, ain't it?" With much grunting and scraping, the sailor raised himself on one elbow and squinted at Kherron. "What's it to you, anyway?" he said suspiciously. "Who are you?"

"I'm . . . a friend." Soothe him with *Challa,* play Eliya's favorite game. It was quite a novelty to sing to someone who didn't seem to know what he was doing, and a grown man at that. Kherron smothered a chuckle. "I can help you with your leg, if you'll help me."

Again, that narrow-eyed stare. Now the sailor was properly

awake, the Song didn't seem to be having as much effect. "And why should I do that, Islander?"

"Because if you don't, I'll report you to the Singers. Then they'll come down here and take you up to the Echorium for Song treatment. And believe me, you don't want a Song, broken leg or not. They mess in here." He tapped his head. "I know, because I've had a few myself. You see, Singers —"

"I know what Singers are, Islander." Death in his words.

Kherron swallowed hard. "Oh? Then you weren't trying to get to the Isle for therapy?" He tried a bit of *Kashe*, and was quite proud of how well it worked. The sailor actually chuckled — a gravelly sound in the bottom of his throat that matched his weird accent.

Then his eyes narrowed again and he grabbed Kherron's wrist. "You mean what you said? About helping me? 'Cause there might be a reward if you can get me a boat."

"You'd need more than a boat to cross all the way to the Mainland in this weather," Kherron said carefully, willing himself not to pull away.

"But it'd get me as far as Metz's ship —"

"There's another ship?"

The dark eyes flashed. The fingers about Kherron's wrist tightened, and the sailor's other hand fumbled for his sword. "I could cut your throat just like *that*, Islander," he hissed. "So don't even think about telling those khiz-interfering Singers of yours about any other ship."

Kherron hummed *Challa* for all he was worth. Plans were whirling in his head. Dangerous, wild, exciting plans. "I won't be able to tell them anything if you take me with you," he whispered, his heart pounding louder than the surf outside. That'd show Eliya. He'd go to the Mainland and practice on men like this. Then he'd come back and show the whole Echorium how good a singer he was.

The suspicious eyes watched him, shadows playing across them. A long way off, in a different world, the storm lashed the cove and wind moaned.

"Why should you want to come with me?"

Kherron took a deep breath. "This island's so small, you can walk around it in three days. I've heard there are towns on the Mainland bigger than that! I want to see the world, but the farthest I'm likely to get is as far as the reef in a fishing boat." It was wonderful how easily the lies slipped from his tongue. No Singer down here to catch him out with truth-listening. Kherron smiled, warming to his story. "And school here is terrible! There's this spoiled little brat in my class called Rialle who thinks she's better than everyone else. Just because she's pretty and has big gray eyes that go all moist whenever she wants something, and a voice sweeter than honey, all the teachers like her. She gets away with murder and I'm the one who gets in trouble for it. Then there's her bully of a boyfriend, Frenn —"

"You've got soft hands for a fisherman," the sailor said, driving the rest of Kherron's story right out of his head.

"Um — ah — well, the school's got this ointment made from fish oil, you see. Our teachers make us use it every day, so our skin stays soft. Besides," he added, quickly changing the subject, "if your leg's broken, how will you manage a boat on your own? You'll have to row in this weather, because it's too wild out there to risk a sail, and you need strong legs for that. If you take me with you, I'll be able to help."

The sailor released him. Kherron rubbed his wrist and breathed easier. He watched the man carefully.

After what seemed an age, a grin flashed in the shadows.

"All right, Islander, you've convinced Cadzi of the Karch! If you can get me off this rock, I'll make sure you get a free passage to Silvertown. Fair?"

Kherron nodded, not wanting to show his ignorance. He'd never even heard of Silvertown.

"Better wait till dark before we set out, though," Cadzi added. "I don't want to run into any of those Singers."

"Me neither!" Kherron said with feeling, and Cadzi threw back his head and laughed.

Kherron's heart hammered. Did he guess the truth? This stupid white uniform and the blue Singer hair dye were dead giveaways. Or was it too dark in here to see? After all, he couldn't see the color of Cadzi's clothes — though judging by the smell of them, that wasn't too surprising.

When Cadzi began to mumble something about khiz-stinking storms and half-brained quests after khiz-crazy half creatures, Kherron seized the chance to back out of the cave. The sailor's injury was obviously making him sick in the head. The Echorium had patients like that sometimes, so badly hurt they went mad with the pain.

Lashing rain brought Kherron to his senses. He eyed the surf breaking over the reef, then lifted his gaze to the massive bluestone building just visible in the clouds that swirled around the highest point of the Isle. Set out in a rowboat in this weather? Was he crazy? On the other hand, Eliya would surely want to reward the novice who warned her about the dangerous foreign sailor. All he needed to do was make sure Cadzi stayed put until he worked out how to handle this.

Kherron glanced back at the cave, and his lips twisted into a small smile. If he played this right, things might work out very well indeed.

*

By the time they reached the gates of the Echorium, the Final Years were soaked to the skin. Rialle, huddled under the goat-hair cloak, was probably the best off, yet she shivered more violently than anyone.

While they waited for the orderlies to let them in, she turned for a last look at the sea. On a good day, you were supposed to be able to see the land that lay beyond the Western Sea, many times farther than the Mainland, so far Rialle couldn't imagine the distances involved. But today, even Harbourtown at the bottom of the Steps was hidden by dark curtains of rain. If Kherron was coming back up, she couldn't see him. Teeth chattering, she clutched the cloak closer. Frenn gave her an encouraging grin.

"Not long now," he said.

As soon as the gates creaked open, Graia sent them all off to the baths with stern instructions to tell the orderlies to heat the water until it steamed. The villagers who'd carried those treasures Singer Graia approved of were escorted toward a slate building huddled in the shelter of the Echorium's east wall. This building was part of a small village that included the Birthing House, the orderlies' off-duty quarters, and temporary lodgings for the families of people brought to the Echorium for Song treatment. Only Singers, novices, and those awaiting a Song were permitted to sleep surrounded by bluestone. There was some superstition Rialle couldn't remember, and couldn't have cared less about as she stumbled toward the baths.

Bathing and changing took enough of her concentration to push what had happened on the beach to the back of her mind. The pain in her head had eased as they climbed the Steps, so by the time she was warm and dry, she felt almost normal again.

But Singer Graia had almost seemed to pity her, and that still left the question of the wild song from the sea.

It was a very subdued class of Final Years who sorted themselves into two lines and filed into the fourth-floor dormitories to await their turn in the First Singer's chamber. Rialle went straight to her pallet and perched on the edge, twisting the hem of her clean tunic. There was no glass in the ancient building, and the gray silk the orderlies had tacked across the windows to keep out the weather billowed as if something were trying to get in. She shivered and avoided the stares of the other girls, trying not to hear their theories about what had made her scream. Most of them seemed to believe she'd been poisoned, and blamed the seaweed salad they'd had for breakfast. It was obviously nobody else had heard a thing.

"Cheer up," a husky voice whispered. "It wasn't your fault."

She glanced up sharply. "Frenn!" she said, unable to hide her delight. "You're not supposed to be in here!"

"No one shut the door, did they?" Frenn folded his legs and bounced onto the pallet beside her. He ignored the whispers and giggles from the other girls and asked, "Can you still hear them?"

"Yes," she whispered back. "Every time I close my eyes, like echoes. *Children eaten* . . . What can it mean?"

Frenn frowned. "Are you *sure* it wasn't your imagination, Rialle? Thunder, maybe?"

"Course I'm sure! Graia knows something, but she won't tell."

"Maybe Eliya will tell you."

"She'll just think I'm sick. I'll get *Challa*."

"Maybe that's best. It'll make you feel better, and *Challa*'s nothing to worry about."

"What if she gives me something else? *Shi*? Or *Aushan*, even?" Rialle shivered again.

Frenn shook his head. "She won't do that to you, silly! You haven't done anything wrong, have you? Kherron might get *Shi* when he comes back, though. He's still out there, you know." He looked thoughtfully at the straining curtains.

"I don't want *Challa*. It makes me forget things. What if you're not around when Eliya's finished with me? I might forget you."

"Why wouldn't I be around?" Frenn stared at her a moment, then pulled off the red bracelet he'd found on the beach, took her hand, and slid the thick metal up her arm. It went all the way past her elbow, and was still warm from his body. "You won't forget me now," he said, giving her that familiar lopsided grin as he scrambled to his feet. "I'd better go now. It'll be my turn soon."

Rialle fingered the bracelet, a lump in her throat. "But what if she gives *you* a Song?"

"*Challa makes you dream, Shi makes you cry, Kashe makes you laugh, Aushan makes you scream, Yehn makes you die.*" Frenn repeated the pallet-ditty, still grinning. "She'd have to give me *Yehn* before I forgot you, Rialle! Look, there goes poor old Gilli. Listen to her, no breath control at all. If anyone's going to get a Song tonight, she will."

It was true. The climb back up the Five Thousand Steps had made Gilli wheeze, and her lungs still hadn't recovered. Rialle felt guilty. Gilli had been given so many Songs, it was a miracle the girl could remember any of the Hums. It'd be awful not being able to breathe, even worse than hearing things in her head.

"Next!" an orderly called from the door, beckoning to Frenn. "Can't escape by hiding in the girls' dorm, you know. Come on, quickly now. The First Singer doesn't like to be kept waiting."

"See you at supper." Frenn winked as he followed the orderly out.

Left alone in the blue storm-shadows, Rialle curled miserably on her pallet. Frenn's bracelet kept slipping down her arm, and she pushed it under her pillow for safety. She closed her eyes, pulled her damp hair across her face, and pressed her hands to her ears. "Go away, whoever you are," she whispered. "Please."

2
ECHORIUM

The First Singer's chamber was chilly and damp. When Rialle slipped inside and shut the door, the tall woman standing at the narrow window did not look around. Rialle smoothed her skirt and attempted to control her hair, which always went frizzy after a bath. "You wanted to see me, Singer?" she said, unable to keep the tremor from her voice.

As usual, the First Singer wore formal dress. The wind blew straight in from the west, stirring the gray silk around her stick-like figure and lifting the wispy hair damaged by years of dye. While Rialle waited, staring at that forbidding back with its severely erect shoulders, she could almost believe the pallet rumors that claimed Singer Eliya had been born before the Echorium was built.

"Tell me what you learned on the beach today."

She hung her head. "I'm sorry I let you down. I felt sick. I know I was supposed to be looking for treasure, but I couldn't concentrate. Then the storm came, and I thought I heard songs coming from the sea. It was silly of me to scream like that. I feel much better now."

"So you learned nothing?"

"I . . . I didn't find anything from the wreck."

"And you think that's the only reason I sent you down there in this weather, do you? Any villager can find bits of wreckage."

"But Singer Graia said —" What exactly *had* Singer Graia said? Use all your senses. Use your ears. "Oh!"

At last, Eliya swung from the window. The skin around her cloudy eyes crinkled into hundreds of tiny lines. "'Oh,' indeed! Come over here and sit down, Rialle. We need to have a little talk."

She patted the cushions piled around the walls of the five-sided chamber. Their rainbow colors glimmered in the light of Eliya's lanterns, making a welcome break from the storm darkness that had invaded the rest of the Echorium. Rialle chose a lavender cushion and crossed her legs. She kept her back straight and folded her hands in her lap. The First Singer lowered herself beside her with great care, joints cracking.

"More comfortable now?" she said.

Rialle nodded, though she wasn't at all comfortable. Novices did not get invited to sit in the First Singer's company unless Eliya was about to tell them something they might not be able to take standing up.

"Good. Then repeat exactly what you think you heard."

Rialle fixed her gaze on the window and took several deep breaths. As well as she could, she echoed the songs that had come from the sea.

Hearing that wild, panicky melody on her own lips brought the whole embarrassing beach episode back again. When she dared look at her teacher, Eliya was sitting very still and stiff-backed. She remained like that for several heartbeats, then pressed a gnarled finger to her forehead and closed her eyes.

Rialle took another breath. "Singer," she blurted out. "What does it mean? Whose children are dying and being eaten? Why can't I hear the songs now? Was it my imagination like Frenn said, or —?"

To her surprise, the First Singer smiled. "Oh, they're real enough. You've sharp ears, Rialle, sharper than the other novices. Sharper than a lot of trained Singers, I might add. You heard the merlee. They're what we call Half Creatures. Half human, half fish, in this case. I used to hear them when I was younger, too." She broke off to gaze at the window. "One loses the trick of it, unfortunately." She looked a bit sad. Then she shook herself. "Actually, quite a lot of people can hear merlee, though most of them think it's the wind or the waves. Very few have the gift of true communication. You're a lucky girl."

Rialle didn't feel very lucky. She had a nasty feeling something more was coming, and she was right.

Eliya patted her hand, an awkward gesture. Her skin felt like withered seaweed. "They're still out there, you know. It's just harder for you to hear them up here — the water helps transmit their songs. Don't worry. Before you go, I'll teach you a technique called farlistening. All Singers learn it. Sometimes it's useful for us to hear what other people are saying when they think we can't. Then you'll be able to hear the merlee whenever you like, talk to them, too."

"But I don't really want to —" She realized what Eliya had said. "Before I *go*! Go where? I don't want to leave the Echorium! All my friends are here."

The smile vanished. "You're in your Final Year, Rialle. Soon you'll have your moonblood and then we expect you to repay us, one way or another, for all the years of training and care. Few Singers remain behind these walls all their lives — though the Birthing House is always in need of experienced women trained in matters of childbirth, so if you don't mind spending the rest of your life up to your elbows in blood —"

The chamber spun. It was too much. What with the merlee and everything else, she missed the subtle *Kashe* in Eliya's final words. Then *Challa* filled the chamber, rippling around the blue walls. The stone at their backs seemed to grow warmer, the colors of the cushions brighter. Rialle relaxed slightly.

"That's better. I won't be sending you to the Birthing House, silly. At least, not until you're older and ready to give us a child of your own. You're going to have a chance novices seldom have. In a few days, when you've learned what you need to, you'll sail on the *Wavesong* with Second Singer Toharo as part of a Singer delegation to the Mainland. You'll persuade the merlee to give our ship safe passage. They'll listen to you, I think."

"Safe passage?" Rialle repeated.

Eliya sighed. "You're confused. It's understandable. I wish we had more time, but we can't afford to delay any longer. These storms must be stopped. No ship has reached the Isle in weeks. High seas mean no new patients, and no patients mean no trade. Our fishermen can't get out and supplies are already running short. Soon we won't have anything to eat but seaweed salad." Again, *Kashe* danced through her words.

In spite of herself, Rialle's lips twitched. "But the storms will stop soon and then ships will come as before — won't they?"

Another sigh. "Not unless we send out the delegation."

"But I don't understand."

Eliya frowned at the window, as if considering how much to tell her. "These aren't natural storms, Rialle."

"Aren't natural? You mean . . . the merlee!" she whispered, in a sudden flash of understanding. "The merlee wrecked that ship! That's why you want me to go on the *Wavesong*, isn't it? So they won't wreck it, too? Oh, Echoes!"

The cloudy eyes narrowed. "Mmm. You are good, aren't you? Not many experienced Singers would have picked that up. Or did you guess? No matter. You're quite right, of course. Merlee can indeed sing up storms when they're frightened enough, and that ship was hunting them, so yes, they wrecked it. The only problem is, they've no control." She eased herself on the cushions.

Rialle stared at the First Singer. She'd never seen her look so old and tired. And Eliya's words contained echoes she'd never heard before. Dark, foreign songs. She waited, twisting her fingers together in her lap, winding them in the ends of her hair.

"You've still a lot to learn about the Echorium and what we do here," Eliya went on. "Healing the people who are brought to us is just a small part of it. Sometimes we have to send Singers to the Mainland to persuade people to change their ways, people who would never come to the Isle voluntarily — these hunters, for example. It won't all be work. You'll get a chance to see Mainland cities. Once the *Wavesong* is safely in Silvertown harbor, Singer Toharo will deal with everything, and you can treat the rest of the trip as a holiday. I know a lot of Final Years who'd jump at the chance."

Rialle considered this. The others were always complaining about having to stay indoors when the sun was shining. Chissar and Frenn spent a lot of time describing the great adventures they'd have just as soon as they were Singers and free. A violent gust blew into the chamber just then, making the lanterns flicker and raising goose bumps on Rialle's arms. She smiled wryly as she imagined her friends' faces when she told them.

Trust her to have her first adventure in the middle of the worst storms to hit the Isle in years.

Eliya had been watching her. Now she nodded and rose in a rustle of silk. "You'll be fine. I've already told the Second Singer you're going with him. He'll probably want to talk to you before you set sail, but don't bother him with too many questions. Ask me if you have any and I'll answer them as best I can. The orderlies will help you pack. Report to my chamber after Morning Hums tomorrow, and we'll begin your lessons in farlistening."

It was a dismissal. Rialle scrambled up, embarrassed to be caught sitting when the First Singer was standing.

Unexpectedly then, more *Kashe* danced around the chamber. "Cheer up, Rialle, I'm sure you'll like the merlee when you meet them. They're playful little creatures when they're not so frightened. Singer Toharo will probably have to drag you away. Now run along to supper. I expect you're starving after all that fresh air, and you've got to keep your strength up. You're an important part of this delegation, don't forget."

*

Rialle left the five-sided chamber, her head in a whirl. She staggered down a spiral staircase, along a shadowy corridor, and into the noisy dining hall without noticing the way the orderlies stared after her.

She searched the rows of blue heads at the tables. The smell of the fish soup reminded her how hungry she was, but her stomach could wait. Above the clattering of plates, a burst of laughter came from the Final Year table where the younger novices had gathered to hear tales of the wreck, no doubt greatly exaggerated by now.

She pushed through the youngsters and tugged Chissar's sleeve, making him spill soup in his lap. "Where's Frenn?"

The boy leaped from the bench. "Watch it! Oh, it's you, Rialle." The anger in his eyes turned to something else. "How did it go?" he said softly. "You were in there for ages."

"Where's Frenn?" she said more sharply, ignoring the disapproving looks from the orderlies on supper duty. The youngsters fell back slightly and stared at her, nudging one another and pointing. Did the whole Echorium know already?

"Didn't you hear? Eliya sent him to orderly training, as of tonight. He didn't even eat with us. It was expected, Rialle. You heard what was happening to his voice —"

"No!" She backed away, tears in her eyes. Then she was running from the hall, through the blue corridors, up the steep, winding stairs. Her leg muscles screamed after all the unaccustomed exercise they'd had already today, but she didn't stop until she reached the boys' dormitory on the fourth floor.

It was empty, gray silk hissing at the windows, dirty uniforms lying in crumpled heaps as if the storm had been inside. Frenn's pallet was stripped bare.

She left the room in a daze, and reached the girls' dormitory before her legs finally gave way. She crawled to her own pallet, slid a hand under the pillow, and clutched the bracelet he'd given her. "Frenn," she whispered. "Oh, poor Frenn."

*

In the days that followed, she had little time to miss Frenn — or anyone else, for that matter. Her new lessons were far too exhausting, and there was so much else to think about. With the orderlies' help, she packed a traveling chest to be taken down the Five Thousand Steps and stowed on board the *Wavesong*. This contained clothes woven from goats hair, all in Singer gray, and several thick, heavy cloaks she couldn't imagine wearing on the Isle, even in a storm. When she tried them on in the girls' dormitory, she started sweating immediately. There were long fluffy wraps, bags that imprisoned her fingers, and — worst of all — boots that made her feet feel like the weights Isle fishermen used to make their nets sink. The orderlies chuckled when she complained and told her she'd be glad of them where she was going.

"Why? Is it cold on the Mainland?" she asked them.

But they just smiled and said if the First Singer hadn't told her, then they couldn't, either.

"Waste of time asking. They don't know anything," Chissar said the next morning, while they were waiting for the Singer who took them for rhythm exercises. "I expect you'll find out soon enough, anyhow. You're so lucky, Rialle! I wish I was going."

"If you'd used your ears on the beach instead of messing around so much, you could be going in my place," she snapped. "I wish you were!"

Chissar gave her a sideways look. "Truth?"

Rialle sighed. She shouldn't have snapped at Chissar. It was hardly his fault. "C'mon, Chissar. You're a good enough singer to know when I'm lying."

Chissar's eyes sparked briefly. "Teach me, then."

"What?"

"I'm serious. If you teach me how to farlisten, I'll ask Eliya if I can go with Toharo instead of you. Then you can stay here and wait for Frenn to come out of orderly training. Simple!"

Rialle stared at him. Why hadn't she thought of that? She glanced around the teaching chamber to see if anyone had heard, then clutched Chissar's hand, her eyes unexpectedly filling with tears.

He colored. "Aw, Rialle . . . I want to go, remember? And it's not fair of her to send you away without even giving you a chance to say good-bye."

She spent the rest of what little free time they had that day trying to teach Chissar how to hear the merlee, but he seemed deaf to everything except the storm. Then the orderlies took Gilli and a couple of the other girls away to the Birthing House to begin their training, reminding her of the First Singer's half-serious threat, and she stopped trying. Chissar seemed disappointed but shrugged and made a joke of it, saying the clothes she'd packed would never have fit him, anyway. Rialle sighed. It had been a slim hope. Besides, maybe she'd be back before Frenn got out of training. It wasn't as if they were crossing the entire Western Sea. How long could it take to sail to the Mainland and back again?

Strangely enough, as she grew better at farlistening, her head-aches grew less frequent. Soon she could hear the merlee simply by closing her eyes and thinking of the sea. She began to look forward to seeing them in the flesh. Eliya's descriptions were far too vague. Rialle wanted to know what color their eyes were, if they had scales, what they ate and drank, where they slept, what their children looked like. All the First Singer would tell her was they had gills like fish so they could breathe underwater as well as on the surface. "Wait and see," was all she'd say. And, "I'm sure you'll like them."

The days raced by, and soon the time came for her final lesson, when Eliya had promised she'd show her how to talk to the merlee as well as hear them.

*

Rialle made her way to the First Singer's chamber right after Morning Hums. She was half excited, half apprehensive. What if she couldn't do it? Now that everyone knew she was going, it would be an anticlimax, to say nothing of embarrassing, to be left in the Echorium when the *Wavesong* sailed. She walked with her eyes half-shut, thinking of the sea. Then her attention returned to the corridor with a start, and her heart missed a beat.

She knew that voice.

She hesitated. No one had seen Kherron since he ran off along the beach, and none of their teachers would mention him. There had been plenty of speculation, of course. Chissar said he'd been given Songs to cleanse his memories and sent away in disgrace to Windy Corner, the most remote and inhospitable of the Isle villages. The very day the orderlies came to take her to the Birthing House, Gilli had giggled and said good riddance, maybe now they'd all get some peace. With so much else to think about, Rialle hadn't really thought about Kherron. It had been a relief he wasn't around to give her a hard time about the merlee, but that was all.

She heard the first shout because it carried through Eliya's closed door and along the corridor. But then his voice lowered until she couldn't make out the individual words. Unless . . . She glanced around and edged closer to the door, her heart thumping.

"Practice whenever you can," hadn't the First Singer told her? "Practice makes perfect."

Rialle rather doubted she'd meant this sort of practice. But she closed her eyes, took a steadying breath, and thought hard of the First Singer's five-sided chamber with its rainbow cushions. Storm winds blowing straight in from the west. Two people, breathing. A single flapping curtain —

The by-now-familiar jerk, and she was *there*.

"How do you know about this ship?" Eliya was saying, very softly.

"Does it matter how I know? The Isle's in danger." Kherron. "There are warriors on board, with swords of red metal. They don't have much love for Singers. What if they attack us? You should prepare."

"I ask you again, how do you *know*?" *Aushan* in that, low and dangerous. Rialle shuddered, even though the Song wasn't aimed at her.

She heard Kherron swallow. "Isn't that why you sent us down to the beach? To find out things? Grai — Singer Graia said to use our ears, so I did! Haven't I done well?"

The *Aushan* hum increased. "You disobeyed Singer Graia. You didn't return to the Echorium when instructed. You stayed four nights outside these walls, which is forbidden for a novice. You know you won't be able to lie to me, so you refuse to answer. Now. *Who told you about this ship*?"

Kherron was silent so long, Rialle thought she'd lost the trick of it. Then Eliya sighed softly. "Very well, Kherron. Have it your own way. Report to the cells immediately. I'll see you afterward, when maybe you'll be more willing to talk."

Kherron's next words were so faint, they seemed like pale smoke. "I'll tell you if you let me sing on the Pentangle. My voice is strong. It's not going to crack like the other boys'. I can do it, I know I can —"

"Enough!" The First Singer's hum was terrifying. What was it? A mixture of *Aushan* and *Shi*? "How dare you come up here and bargain information with someone who's taught you all you know?"

The hum relented slightly and Rialle heard the First Singer take a deep breath.

"As for your voice, Kherron, it's still a child's. I hope it does survive, because the Echorium needs male Singers. But you're not ready yet, and the more punishments you bring upon yourself, the less chance you have. Go. And while you're recovering, you might like to think about what I said."

Rialle drew back from the door as it was flung open. But Kherron's next words, tight with fury, could be heard easily without her new skills. "I come to warn you, and all you do is punish me! You're a —" Apparently, even Kherron thought the better of insulting the First Singer to her face. "— not being fair."

"You brought no warning."

This stopped him. "Do you think I'm making it all up? I thought you Singers were supposed to hear truth!"

"I already knew about the ship, Kherron."

"But, how? How did you know?" Confusion now.

"Rialle told me four days ago." Her voice turned cold. "I haven't time for this right now. Go to the cells, Kherron. Speak to no one on the way. And get yourself properly cleaned up before you come in here again. I don't know where you've been sleeping, but you smell like a sewer."

Kherron shut the door with deliberate control, then whirled and kicked the wall. Rialle winced. His face was scarlet under the dirt, his teeth bared. She'd never seen him so scruffy. He looked like one of the Crazies. She stared a fraction too long. When Kherron gave the wall a final thump and turned to leave, it was too late to duck around the corner.

A shadow rippled across his eyes. His lunge came so fast, the bracelet Rialle had taken to wearing since Frenn went into training slipped from her arm and clattered at her feet. Kherron kicked it aside, grabbed her wrists, and pressed her against the wall. A lump of stone dug into her back.

"You little tattletale," he hissed.

Scream, she thought. Call Eliya.

"Kherron," she whispered. "Don't make things worse for yourself. She'll be listening —"

He pinned her arms above her head with one hand and leaned closer, his breath hot on her face. "How worse can it get? It's all right for you, isn't it? You don't have to worry about *your* voice cracking. But you had to spoil my chances, didn't you? You'd love it if I ended up in orderly training."

He was panting almost as much as she was, and sweating, too. His words contained traces of *Yehn,* but he was too worked up for the Song to have much effect.

"That's not true! I didn't know you'd heard the merlee, too. Why didn't you come back when you were supposed to? If you'd told Eliya earlier, she might have let you go instead." It was an effort, but she steadied her voice, even managed a little *Challa.* "If you don't let me go, I'll tell Eliya. Stop it, Kherron, you're acting like a Crazy."

"Crazy? You don't know what crazy is!" He gave her wrists a final squeeze, then mercifully stepped back. Light and air swirled around Rialle's head — and tiny stars.

"She's never going to let me sing anyway," Kherron said. "So go ahead, tell! It doesn't matter now."

He glanced down at the bracelet, and his lips twisted at one corner. He picked it up and weighed it in his hand. "Where did you get this, Rialle? You can't wear jewelery on the Pentangle, you know — interferes with the Songs, doesn't it?" He grinned and thrust the bracelet up his arm.

Rialle's stomach twisted. She whispered, "Give that back. Please, Kherron. It was a present from Frenn."

He laughed. "That *orderly?"*

On his lips, it was the worst insult in the world. She wanted to tell him Frenn was twice the singer he'd ever be, and she hoped Eliya gave him *Aushan* until he screamed — but before she had a chance to recover her breath, Kherron was gone.

*

She was still trembling when Eliya's door opened and the First Singer looked out. But Eliya seemed distracted, and didn't notice her flushed cheeks and mussed hair. "Hurry up, Rialle," she said. "We haven't got all day. Singer Toharo wants to catch the evening tide."

"Tonight? We're going tonight?" Now the time had finally come, she didn't feel at all ready.

"Provided the merlee listen to you, yes. I'll help you this time. When you're on the *Wavesong*, you'll have to do it by yourself, but you'll be closer to them then, and surrounded by water besides. You shouldn't have too much trouble once you get the trick of it. Come on, quickly — no, not that way. We're going to the Pentangle."

Rialle hurried after the First Singer, doing her best to catch her breath. The Pentangle! She couldn't help a shiver of excitement. When she'd entered these midnight shadows before, she'd either been up on the viewing balcony that ran around all five walls of the windowless chamber or seated on the stool, dreamy with Song-potion. Then the Pentangle had been full of Singers, whereas now it was empty. This was the first time Rialle had really had a chance to examine the five-pointed star carved into the bluestone floor.

She stopped and looked down, shivering a second time as her toes touched one of the deep grooves. Pallet rumor said old Songs collected in these grooves, and if you stopped on one, the echoes would rise up and get into your head. There might be *Aushan* here, or even *Yehn*.

Eliya swung the doors shut with a clang that echoed in the high ceiling. The lanterns near the door flickered behind their blue silk shades, and Rialle jumped as her shadow swung around the vast space like a drunken ghost.

"Don't be nervous, Rialle." The First Singer unbent a little and came back to take her hand. She led her to the stool, sat her down, and smoothed her hair behind her ears, putting one gnarled hand on each side of Rialle's face. "This is the heart of the Echorium, remember? It's where our power is strongest; nothing can hurt you in here. Sit down, that's right. Now close your eyes and tune your ears as I taught you. Think of the sea."

It was easier than it had ever been. She still couldn't see the merlee, beyond vague shadowy outlines of fish tails and human torsos. But their songs were as clear as if the creatures were inside the chamber with her. Blue shadows swirled around her like deep water. The familiar jerk, and she was *there*.

Strange ships sailing . . . nets . . . fear . . .

"Now ask them," Eliya murmured. "Ask them to make the storm stop."

Rialle wrinkled her brow. Her head began to hurt, and she felt Eliya's bony hands squeeze her cheeks. "I — I can't. I don't know how!"

"You're trying too hard." The words were laced with *Challa.* "Just speak to them as you'd speak to me. Sing something if you like."

There was a rustle of silk as Eliya released her. The blue shadows spun. Beneath her thighs, the stool began to vibrate. Rialle began to feel sick. *Challa,* she hummed, picking up the First Singer's prompt. *Challa* makes you dream. . . .

"Good," Eliya whispered. "Now ask."

"Merlee? Can you hear me?" Rialle said, feeling a bit foolish.

"You've got to let the *Wavesong* sail tonight, so we can help your children."

The merlee's songs stopped. The shadows spun faster, and she thought she'd lost the contact. Then the songs came again, only changed.

Stone-singer! The delighted welcome was like lightning flashing in her head. She had a brief glimpse of floating silver hair, a rainbow tail splashing in the surf. *Come swim with us!*

"I'm coming!" she replied. "We're coming to help you."

The tails glittered, filling her head with tantalizing glimpses — here a slender green arm, there the silver curl of a beard — but before she could see them properly, the stool stopped spinning and the magical vision faded. She tried to go back, but a stern voice said, "Enough!"

More tired than she realized, Rialle staggered from the stool, and someone caught her. At the contact, her eyes snapped open. The floor was solid once more. The walls shimmered into focus. The doors were still sealed. With a start, she realized she was in the First Singer's arms and backed away, cheeks hot. "I'm sorry —"

But Eliya was smiling down at her. "You did well. They heard you, I think."

"They did! It was like they knew me!"

She stared around the Pentangle, her mouth stretching into a smile. "They wanted me to swim with them." Then she remembered the fate of the merlee children, and for the first time it seemed real, as if the hunters had sailed into the Isle harbor and taken children from the Echorium dormitories. She shuddered slightly. "I think we should hurry."

Eliya nodded. "Yes, we've been in here quite long enough.

We've missed lunch, I'm afraid, but Singer Toharo will make sure you get something for supper. Don't forget merlee have short memories — you'll need to keep reminding them about the *Wavesong*." She opened one half of the big double doors and held it for Rialle to pass, the lines of her face very deep in the shadows. "Good luck, Rialle. Come back safe."

Rialle's legs still felt a bit shaky, but she made an effort to walk in a straight line and hold her head high, as Eliya would expect a member of the Singer delegation to behave. Just before she rounded the corner, she looked back. Eliya was leaning against the door, eyes closed, the heel of one hand pressed to her forehead. Rialle frowned and hurried to collect her things.

*

Kherron didn't go to the cells. Nor to the baths, though the thought of being warm and clean after all that creeping around in wet caves was very tempting. But once the orderlies got their hands on him, they'd drag him to the Pentangle stool, willing or not. They'd give him the Song-potion, and that would be that.

So he was careful which stairs he took, and which corridors he chose. There were back ways out of the Echorium, tunnels that led under the walls. Novices weren't supposed to know about them, but this had never stopped Kherron before. A final look around to check he wasn't being observed, and he let himself out a side door into the storm.

He headed south, following the stream that tumbled through the goat pastures to the coast. The village of Surfover was shut up like a clam, its doors latched against the wind, its boats pulled high on the shingle out of reach of the storm waves but not of desperate hands. Kherron allowed himself a tight smile as he slid down the steep cliff path, into the cove where he'd left

Cadzi. This weather was good for something, at least. It made moving around the Isle without being seen ridiculously easy.

He ducked into the cave, wiped his hands on his tunic, and quietly began to pull strips of camouflaging seaweed from the boat he'd stolen before he went to see Eliya. He hadn't wasted his four days of freedom. Even if most of his preparations had been to keep Cadzi quiet while he worked up the courage to confront the First Singer, everything was ready for two people to flee the Isle. All they needed now was a lull in the storm long enough to row out past the reefs.

"I won't let you make me into an orderly," Kherron said through gritted teeth as he lit a lantern. "If I can't be a Singer, I'll be something better."

He rummaged under the seat. When his hand found the dagger he'd hidden there, his lips twisted into a small smile. His blue Singer curls came off first. He examined the result in the blade. Not pretty, but it would do. Next, he changed his stained novice's uniform and sandals for stolen villager clothing and a pair of stout fisherman's boots. He laced these with angry jerks, imagining his ankles were Eliya's throat. The dagger fit through his belt. As a final touch, he added the bangle he'd taken from Rialle, smiling when he remembered how he'd scared her. Then he took some of the smoked fish he'd stored in the boat and went to find Cadzi.

He tossed Cadzi the fish. "I've done all I can. We're ready to leave as soon as it's safe."

The sailor gave him a long stare. "You look different, Islander."

Kherron twisted the red bracelet farther up his arm, pushed the dagger farther into his belt, and grinned. "I feel different! How's your leg?" Under Cadzi's instruction, he'd splinted it as best he could, using a piece of timber from the wreck and a strip hacked off the hem of Cadzi's tunic and washed in the sea. The sailor had yelled like a Crazy, but seemed in less pain afterward.

"It'll do." Cadzi began to smile, then glanced at the cave mouth and frowned. At first, Kherron thought it must be his leg hurting him. But the sailor heaved himself on one elbow, his other hand fumbling for his sword. "What's that noise? If you've betrayed me, Islander —"

Heart racing, Kherron blew out the lantern. "I haven't told anyone you're here, I swear!" For once, it was the truth.

"Shh!"

Both of them listened, Kherron's nerves tighter than harp strings. He hadn't seen anyone, but what if Eliya had had him followed? It was just the sort of sneaky thing she'd do, wait until he led her to his hideout before she made her move. He'd been stupid to think he could bargain with her, stupid to go back at all. A weird moaning came down the tunnel, distorted by echoes. Like the wind, only much creepier. The very rock around them began to vibrate, and dust trickled from the roof like blue smoke.

It took Kherron a moment to realize what was happening, for he'd never experienced such a thing outside the Echorium before. When he worked it out, he laughed. "Relax! Someone's singing on the Pentangle, that's all. They say you can hear it from Shell Island on a clear day. I'm surprised it got as far as down here in this weather."

Cadzi put his sword away. "Oh, I don't know . . . looks a bit brighter out there to me. Go take a look, Islander. The sooner we're off this khiz-cursed rock, the happier I'll be."

Kherron couldn't agree more. Avoiding the mini-avalanches, he crept past the boat and peered out. Cadzi was right. The rain was easing. A strip of crimson and orange glowed on the western horizon. He could almost see the waves getting smaller as they broke on the rocks. Beyond the reef, the sea was like glass.

Shivering with excitement, he hurried back. "The storm's blowing itself out!" he said. "I'll get the boat ready. Soon as it's dark, we can start looking for that ship of yours."

He whistled as he stripped off the rest of the seaweed. That little tattletale Rialle had done them a favor. At least they now knew there was a ship to look for.

3
STORM

The *Wavesong* sailed at sunset in a blaze of scarlet and gold, shouts from the loading crew, and last-moment rush. There was hardly time to be nervous before the ship was sliding past purple cliffs, and they were heading east toward open sea. While the sun sank slowly into a cloud bank astern, Rialle watched the orderlies raise the sails one by one, transforming the masts into a billowing confusion of ropes and gray canvas that creaked and snapped intriguingly in the stormy red light.

It was all so new and exciting, she was determined to stay awake all night. But soon after they left the shelter of the headland, she began to feel queasy, and Singer Toharo sent her to her cabin with strict orders to lie down. She'd secretly been hoping the merlee would appear, but the creatures stayed hidden, and the very thought of farlistening to see how close they were made her feel worse.

By morning, even if a merlee had popped its head up at the

porthole, she'd have turned over and groaned. The spray kept up a constant rattle against the glass, her bunk tipped first one way then the other, and her teeth wouldn't stop chattering, even though she'd kept all her clothes on and rolled herself in two of the thick cloaks the orderlies had insisted she pack. She failed to hear the first tentative knock on her cabin door. Then it came again, more urgent.

She opened one eye. The floor of the little cabin was littered with garments, heaped like dead things in the faint gray light coming through the porthole. She'd pulled them all out during the search for the cloaks, but had been too ill to think about putting them back. Singer Toharo would be furious.

She swung her feet to the floor, and promptly collapsed in the middle of the pile. She held onto her stomach and stifled a groan.

"Rialle?" came a whisper. "Rialle? You in there?"

That wasn't Singer Toharo's voice.

"Go away," she moaned in relief. "I'm sick."

The door opened, and a thickset boy in an orderly's uniform slipped inside. His hair had been shaved close to the skull, showing a couple of places where the blade had nicked him. He stared at her a moment from nice blue eyes, then put a hand to his mouth and spluttered. At first, woozy from lack of sleep, she didn't recognize him. Then he removed the hand, revealing a familiar lopsided grin.

"Frenn! What happened to your hair?" The rush of pleasure and surprise quickly turned to guilt. "I lost your bracelet, I'm sorry."

He helped her back onto the bunk. "Don't worry about that now. Echoes, Rialle! Whenever I see you lately, you look like something's chewed you up and spat you out. What you been eating this time, then?"

"Don't talk about food, Frenn, please."

"But that's why I've come to get you. Singer Toharo says you've got to come and eat something or you'll feel even worse. He says we're both to come up to the main cabin for breakfast. Oh, and he wants you to sing to those merlee-things again, because it's getting pretty rough out there."

"You don't have to tell me." Rialle leaned her head against the wall with another groan. It was hard to think with the cabin rolling around so much, but she had a feeling Frenn wasn't supposed to be on board.

"I didn't think trainees got off the Isle so soon," she said. "How did you persuade Eliya to let you come?"

Frenn grinned. "Oh, I didn't, not exactly. I stowed away in one of the orderlies' clothing chests. Couldn't let you and Kherron have all the fun, could I? I figured if I waited till we were far enough from the Isle, old Toharo wouldn't turn around just to take me back, and looks like I was right. I meant to stay hidden a little longer, but he went through the whole ship last night, tappin' things, and dragged me out. Just as well, really. It was getting pretty uncomfortable in that chest. If I'd still had hair, I wouldn't have fit." He touched one of the cuts and winced.

Rialle turned cold. Even her sickness faded for a moment. "Kherron? He's not —"

"Don't panic! He's not on board — though he's the real reason Singer Toharo was looking, I think. You should've seen his face when he saw it was me crammed into that chest! I'm lucky Kherron ran away like he did. Old Toharo's so bent on finding him, he forgot to be angry with me. He's up on deck now — in this weather! — listenin' over the side. I'll bet Kherron's still on the Isle. Even he wouldn't be so crazy as to set out on his own in this storm."

"I wouldn't be so sure." She looked at the little round window with its spots of spray and thought of the last time she'd seen Kherron, in the corridor outside Eliya's chamber.

Frenn laughed. "If he's out there, then I hope we do find him, 'cause he's in serious need of therapy!" His expression grew more serious. "Can't say I blame him for running away, though. Eliya did have it in for him, didn't she?"

"I suppose."

"It's a shame. He'd have made it, I think, if only he'd been a bit less stupid." He looked at the porthole, too.

"What if we catch him?"

Frenn shrugged. "He's blown his chances now, that's for sure. Eliya might make him an orderly, I suppose — though Songs never seemed to work too well on Kherron and he'd have to be cleansed first. Look, Rialle, are you well enough to come up now? I think you'd better sing to those pets of yours pretty quick, 'cause all this tossing around is beginning to make me feel sick as well. We can't all be throwing our guts up, or who'd be left to sail the *Wavesong*?"

Keeping one of the cloaks to hide her crumpled uniform, and hoping Frenn wouldn't get into trouble for stowing away, Rialle followed her friend up a dangerously swaying ladder to the main cabin, where Second Singer Toharo was waiting for them. Though it was morning, he'd lit the lanterns, which swung from hooks as the ship rolled. Their unsteady light made the cushions piled around the cabin shimmer, while the wall carvings of sea creatures came alive as shadows moved around them. Rialle was careful not to look at them too long.

A tall Singer, Toharo had to stoop to avoid hitting his head on the lanterns. His eyes were very dark, and the lines in his face deeper than she remembered from the Echorium. His robes were black with the soaking they'd received on deck, reminding Rialle of Singer Graia on the beach. His blue hair, stiff with salt, stuck out in all directions.

"Ah, Rialle," he said, frowning at her. "How are you feeling?"

She pushed her hair out of her eyes. "Not too bad, Singer." Spotting the plates of shellfish and cakes laid out near the cushions, she added quickly, "I'm not hungry, though."

"Nevertheless, you're going to eat — just as soon as you've spoken to the merlee again. For now, just water I think." He handed her a goblet fashioned from a shell. "Drink it all, there's a good girl. And you — Frenn, isn't it?" The boy nodded. "Seeing as you've taken it into your head to join us, you can make yourself useful and go fetch Rialle some more practical clothes and a pair of boots from her cabin. Quickly! The girl's fit to faint."

"I'm all right —" Rialle started to say, but Toharo shut her up with a look. Frenn gave her a wink as he ducked back down the ladder.

"Now then," Toharo said when the boy had gone. "Sit down a moment, young Singer. It's time we had a serious talk."

To Rialle's acute embarrassment, he knelt in front of her, took her hands, and rubbed them between his. He did this quite roughly, and the calluses on his palms hurt. "Ow!" she said, surprised by the rough skin.

Toharo rubbed harder. "You're freezing. The sickness does that sometimes. You should have changed. The orderlies packed plenty of warm clothes for you, yet here you are, dressed in next to nothing. You're not in the Echorium now, you know."

"I have a cloak on," Rialle pointed out. "And there's only one skirt —"

"For good reason. Now, listen. I didn't want to bring you on this trip, but now that you're here you're in my care, so you'll do things my way. I don't suppose Eliya thought to tell you anything about Mainlanders?"

Rialle shook her head.

Toharo grunted. "There are good reasons we don't take novices on voyages like this, but it'd take too long to explain now. You'll just have to trust me when I say it'll be much safer if you change out of your uniform right now, pack it away at the bottom of your chest, and forget you've ever sung on the Pentangle. And you're not to dye your hair until we return to the Isle. I'd shave it off like Frenn's, but —"

"No!" Rialle said, snatching her hands away.

He chuckled, and fingered a long blue curl. "I guessed that was what you'd say. When the roots grow out a bit, I might trim it, we'll see. Until then, you'll just have to pull your hood up whenever I tell you to, and be discreet. Tie it back, or something. Most Mainlanders don't realize only Singers have blue hair, so you should be safe enough, particularly if you're dressed like an orderly."

"But why?" It was a bit disappointing to learn she wouldn't be able to act the Singer on the Mainland.

Singer Toharo sighed. "We've an important task ahead of us, and I don't want any unnecessary distractions. Keep your head low and stay out of trouble, that's all I ask. Anyway, from what Eliya told me, I thought you were as keen as anyone to stop this merlee hunting?"

"I am. It's just —"

The ship, heaving up at the bow, stopped the words in her throat. Everything began to slide toward the back of the cabin. Then the bow bounced back down, throwing them both flat into the cushions, and sending all the plates and goblets rattling against the door. Rialle curled up in terror and clutched her stomach, but Toharo grabbed her wrist and dragged her to her feet.

"Come on!" he said. "I only hope you feel well enough to sing. Hold onto me."

She was far too miserable to listen for the undercurrents in his words, but she thought the Second Singer sounded angry. With her? With Kherron for running away? With Frenn for hiding in the chest? With the merlee for singing up the storm? Impossible to tell.

Toharo dragged her to the mainmast and held her tightly, while spray and rain lashed them like whips. Though it was morning, the sky was still black. The sails, which the orderlies had tied around the boom so they wouldn't be torn to pieces, struggled against their bonds. Vast walls of water kept breaking over the rail, foaming around Rialle's ankles, before the deck tipped again, and the dark wave slid back into the sea.

Rialle stared at all the water in dismay. There was no sign of land, either the blue cliffs of the Isle, or any other sort. The sea was so huge and wild, and the *Wavesong* so tiny, like a petal blown upon it by the gale. Any one of those waves might scoop them up and smash them onto a hidden rock, and then the black water would close over her head, and —

Toharo shook her. "Do it!" he shouted into her ear. "Or I swear I'm turning around and taking you back to the Isle right now, merlee or no merlee."

She took a deep breath for courage, then another. She closed her eyes and, though it was the last thing she felt like doing, thought of being out *there*.

Her head throbbed, her stomach heaved, the waves kept crashing down. If there was a jerk, she missed it. All she could hear was the noise of the storm.

"We're coming," she shouted into the wind and the spray. "We're coming on a ship with gray sails. Don't sink us! We're coming to help you, to help your children —"

This time there was no burst of welcome, no way of telling if she'd got through to them. She collapsed against the Second Singer with a little moan. "I'm sorry," she whispered. "They're so frightened and so far away. I don't know if they heard me."

Toharo's arms tightened around her. He half carried her back to the cabin, pushed her inside, and slammed the door shut on the storm. "Never mind," he said. "We'll get through it. The orderlies are all experienced seamen, and I've sailed through worse weather than this."

"You're lying," Rialle whispered, then slammed a hand to her mouth. The cushions Toharo had dropped her into were soft; the lanterns filled the cabin with a golden glow. She could only suppose the relief of escaping the terror on deck must have made her think for a moment she was back in the pallets.

The Second Singer stared down at her, something she couldn't read in his eyes. "That does it! Seasick as I've ever seen anyone, frightened out of your little head — don't try to deny it, I can always tell — and you dare accuse the Second Singer of the Echorium of *lying*?"

"I'm sorry."

But to her surprise, Toharo chuckled. "Don't be sorry. It's my own fault for not being more careful. Eliya warned me you were good, I just didn't realize how good. So I lied, did I? It's a rare novice who has the gift of truth-listening. Maybe you'll be some use on this trip, after all."

Rialle hung her head. "I failed to get the merlee to stop the storm."

"Oh, I wouldn't worry about that too much. To be honest, I

never expected you to. Merlee are strange creatures and they have their own ideas. Anyway, as you said, they're still a long way off. You can try again when you feel better."

Toharo's admission made her feel worse, not better. Now there was more chance than ever they might sink.

Just as her stomach was starting to churn again, Frenn came clattering up the ladder, gray goat hair spilling from his arms, his grin stretched from ear to ear. "You did it, Rialle!" he said. "There's a line of clear sky on the horizon, and if you look out the portholes you can actually see the waves calming down. The orderlies are talking about breaking out more sail. The wind's gone around, they say. Oh, yes, and the captain said to ask you, Singer, should we keep goin' for Shell Island as planned, or head straight for Silvertown now we got the wind?"

Toharo's lips curved — the first time Rialle had seen him smile. "Silvertown, of course. Bring those over here before you drop them, and go tell the captain I said you can share Rialle's cabin. Tell him, from now on, she's to be treated as a trainee orderly, and it's particularly important they remember not to treat her any differently when we land. Understood?"

Frenn's eyes widened. He was clearly dying to ask why, but at Toharo's frown he hurried from the cabin.

"I trust you've no objections to sharing?" Toharo asked, almost as an afterthought, when they were alone again. "I know it's awkward with you being a girl, but we're fully crewed and there just isn't anywhere else. You can always take turns changing, and shut your eyes when you're in your bunks." He gave a little cough, as if this embarrassed him. "I'm sure you'll work it out."

Rialle looked at him curiously. She supposed a potential Singer might have cause to complain at being forced to share a tiny cabin with a trainee orderly just out of the pallets, but she had trouble hiding her smile. "Can I ask you a question, Singer Toharo?"

He grunted.

"What'll happen to Kherron if we find him?"

The Second Singer had been picking up the spilled shellfish and cakes, brushing bits of grit off them and putting them back on their plates. He looked up from his task with another frown. "Who told you I was looking for Kherron?"

"Well, you are, aren't you?"

He sighed. "No point trying to lie to you, I suppose — you've already made me look stupid once. Yes, finding the runaway is one of my duties this trip — and an extra worry I could have done without, I might add. If he hasn't drowned or otherwise come to grief, Kherron will be returned to the Echorium, where the First Singer will decide what to do with him. She'll probably have to give him *Yehn,* anyway, so it'll be a lot easier for everyone concerned if the sea has claimed him."

Rialle stared at the Second Singer, not sure she'd heard right. "*Yehn?*" she whispered. "You mean . . . kill him?"

Toharo watched her closely. "After a fashion. '*For death of deepest midnight shade,*' as we say."

"But . . . but others leave the Echorium, don't they? Orderlies and people from the Birthing House? It happens all the time — or, at least, that's what I heard in the pallets. . . ."

"You heard right. Orderlies leave us all the time. We can hardly prevent it, since they visit the Mainland so much, and besides, we wouldn't want to be served by anyone with a grudge. Experienced Birthing House staff are a bit more precious to us, but once they've repaid us for their keep and training, they have a choice, too. Girls like Gilli will look after Singer babies while they're still young. Then if they want to leave us and start a family of their own, the Echorium pays for their passage on an outbound ship. You might be surprised, but a lot of people decide to stay. We have orderlies who've been in the Echorium all their lives and can cook fish dishes that put Silvertown chefs to shame, and women too old to have children of their own who love their work in the Birthing House. Kherron, however —" He pressed his lips together. "Kherron's different. Our Songs are very powerful, remember. In the wrong hands, even *Challa* can become a weapon."

Rialle hugged her knees to her chest. "It doesn't seem fair. He only wanted to sing, that's all, but Singer Eliya wouldn't let him, and —" She had a horrible thought. "What about Frenn? Will he be punished, too?"

Toharo chuckled at this. "Oh, I don't think Frenn has any intention of leaving us, do you? But even if he did decide to run off, it wouldn't matter." He gave her a dark look. "I think it's time you learned the real difference between Singers and others who serve the Echorium. Change out of those wet things, and try to eat something. I won't be long."

Eat? How could she eat after what the Second Singer had just told her? But the ship was sailing more smoothly now, and by the time she'd struggled out of her wet skirt and tunic and put on the dry clothes Frenn had brought for her, the smell of the honey cakes was making her empty stomach rumble. She snatched one, and nibbled at it while she rubbed her damp hair with the cloak. The cakes were was as good as they looked, so that by the time the Second Singer returned with Frenn, she'd almost forgotten she was on a ship racing away from the Echorium.

Frenn looked a bit worried when he was ushered through the

door, but grinned when he saw Rialle curled in the cushions, dressed like an orderly in gray leggings, tunic, and boots, gorging herself. She quickly swallowed the mouthful she'd been chewing and started to scramble up, licking her fingers.

"Stay where you are, Rialle," Toharo said. "Frenn, stand over there and do your breathing exercises."

Frenn frowned, but did as he was told. Meanwhile, Toharo seated himself and started on the food Rialle had left, which wasn't very much.

"You look much better," he said, appraising her. "Those clothes suit you."

Rialle felt herself blushing.

"Now then, pay attention. Frenn, if you're ready, will you hum us some *Challa* please? Just a few bars will do. We don't want to be falling asleep in here."

Frenn shifted his weight from foot to foot and glanced at the door, as if he'd much rather be somewhere else. But a trainee orderly couldn't refuse the Second Singer. After a moment, he began to hum.

Rialle listened, appalled. *Challa* was the first Song novices learned. To hum a few bars was as natural as breathing by the time they'd passed their first year, and she'd heard Frenn sing the entire *Challa* many times, note perfect. So what was wrong with him? It wasn't so much his voice, though this did crack a bit in the higher registers. But the pitch, timing, and rhythm were all wrong. Further proof, as if they needed it, was the Song's effect. She didn't feel at all calm or dreamy — quite the opposite, in fact.

Toharo glanced at her, then smiled tightly and said, "All right, Frenn, that's enough. Try *Kashe* now."

Frenn hummed. No one in the cabin laughed.

"And *Shi*, please?"

Another mutilated Song left Frenn's lips — and though this time Rialle saw tears in his eyes, she knew it wasn't the *Shi* putting them there.

"Stop!" she said, jumping to her feet. "Oh, please let him stop! This is cruel."

She stared at her friend, wanting to rush across and comfort him, only that would embarrass him before Singer Toharo. Frenn avoided her gaze and looked instead at one of the wall carvings, his big hands trembling slightly. She'd never seen him look so vulnerable and defeated.

At last, Toharo nodded. "All right, Frenn, we've heard enough. You can go."

The boy left the cabin in silence, his shaven head hanging and his shoulders bowed. Rialle bit her lip and turned on the Second Singer. "Why did you do that to him? Was it because he stowed away? He meant no harm —"

"Hush, young Singer. I didn't do anything to him that wasn't already done. It was merely a demonstration for your benefit. When novices are sent for orderly training or to the Birthing House, we do two things. First we shave off their blue hair. Then we give them a mild form of *Yehn* to protect the Songs. Both are painless, and both help them forget. They can still *sing*, of course — even someone like Frenn will have a fairly pleasing adult voice. They just can't manage Echorium Songs, ever again. Now perhaps you see why Eliya's so anxious to find Kherron? And why I want you to travel in disguise? On the Mainland, there are certain people who would dearly like to use us if they could."

She frowned. "But couldn't Frenn learn the Songs again?"

"No. *Yehn* does more than make people forget the Songs — it ensures they can't be relearned. Think of it as a room, built around the place where the Songs are stored. When you're a First Year, this room is empty. But the door is open, so the Songs can get in. When you sing properly, they get out through the windows. We've locked Frenn's door and shut all his windows. He still has the room in his head, but he can't get into it."

"You put his Songs in prison?"

Toharo smiled. "I wouldn't put it quite like that. More like locked them away for their own protection." He climbed to his feet with a sigh. "Now go below and get some rest, Rialle. I might need you to sing to the merlee again, and I don't want you so tired you can't keep your eyes open. We still have a long way to go."

She worried about Frenn after that, but now that he was no longer expected to sing, he didn't seem to mind about not being able to use the Songs anymore. In fact, he didn't seem to remember the Second Singer had asked him to try, and frowned every time Rialle brought up the subject. In the end, she stopped mentioning it, though the locked room in Frenn's head made her wonder what Eliya was going to do to Kherron if they found him. After what Singer Toharo had said about *Yehn*, she had the feeling it wouldn't be pleasant.

"Run, Kherron," she whispered. "If you're out there, keep running."

4

THE HUNTERS

Kherron had never rowed a boat before, but he knew the theory, and was doing his best to get himself and Cadzi away from the Isle as fast as possible. Only, like so many times in his life, everything and everyone seemed determined to make sure his best wasn't good enough.

Things had started to go wrong at moonrise on the night the storm stopped, when he and Cadzi had dragged the boat out of the cave. No sooner had they launched it in the shallows, than Cadzi discovered he couldn't climb over the side with his bad leg. The sailor had splashed and cursed so loudly, Kherron's heart was in his mouth the whole time, thinking someone from the village would hear. Once Cadzi was aboard, dripping wet and in a foul temper, the boat had proved a lot harder to control than Kherron had anticipated. Every stroke dragged at his arms, while the oars rubbed his palms raw. Then, when they finally got beyond the reef, and Kherron was just beginning to wonder how they were going to find Cadzi's ship in the dark, the sailor fell asleep.

Kherron rowed a bit longer, then shipped the oars and let the boat drift. Was it his imagination, or had he heard a creak out in the dark?

"Cadzi?" he whispered, blowing on his blisters.

No answer.

"Cadzi! Wake up!" He stretched a foot and nudged the body propped in the stern. Though it was tempting to kick the sailor's injured leg, he remembered whose ship they were looking for, and aimed for Cadzi's good ankle instead. The sailor groaned, but still refused to wake.

Kherron bit his lip and examined the horizon. Black and silver water glittered on all sides, as if the stars had fallen from the sky and were drowning in the waves. Past Cadzi, he could just make out the jagged teeth of the reef that made approaching the Isle from the south so treacherous. When he twisted his head, nothing but waves and the huge, spangled sky. He took a firmer grip on the oars, closed his eyes, and listened. In the pallets, they'd always been taught to trust their ears above their eyes, especially at night.

There it was again. A creaking that had nothing to do with his aching back and arms.

Now that he'd stopped rowing, the little boat seemed to have a life of its own, lifting them over black hills and plunging them into watery valleys. Wincing, Kherron picked up the oars again. He headed in the direction of the last creak, humming *Challa* under his breath.

"There! It's coming from over there, I tell you. You must've heard it this time!" The shout sounded as if it were right on top of them.

Kherron twisted around, and an oar slid out of his hand and was carried away by the next wave. "Echoes!" he hissed, then swallowed the word. Stupid. Sounds carried a long way across water, everyone knew that.

He took a more careful look around, moving slowly so as not to capsize the boat. His heart was just about back to normal when the waves lifted them up again, and a ship appeared as if from nowhere, pushing ahead of it a black bow wave twice the height of a man.

Kherron paddled madly with his one remaining oar. Just in time, the little boat spun to one side, and the towering hull plunged past. For a sickening moment, they were caught by the bow wave and tossed up and down like a fly. Then the ship swung into the wind and stopped altogether, her sails flapping in the night.

Kherron fended off the hull with his oar and looked up. Leaning over the rail silhouetted against the stars, were three figures with many thin braids flying in the wind and swords swinging at their hips. One held a lantern over the side, yellow light pouring into the water just short of where Kherron and Cadzi crouched in the boat.

"Hear what?" demanded the biggest of the three, leaning so hard on the rail the wood groaned. "I don't hear a khiz! Your ears playing tricks on you again, Ortiz? Eh?"

There was coarse laughter, laced with tension. Not good. Such men might kill first and ask questions later. Kherron prodded Cadzi hopefully with the oar, but the sailor only moaned.

"But I thought I heard —"

"Don't think, Ortiz. You'll hurt yourself."

Kherron made a mental note of the name. Ortiz. Three men on deck, and more below, no doubt. It was a big ship, bigger than

most of those he'd seen in the Isle harbor. He let the little boat drift
closer. A sour rotting-fish odor wafted down, turning his stomach.

He hummed some more *Challa*.

"Hear that?" shrieked Ortiz, swinging the lantern in a wide
arc that sent sparks raining into the boat and Kherron ducking
for cover. "It's right below us! There! I see it!"

"Get the net, then," the big man hissed. "Quick, you fools,
before it tries its magic on us."

Desperate now, Kherron changed his hum from *Challa* to
Aushan, and the men froze — the big one with sword half drawn,
the others caught partway across the deck.

"I've brought your friend!" Kherron called, his heart still
thumping. This wasn't exactly the sort of welcome Cadzi had led
him to expect. "Have you got a ladder? He's hurt his leg, and I'm
pretty tired after rowing all the way out here. I don't think I've
got the strength to lift him up there just now." A little *Kashe* in
this, to make them laugh.

Which they did.

"That's no fish-man, Metz!" the third man said. "Looks like
one of ours. Oy, lad! What's your name? Were you wrecked?
What happened to the others?"

"All drowned," Kherron called back.

"It's a trick," the big one, Metz, muttered, squinting at Kherron. "Where's his death braids, eh? No self-respecting karchholder would cut his hair short like that. Ready that net! He's
probably got a whole army of them wild fish-men down there."
He leaned over the rail again and bellowed down, "Stay right
where you are, boy! And throw your weapons up here!"

Kherron thought fast. Until Cadzi woke up, his best bet was
probably to play along. He tossed his dagger onto the deck,
heard it fall with a clatter, and saw Metz bend to pick it up.

"And the rest!" the big man called.

"I don't have any more. Why would I need weapons? I'm not a warrior." More *Kashe*. Keep it light.

"No, I can see that!" The big man shook with laughter until the bones in his hair rattled.

More of the fishy stink wafted over the side. Kherron closed his nostrils and breathed through his mouth, hating to think of that stench polluting his lungs. Against the stars, the dark mesh of their net hung over the boat like a sea-eagle hangs over its prey. He wondered if they were going to use it to haul Cadzi aboard. But they were still staring into the sea as if they expected it to erupt with monsters at any moment.

As the *Kashe* wore off, Metz's eyes narrowed. "So what are you, then? A spy?"

"Don't be stupid —"

The eyes became slits.

Kherron forced himself to unclench his fists, take deep breaths. "Look," he tried again. "You can see your friend is hurt, and he's getting tossed around down here. Why don't you bring us up? What are you afraid of?"

The big man frowned. "Why would you help a karchholder?"

Kherron sighed. This was getting silly. Were all Mainlanders this suspicious? He paddled to keep the boat close to the hull while he repeated word for word what he'd told Cadzi in the cave, and what Cadzi had said.

"Free passage to Silvertown?" said Metz with a guffaw. "Are you an escaped Crazy? Know anything about Singers, do you? Know what they did last time they discovered a ship with an unauthorized cargo of pale-skinned Islanders?"

At the mention of Singers, a coldness ran down Kherron's spine. He shook his head.

"No, you wouldn't, I s'pose. You're too young. Go home to your father, boy. If you're very quick, he might not beat you for stealing his boat. Though if you were mine, I'd string you up by your toes for a week."

Kherron's blood ran hot. He raised his chin. "I'm old enough to rescue a karchholder from these Singers you seem to fear so much!" he said. "And I'm not going back now. If you won't help us, we'll row to the Mainland ourselves." Difficult with only one oar, but hopefully they wouldn't notice that.

Though he hadn't used a Song this time, all three men laughed. "He *is* crazy, Metz!" said the one he didn't yet have a name for. "Do you have any idea how far it is, lad?"

"Look," Kherron said, trying a new tack. "I have certain, um, gifts. If you take me to Silvertown, I could help you."

There was a muttered consultation on deck, which Kherron picked up in snatches.

". . . take the risk . . ."

". . . who's to know? . . ."

". . . extra pair of hands might come in useful in the next hunt."

The consultation ended in more guffaws. Then a knotted rope came swinging over the side.

"Tie it around Cadzi first," Metz instructed. "We'll haul him up then send the rope back down for you."

Did they think he was stupid?

Kherron shook his head. "No!" he said. "I come up first, then you lower one of your men to get Cadzi."

This earned him another laugh. "You hear that?" Metz said. "The boy learns fast. All right, up you come."

Kherron gripped the rope as hard as he could with his ruined hands, but luckily he wasn't expected to climb. While he kicked and scrabbled at barnacles, too out of breath to hum a note, the men hauled him up. They almost tore his arms from their sockets. Then, just when he thought he could hold on no longer, strong hands reached over the rail and lifted him aboard, while Ortiz shinned back down the rope to collect the injured man.

As his feet touched the deck, Kherron's mouth stretched into a grin. He'd done it, escaped Eliya for good. But his triumph was short-lived. Without letting go, his rescuer twisted his arms behind his back and made him stand before the big man.

Small black eyes studied him, while Kherron glared back, trying to look braver than he felt. Metz's braids — at least a hundred of them — were gray and straggly and looked as if they hadn't been washed in weeks. His lips and fingers bore green stains, luminous against his dark skin. He weighed Kherron's dagger in one hand, while seeming to weigh his story in his head.

"So, boy," he drawled. "What you plannin' on doing when you get to Silvertown, eh?"

Kherron licked his lips and tried not to think about the pain in his arms. "I don't know, travel a bit, see the world."

"Join the Karchlord's great army, perhaps?"

"Um — if that's who you serve?"

It seemed a good guess, but Metz threw back his head and roared. Kherron slid his eyes sideways and saw Ortiz bring Cadzi aboard, slung over his shoulder like a sack. Wake up, he willed. Wake *up,* you fool.

They weren't the only ones on deck, he saw now, but the other sailors were pointedly ignoring the activity by the rail. Must be lowlanders, he decided, remembering what Cadzi had said in the cave. They obviously weren't going to be of much help. His attention snapped back to Metz, who had drawn the dagger out of its sheath and was testing the point with a green thumb.

"Will you look at the boy?" he said. "Pale as a fish-man! Maybe we should throw him overboard on the end of a rope and see how well he swims?"

The other two glanced at each other.

"Or maybe our young Karchlord would 'preciate a bite of tender Islander meat," Metz went on, still fiddling with the dagger. "Rare enough in the Karch, ain't it?" He bared his black teeth and slid the edge of the blade down Kherron's cheek.

Enough was enough. Kherron raised his chin, stared the big man in the eye, and with a strong undercurrent of *Yehn* hissed, "If you touch me with that once more, you're dead."

The black eyes sparked briefly, then went dull. Metz backed off, frowned at the dagger in his hand as if he couldn't quite remember how it had got there, then licked his lips and glanced around. "Well?" he demanded. "Why are you two still hanging around up here? Let the boy go, Malazi! You an' Ortiz take Cadzi below and see to his leg while I show this island boy how he's going to pay for his passage."

Dawn had crept upon them while they were arguing. By its light, the men were breaking out more sail, which billowed overhead in orange clouds. Daylight also revealed the source of the rotten smell. Piled on deck in an area strictly avoided by the lowland sailors were about twenty fish carcasses, each as large as a man.

Kherron crept closer, curious. Back in the Echorium, the orderlies had never served up fish as large as this. There was a lot of what could only be blood, glistening in pools on the deck, though it was the strangest colored blood Kherron had ever seen — bright green. Each carcass had been slit open from tail to — He took a step back, unsure of what he was seeing. Did those fish have human torsos? Or were there human bodies mixed in with the pile?

He suddenly became aware of the big man's scrutiny. Metz had hooked his elbows over the rail and was leaning against it so he could observe Kherron.

"Not all of them are pregnant, of course," he said. "Unfortunately, we've no way of telling beforehand. They all look the same to me." He chuckled. "Course, we'd have to kill them all anyway. They wail something awful when you net them and keep on doing it even if you put them back in." He unhooked his elbows and swaggered across. "You want passage to Silvertown, boy? So make yourself useful! Get your hands inside that lot and find the Karchlord some more of them sweet little green eggs he likes so much."

Kherron stared into the lifeless eyes of one of the creatures, and turned cold as he realized it was at least as much human as fish. Its skin was pale green, with darker veins showing through like ripples. It had a human face, smooth as a First Year's. Limp silver hair plastered the cheeks and clung to its body, which was also a bit like a First Year's — shapeless and blubbery with no breasts, only an ugly flap of skin he'd mistaken at first for another cut. Its tail was dull and badly damaged, though colors glimmered faintly where the scales had survived. He shuddered. There'd been rumors of such creatures in the pallets, of course, but he'd never really believed them. There were always rumors in the pallets, a lot of which Kherron had started himself. If half the tales were true, these strange half-fish were singers of a sort.

He felt a bit less sorry for the creatures. Dead singers.

"You'll need this," Metz said, tossing him the dagger. "Get on with it, boy, then we can chuck this lot overboard. There's a bucket over there for the eggs. Just toss them in and put the lid back on when you've finished. Mind you don't split 'em, though! Make a khiz-stinking mess they do, believe me."

Kherron did believe him. Trying to hide his disgust, he knelt beside the first carcass and clutched the dagger tightly. It'd be no match against a sword, of course, but it made him feel a bit safer.

Metz stooped and plucked an egg out of the bucket. He bared his teeth at Kherron, popped the green slimy thing into his mouth, and swallowed it in one gulp. "Delicious!" he said.

Kherron fought down a wave of nausea. But even as he bent to his vile task, he was learning things about these men. Though Metz kept his grin, the undercurrents in the big karchholder's voice shouted: *lie, lie!*

*

Scooping out those eggs was the most horrible thing Kherron had ever done. The creatures' dead eyes stared accusingly at him, and he was sure his hands would never be clean again. But, finally, the deck was clear of carcasses and Metz showed him to a tiny store cabin in the bowels of the ship. He watched while Kherron carried the buckets of eggs down, then flung him a couple of filthy blankets, told him to make himself comfortable, and stumbled off to his own cabin, from which he didn't emerge for several days.

With Metz out of the way, the entire crew woke up as if they'd all been given *Kashe*. The lowlanders sang at their work — if you could call their rough, out-of-tune voices singing. Ortiz and Malazi spent most of their time on the poop deck, playing a complicated game involving the small bleached bones at the ends of their death braids, while Cadzi stayed in his bunk. Kherron supposed it was the safest place for a man with only one leg on a ship that seemed always to be rolling at the edge of a storm.

No one much bothered Kherron, which gave him plenty of time to explore. He discovered where the supplies were kept, helped himself when he was hungry, and spent a lot of time listening with his ear pressed to cabin doors. This yielded fascinating scraps about the Mainland, which he filed away for future use even though he didn't understand half of it.

Metz seemed to have lost interest in him but Kherron was taking no chances. The store didn't have a lock. So, each night before he slept he left one of the full buckets with the lid loose just inside the door where any intruder would knock it over as he blundered in.

For three nights, the eggs remained in the bucket and he started to think these karchholders weren't as tough as they liked to make out. Then, early on the fourth night, he woke to a faint scratching noise.

He sat up with a start and groped for his dagger. In the light that seeped around the badly fitting door, he could just make out the bucket of eggs, rocking wildly. His heart hammered, but the voice that called out softly didn't belong to Metz.

"Islander? You in there?"

Kherron fought off the blankets, dived across the tiny cabin, and slid the bucket out of the way. Only just in time. The door burst open, and Cadzi lurched in.

Kherron eyed the injured karchholder with mixed feelings. He hadn't seen Cadzi since Ortiz and Malazi had carried him below that first night. Though the man was as dirty as ever, his leg had been freshly splinted and bandaged, and the fever had gone from his eyes. He held onto the door frame, swaying unsteadily, one hand pressed to his nose as he surveyed the store.

"That crafty devil Metz found a job for you, I see."

Kherron kept hold of his dagger and watched the karchholder warily. "You said I'd get free passage."

Cadzi's eyes shifted. "Ah, I know. But this is Metz's ship. I'll make it up to you when we land, promise. I came to say thanks. I must've passed out before I could tell you 'bout the signal, but I see you worked it out for yourself."

Kherron frowned. "What signal?"

"The lantern, of course. Flashes. Two long, two short. You mean you didn't use it?"

"I don't know about any signal, but Metz virtually ran over us. Must've heard me sin — must have heard the oars, or something." Fine time to tell me now, he thought. Signal, huh.

Cadzi looked at him strangely. "That was lucky."

"Yes it was, wasn't it?"

Cadzi scratched beneath his bandage. He gave Kherron a long look, then seemed to decide on something. "How are you getting on, then? Metz told you anythin' of his plans for you yet?"

Kherron had to laugh. "Apart from gutting fish-people, you mean?"

Cadzi's already dark skin turned a deeper shade. "Look out for yourself, Islander, that's all I'm saying. Metz ain't a good sailor. He's probably too sick at the moment to think about much except staying as far away from this stink as possible, but things will be different when we land, mark my words. You're a long way from home, and Metz is Frazhin's man, every last braid of him."

Something deeper in that. "What do you mean?" Kherron said, his skin prickling.

But before Cadzi could answer, a sudden heave of the ship rocked the bucket with the loose lid. Some of the eggs slopped over the side. Cadzi lost his balance and slipped in the slime.

"Khiz!" he swore. "Khiz-stinking fish-people eggs! No wonder the Karchlord's goin' crazy like he is!" He was still cursing as he lurched off along the narrow corridor that ran bow to stern belowdecks.

Kherron stared after the injured karchholder in confusion. Metz sick? That would explain why they hadn't seen the big man on deck the past few days. He nudged the red bracelet farther up his arm and scowled at the skin beneath. It was still faintly green, despite repeated scrubbing in the buckets of salt water the lowlanders heaved over the rail each morning for what passed as baths on this ship.

Then he smiled and hooked his thumbs into his belt. Metz sick. What if it wasn't the sea making him ill?

"You touch me, you're dead," he whispered with a bit of practice *Yehn*, and smiled again as the echoes rolled darkly around the store. Eliya must be wrong. His voice was a lot stronger than she thought.

5
MERLEE

Once the danger of sinking was past, and Rialle's stomach settled down, sailing became quite boring. She and Frenn spent most of their time on deck, enjoying the sunshine and fresh breeze that had sped them on their way since the storm. Meanwhile, the Second Singer stayed below, polishing all the gifts he'd brought for the Mainlanders he wished to talk to. He had an entire silk-lined chest of bluestone jewelry set in silver, everything from chunky necklaces to tiny earrings, so the polishing took ages. He didn't trust any of the orderlies to work with them, and snapped if Rialle or Frenn so much as touched the lid.

"He's probably as bored as we are," Frenn whispered one morning, as they watched the Singer open his chest and take out the pieces, one by one, frowning at each. "At least I didn't get landed with the job! C'mon, the captain's promised to teach me how to steer the ship today. Wait till Chissar hears!"

Rialle smiled at the pride in his voice. It was their seventh day at sea and ever since Toharo had run out of jobs to keep him busy Frenn had taken to following the crew around, asking endless questions. She suspected the captain had made his promise to stop the boy from driving him crazy. Once, she would have teased him for it but she didn't say a word. Frenn can't sing, she reminded herself. Steering a ship is the most fun he's likely to get from now on. She got a lump in her throat at the thought and had to turn away quickly before he noticed her expression.

She settled in the shade of the fringed canopy the orderlies had erected to give them all some relief from the sun. From here, she had a good view of Frenn at the wheel, legs braced and jaw clenched as he struggled to hold the course to the captain's satisfaction. He was concentrating so hard, he'd forgotten she was watching, so she didn't feel embarrassed about looking. Frenn's hair was beginning to grow out, a black fuzz that would soon cover the scars made by the orderlies' blades, and muscles were forming under his sunburn. He seemed a lot less awkward out here than he had in the Echorium, and his big hands looked right on the wheel. She began to feel a bit better about him not being able to sing.

Idly, she pulled a strand of her own hair into view but still couldn't see what color it was under the dye. She wondered if Singer Toharo would let her have a mirror from his chest. She'd seen some designed to be held in the hand, their polished silver circles ringed by tiny bluestones. Probably not. He guarded that chest closer than his life. She sighed and flicked the hair back. The silk canopy fluttered above her. The sails creaked and snapped. Waves hissed past. Though there was no need, she decided to try contacting the merlee again. If she went back to the pallets without even seeing one, she'd never live it down.

She made herself comfortable in the cushions and closed her eyes. Now then, where would they be? Water, waves, sunlight, spray . . . She was getting quicker at finding them every time. She was just about to make the final jump when Frenn's shout jerked her back.

"Look!" he called, letting go of the wheel to point. "What's that?"

Rialle scowled at him.

Sails flapped crazily as the ship veered off course, bringing the captain across deck with a yell. "Never trust a trainee!" he said, but he was grinning as he relieved Frenn. "Your arms getting tired, young one, eh? Go on then, shin up the lookout. Your eyes are obviously sharper than your hands today."

Frenn scrambled up the rigging. He squinted at the glittering waves a moment, then twisted around so fast he almost fell out. "Rialle!" he called down. "I think it's the merlee! Hundreds of 'em — to port, Capt'n!" he added, belatedly remembering his seamanship training. "'Ware, merlee to port!"

By this time, Rialle was out of the cushions and clutching the rail. At first she could see nothing but the bright flash of sun on water. Then she remembered and shut her eyes.

It was easier than it had ever been. Barely a flicker, and she was *there*.

"Merlee!" she called.

They replied at once. *We're here! We're here! Come swim with us, stone-singer. Be warm and safe in the shoal.*

Trembling with excitement, she opened her eyes. At first, they were only shadows under the surface, dark blurs that glimmered silver and green around the edges as they rippled closer. Then about fifty of them broke the water at once in a fountain of spray and flashing rainbow tails. Rialle caught her breath. They were even more beautiful than she'd imagined. Their hair trailed behind them like liquid moonlight as they beckoned her in. Eliya had omitted to tell her their skin would be green, but it was luminous as sunlight trapped in the shallows, as if they were lit up from inside. And their songs — oh, their wild, haunting songs!

Before she knew she'd even moved, she had stripped down to her undergarments. The dive over the side drove the breath from her lungs, and only as she broke the water with her fingertips did she remember she didn't know how to swim. But after a few floundering strokes, it felt natural to be surrounded by water, and she relaxed. She breathed normally and let her legs and arms do what they wanted. This was easy. And the merlee were right. There was a pocket of warm sea here. Her hair floated lightly around her like a blue version of the merlee's, and the water, silklike, caressed her skin as she swam out to join the shoal.

So glad you came.

Close up, the adults were bigger than she'd thought, yet she felt no fear. Strong fingers plucked at her hair, and muscular tails curled around her legs. There was some merriment over her strange coloring. But their songs were of gladness and welcome, overlaid by faint playful melodies. It took her a moment to realize these were coming from the almost transparent merlee children, whose tiny tadpolelike bodies emerged in clouds from the chest pouches of some of the females.

The children tickled as they swarmed closer to see this strange land creature with four limbs and no tail, and Rialle cupped some in her hand and looked at them in amazement. They were mostly tail and head, but she could see miniature lungs and hearts developing inside some of their bodies, and a few of the bigger ones had the stubby beginnings of arms.

The mothers floated closer, watchful. Rialle smiled and let the tiny, unformed merlee trickle through her fingers. "I won't hurt them," she said.

She rolled on her back and gazed at the sky, paddling with her fingers to keep herself afloat. So peaceful out here, safe from humans who walked on two legs and were afraid of the sea. . . . As the merlee splashed around her, and their children played games in her hair, the *Wavesong*, Singer Toharo, even Frenn, leaked out of her head, to be replaced by the pleasures of plankton on the tongue, of surfing a deserted beach under a full moon.

Then a large male with a curly silver beard swam up beside her and stared at her with his turquoise eyes, the gills beneath his ears opening and closing as the waves lapped his neck. He swept away the children who were playing in her hair, and stared at her again.

"What is it, shoal-father?" Rialle asked. She wasn't sure why she used that form of address, only that it sounded right. "They weren't hurting me."

The male made a low sound in his throat, almost *Aushan*, and drove the other adults away with his powerful tail. Rialle twisted in the waves, a little disturbed.

"It's all right. . . ." she said again. But the words died in her throat when the male seized her hands in a strong grip.

Stone-singer remember! Nets took friends. Many cut! Some taken alive to cold prison, can't breathe. . . . Need help!

How could she have forgotten?

"I know you do, shoal-father," she said, full of remorse, stroking his agitated tail as it churned around her. "I'm sorry I forgot. We'll help you now, I promise. That's what we've come for."

Reluctantly, she looked around for the *Wavesong*, rather disconcerted to see how far away it was. Her limbs felt heavy and tired now, after so much unaccustomed exercise. She caught hold of the shoal-father's slippery tail. "But you'll have to help me back to my ship," she added with a little smile. "I'm afraid my swimming is not as strong as yours."

He didn't seem to be listening — or, at least, he *was* listening, but to something else.

Then Rialle heard it, too. Terror, rippling across the ocean like a huge wave, growing as it came.

Stone-singer betrays us!

The water boiled with rainbows as the mothers scooped their children into their chest pouches and dived. Rialle lost her grip on the shoal-father's tail, but found herself being pushed and pulled through the water by hundreds of green hands. The waves were growing by the moment, the sky darkening, yet she still wasn't really worried. They think I'm one of their own children, she thought with a giggle. Only I'm too big to fit in a pouch.

With the larger waves, she quickly lost sight of the *Wavesong*. Surrounded by agitated merlee, it was difficult to tell where she was, though at some point she realized the school had left the warm pocket and carried her into water so cold, it stopped the breath in her throat. Then there came an alien echo, of water slapping wood. Ship.

Rialle smiled. She couldn't wait to tell Frenn all about her swim. She was just imagining his face when she told him about the tiny children in their pouches when the large male came back, took a firm grip on her hair, and without warning dived straight for the bottom.

At first she was too surprised to do anything, and let him pull her into the murky depths, blinking at the strange feel of water against her eyeballs. Then the pressure on her chest brought her to her senses, and panic set in.

No!

Lungs bursting, she ripped her hair free, leaving what felt like a good chunk of it behind. She fought her way out of all the clutching hands and kicked desperately toward the light. If she could just hold her breath a few moments longer, just a few more beats of the rhythm drum . . .

She was almost clear when a tail struck her on the side of the head — slap! The last of the air was knocked from her lungs, and they refilled with seawater. Bubbles surrounded her, a silver storm of bubbles. She had time to feel afraid.

Then everything went black.

*

"Fish-people!" cried the lookout, making Kherron jump.

He'd been trying to work out the rules of the bone-game Ortiz and Malazi kept playing, but they seemed to change them every time, and after several days of peering over their shoulders, Kherron was no wiser. Now the two karchholders looked up in annoyance as a lowlander pounded past and hurried below, echoing the message.

"Fish-people hunt! Fish-people hunt!"

The karchholders sighed, pocketed their bones, and scrambled to their feet.

"What's happening?" asked Kherron. "What do I do?"

Malazi frowned, as if surprised to see he was still there. "I'd keep out of the way, lad, if I were you. Stay below, and he might not remember you —"

Too late. Grumbling and squinting, Metz heaved his bulk up the ladder into the sun.

"Nets!" he roared. As Ortiz and Malazi hurried to obey, Metz's small eyes peered around the deck. "Boy! Where are you?"

Kherron stiffened. He couldn't see the school from where he

was standing, but there was a strange vibration in the air. He frowned at the sea. Ahead, the skies were clear. But behind them, dense clouds boiled across the waves, eating the water like night.

One of the lowlanders pointed this out. In answer, Metz drew his sword and speared the lowlander in the thigh.

There was a heartbeat of silence before the unfortunate man fell to the deck, clutching his leg and screaming. No one else moved.

"Any other suggestions?" Metz said, wiping his blade.

There were none. Kherron's stomach clenched as he watched the lowlander crawl away, leaving a trail of blood across the deck.

"Boy!"

"I'm here, sir." *Challa*, shh, calm . . .

Metz whirled, his blade leaving a red arc in the air. When he saw Kherron, he snorted and sheathed the sword. His hand shot out and tightened about Kherron's elbow. "C'mere, boy. Time for work. You see them there nets?"

Kherron nodded. The nets in question were being winched over the side by Ortiz and Malazi, who worked the handles as quickly as they could, muscles bulging beneath their dark skin.

"You wait right over there with your bucket. When we draw them in, there'll be all sorts of wailing and shrieking. Don't you take no notice. Soon as we toss you one of the fish-people, you get right in there with your knife. No need to wait for 'em to die first. They ain't got no feelings like we humans do. Got that?"

Kherron nodded again. While Metz went to join Ortiz and Malazi at the rail, he surreptitiously rubbed his elbow. The thought of gutting more fish-people carcasses made him feel ill.

But he gritted his teeth, drew his dagger, and crouched obediently beside the empty buckets. He consoled himself with the thought that it couldn't be worse than last time.

What he hadn't counted on was the songs.

The fish-people didn't just wail. They screamed. As the net closed around the school, the air filled with wild animal terror, invading Kherron's head like a Song. The dagger slipped from his limp fingers, and he slammed his hands to his ears. He was beginning to envy Cadzi, laid up in his bunk.

The three uninjured karchholders were too busy hauling fish-people over the rail to notice, slashing pale throats with their red swords, and slinging the bodies onto the deck. Glistening with seawater and green blood, the wounded creatures slid toward Kherron and fetched up against the mast. Very few were properly dead. Soon he was surrounded by flapping rainbow tails, coils of silver hair tangled with seaweed, gaping mouths and gills, reaching hands, wet pleading eyes — and those terrible, terrible songs.

Help us, they seemed to say.

He shook his head. "I can't help you," he whispered.

"What you doing, boy?" Metz's roar sent the dying creatures into a fresh frenzy. "Pick up that knife and gut 'em, or I'll cast you overboard and let the rest of 'em down there eat you alive."

Kherron watched his hand fumble in a pool of green slime and close on the dagger. He began to hum softly. *Challa*, shh, *Challa* makes you dream. . . .

The creatures' struggles grew less violent. One by one, their arms and tails flopped to the deck, and their luminous eyes closed. Kherron opened their guts as swiftly as he could, and tried not to think what he was doing as he scooped out handfuls of their unborn children. It helped if he didn't look at their faces. That way he could pretend they were just fish.

There were so many to gut this time, his partly healed blisters broke open again, and he couldn't be sure if the sticky blood on the handle of the dagger was theirs or his own. He'd filled three buckets and started on a fourth before the storm forced them to abandon the hunt. The lowlanders were finally allowed up the rigging to rescue their sails, while Ortiz and Malazi wound in the empty nets. Metz vanished below, clutching his stomach and looking greener than the fish-people's blood.

Kherron dropped to his knees amid the pile of carcasses and let the dagger clatter to the deck. He felt numb inside, as if someone had gutted *him*. Some of them weren't even female, for Echoes' sake. As he fingered the long, curly beard of one of the males he must have gutted without noticing its sex, the deck heaved and the creature's hand flopped open. Kherron stared at the blue strands wound around the fingers. The color touched something in his memory and he bent for a closer look, but just then a wave foamed across the deck and washed the blue strands over the side.

He shook his head angrily. Now he was seeing things. Probably seaweed.

6

LIES

Rialle's dreams churned with rainbow tails and wild songs.

Stone-singer, cold prison, can't breathe —

She sat up in a panic, fighting off blankets, and her head connected with something hard. Stars fizzed before her eyes.

"Steady, Rialle! You tryin' to knock yourself out again, or what?"

Firm hands pushed her back down. She blinked, trying to place the voice. Gray light. A round window, spray-splashed. The concerned blue eyes of a boy with a bad case of sunburn and a shadow of black hair.

"Frenn," she whispered in a rush of relief. "What happened?"

"You nearly drowned, that's what. Singer Toharo was furious. The orderlies put out the little boat to rescue you, but old Toharo was already in the water. He was the one who dived down and found you."

"Really?" she said. "The Second Singer dived in?" The image

made her smile. Then she frowned. "The merlee hurt me. I thought they were my friends." There had been something important in their panicky songs, something she couldn't quite remember.

"They vanished pretty quick," Frenn told her. "Maybe they thought we were throwing nets or somethin' when we lowered the boat. Or maybe it was the other ship. Toharo said he saw a mast on the horizon, but we lost it in the storm. Look, I'd better fetch him. He said to tell him as soon as you woke up." He kept darting glances at the door, excited undercurrents in his words.

Rialle frowned around the cabin. Something was different, but she couldn't place it. Then she realized. The ship wasn't rolling anymore.

She scrambled off the bunk, cupped her hands to the porthole, and peered out. Ships at anchor, a harbor wall curling around them like a stone arm . . . Her cabin was on the wrong side for a view of the shore but it was obvious they were no longer at sea.

"We're here!" she said, swinging around in excitement. "How long have I been asleep? Why didn't you *tell* me?"

"Singer Toharo said I shouldn't wake you. We got here three days after you swam with the merlee. He, uh, sang to you, to keep you asleep. If you ask me, he seemed pretty worried 'bout you."

Rialle smiled. "He's just worried he'll be in trouble with Eliya for letting me get hurt. You'd better go tell him I'm awake, I suppose. Is this Silvertown? Have you been ashore yet?"

Frenn made a face as he opened the cabin door. "Not yet. Misery-guts Toharo won't let me. *He* has, though, lots of times. I think he's been talking to people already. He takes them bluestones with him, and sometimes he comes back empty-handed. At the rate he's givin' them away, we'll be broke before we even start." He considered her a moment, then gave her a flash of that lop-sided grin. "Don't look so worried, Rialle! He's calmed down quite a bit."

Rialle dressed as quickly as she could. While she waited for the Second Singer, she sat on the edge of the bunk and teased a comb through her sticky hair, wincing when it tugged at the bruise the merlee had given her. Why did she have to go and get herself knocked out like that? And then to try breathing sea-water, as if she had gills herself. That had been so stupid. But if Frenn's reckoning was correct, they'd made good time to the mainland. The Second Singer ought to be pleased about that, at least.

Remembering what he'd said about being discreet, she decided to try her hair in a braid over one shoulder, like Singer Graia had worn hers on the beach. It still reached way past her waist. The string of pink shells she'd used to secure the end tinkled when she moved. She smiled and was just wondering if she should go up to the main cabin, when the door burst open and Toharo strode in. He looked her over, slammed the door behind him, crossed the cabin in two strides, took her by the shoulders, and shook hard.

"What did you think you were doing out there?" The words thrummed with *Aushan*.

Rialle shrank away from him in surprise.

"You acted crazy!" Toharo continued. "Stupid! You might have been killed! What were you thinking of, girl?"

"You said I was supposed to be an orderly on this trip," she whispered. "Orderlies swim, don't they?"

He stared at her a moment, then let go. "Not with merlee,

they don't. Good thing you've got Singer lungs, otherwise they'd have drowned you for sure." His chuckle ruined the rebuke.

Rialle relaxed slightly. "Something frightened them," she said. "Singer Toharo, have you found out who's netting them yet? One of them told me some of the school had been captured and were dying somewhere they couldn't breathe. I think that means suffocating." She frowned. "It was very confused, though."

Toharo was immediately serious again. "Captured? Yes, I heard something similar in the town. It looks as if we're going to have to journey inland soon. There's a lordling in the foothills who's supposed to be helping these hunters. I want to question him. Seems merlee aren't the only Half Creatures they've been carrying off lately."

He examined her bruise with fingers that probed mercilessly, holding her still by the braid when she winced and tried to pull away. He grunted. "Could be worse. How do you feel?"

Rialle blinked, determined not to cry. "All right."

He gave her a sharp look. "What's wrong?"

"Nothing. It's just . . . Singer Toharo, they hurt me! Why would they do that? Maybe they *were* trying to kill me?"

He smiled. "Oh, I doubt it. Merlee are strange creatures, more fish than human. I expect they panicked and forgot you couldn't breathe underwater, that's all. I'm going ashore soon to trade for some transport. If you're feeling well enough, you can come with me. It'll be an education." He left before she remembered to ask what "stone-singer" meant.

She took another look out of the porthole. The sun was shining, but the pennants at the tops of the ships' masts were flapping horizontally. Did that mean it was hot or cold? In the end, remembering what Singer Toharo had said about disguise, she snatched up one of the gray cloaks and hurried up the ladder to the main cabin.

Frenn was already there, his belt laden with silk pouches that rattled when he moved. He raised an eyebrow when he saw what she'd done to her hair. "Different," he said. "Makes you look older."

Rialle raised a hand to the shells, but Toharo didn't give her time to think of a suitable reply. He hurried them out on deck, beckoned to two of the orderlies, and led the way across the gangplank onto the quay. Rialle followed close behind Frenn, eyes wide and ears open, determined not to miss a thing.

Silvertown was disappointing. The houses were small and white with no towers or silver roofs, and the people seemed quite ordinary. Their clothing showed more variation than the Islanders', but was for the most part torn and stained, and they scurried about with lowered heads, clutching their cloaks around them as if they all had something to hide. In contrast, the Second Singer's gray robe billowed, his blue hair streamed out behind him in the wind, and he walked with chin high as if he expected everyone to step out of his way — which the townspeople did, falling silent as he passed, and only resuming their conversations when they thought the Singer party was out of earshot.

It was hard not to laugh at their awed whispers.

". . . There! What did I tell you? Singers control the wind, don't they? Told you a little storm wouldn't keep them away for long. . . ."

". . . That dunghill of a Karchlord is in for a big surprise, that's for sure. I'd love to see his face when a Singer turns up on his doorstep. . . ."

". . . Singers will soon stop this nonsense, you'll see. The Karchlord will have to pay up now. It will clean him out, and serve him right. His warriors will run off pretty quick when the gold dries up, see if I'm not right. . . ."

". . . I dunno. Those karchholders are a weird bunch. There's some who say they don't get paid in gold but in coins of ice, and they can't ever leave the Karch because their ice coins would melt and they'd all be poor as Half Creatures. Besides, what can one man do against an army?"

". . . One *Singer* . . ."

Toharo didn't give any sign he'd heard. But if Rialle could hear the whispers, then the Second Singer certainly could. Even Frenn picked up most of them, to judge by his grins and winks. A few of these, Rialle noted with disgust, were directed at pretty girls in the crowd.

The orderlies strode shoulder to shoulder, a little behind her and Frenn. They chatted as they walked, and they seemed relaxed, but Rialle couldn't help noticing their hands were never very far from the short swords strapped to their hips.

"What'll happen if someone tries to attack us?" she whispered to Frenn.

"They won't," he said. "Wouldn't dare."

"Yes, but what *if*?"

"Don't worry, Rialle! We learned it all in orderly training. Mainlanders are terrified of Singers, which makes them easy to control. All Toharo has to do is start humming, and they'd flee. I can't wait to see him work on this Karchlord everyone's talking about."

Rialle fiddled with the shells in her braid. It was impossible trying to talk to Frenn, who'd gone back to winking at girls. This obviously wasn't the time to point out he'd hardly stayed four days in orderly training.

Singer Toharo stopped outside an elegant stable yard, separated from the street by high gates of twisted black metal. He had one of the orderlies draw his sword across the bars. The glissando echoed around the buildings, silencing everyone who heard. Rialle recognized it as one of the tricky exercises Eliya used to wake up their voices after Morning Hums, and looked at the orderly in surprise.

A fat man dressed in green velvet puffed up to the gates. "Get away from there! I've told you before, I have no carriages to spare. . . . *Singer*?" The final word was a whisper. With shaking hands, he hurried to unlock the gates with a key he carried on a long chain around his waist.

"I need a carriage with a hood to keep off the rain and plenty of room for our luggage, six fast horses to ride escort, and an experienced driver," Toharo said. He beckoned to Frenn and relieved him of one of the pouches. "This should cover the hire. If we're away longer than I anticipate, I'll pay you the rest when we get back." The Second Singer smiled as he extended the pouch, standing there as if he owned the entire town, blue curls blowing softly against his dark cheeks and the scent of the sea on his robes.

The man in green velvet swallowed, greedy eyes on the pouch. "I suppose I might be able to find you a few of my reserve mounts."

"Pay the man, Frenn," Toharo said, handing the pouch back to the boy. "Make sure he's quite happy with the value of the pieces, won't you? Meanwhile, we'll go look over the horses." He beckoned Rialle and one of the orderlies to follow, and strode off toward the stables.

Looking back, Rialle saw the man in green fidgeting from foot to foot. He looked as if he longed to rush after the Singer, but was held in place by the bluestone jewelery Frenn displayed across his large palms, piece by slow piece, while the remaining orderly watched the process with one hand resting on his sword. She smiled. It seemed there were ways other than Songs to control these Mainlanders.

As he strolled down the rows of stalls, Toharo stopped to exchange a few words with the stable hands. This surprised Rialle, until she realized his casual questions had a purpose. Then she turned cold inside.

"Any new boys started work here recently?" Toharo asked, and the boy he was speaking to replied, "Only young Lupi."

"Which one's Lupi?" Toharo asked. "Can't sing, by any chance, can he? We could do with a few more boys in the Echorium."

At this, the stable hands laughed. "Lupi? Come over here and give the lord Singer an audition!"

A small boy, maybe five or six, crawled out of one of the stalls to stand trembling before Toharo, obviously too terrified to make a sound. The Second Singer ruffled the boy's hair and hummed a note or two of *Challa* before moving on.

To another boy, he said, "I expect you travel a fair way with your horses, don't you?" When the boy proudly replied yes, he did, Toharo asked what sights he'd seen, and the boy launched into an enthusiastic account of his travels.

Casually, the Second Singer inquired which was the fastest horse in the stables, which started a fierce argument among the stable hands over whose charge was best. The argument got quite heated and ended with two of the boys in the water trough, splashing and taking swings at each other, while the horses whinnied nervously and the other boys whistled and cheered. Toharo smiled, then beckoned Rialle and the orderly outside once more.

"Well?" he said as they stepped into sunshine, almost colliding with the man in green velvet, who was rushing in to see what all the fuss was about. "What did I learn in there, young Singer?"

Rialle took a deep breath. *Undercurrents.* Good thing she'd been paying attention.

"You found out which were the fastest horses in the stable, quite a lot about horse thieving farther up the coast, discovered one of the boys is part of a secret group that plans to — um, assassinate the Karchlord? — but in the meantime goes around writing slogans on walls, and —" She bit her lip.

"Go on."

"And Kherron's not here."

Singer Toharo nodded. "Not bad for a first attempt. Interesting you picked up on the assassination plans; they were really quite subtle. Doomed, of course, if not unexpected. I also discovered the manager is a crook, does regular deals with the karchholders, and as soon as we're gone will send a messenger to the mountains to warn the Karchlord of our arrival. He'll do this not because he thinks he'll get paid but because the karchholders have told him if he cooperates, they'll leave his horses alone so he can continue in business. He also thinks that when the karchholders have forced every other carriage-hire company in Silvertown out of business with their raids, he'll be able to charge whatever he wants and get rich. He's a fool. That last conclusion's my own, but everything else comes from what he told me."

Rialle stared at the Second Singer in amazement. "When did you hear all *that?*"

Toharo smiled again. "Almost as soon as the manager came to the gate. You forget I've had a lot of experience with these Mainlanders. Mostly, they lie whenever they can, and tell the truth only when there's no alternative. The trick is working out if what they think is a lie is actually false, or if it's really true. For example, the carriage manager *thinks* the karchholders will allow him to get rich by letting him continue in business, but how does he know they're not lying to him? I think they probably are, but I won't know for sure until I talk to them. And then I'll have to work out if what they think is a lie is false, or if it might be true — in which case the manager's belief might be true after all. See?"

By this time, they had left the stables and were retracing their steps to the harbor. Frenn shook his head. "I don't see at all! Who's this Karchlord everyone's talkin' about, Singer? And what are karchholders? Why are they stealing horses, and why don't the townspeople like them?" He gave Rialle a sly sideways look. "I'm glad *I* don't have to sort it all out."

Rialle shook her head, too. "It makes me dizzy just to think about it! You were truth-listening, weren't you? Do Singers have to do that all the time?"

Toharo chuckled. "Not all of them, no. Some of us are better at it than others. But since you're here, it'll do you no harm to practice. You did all right back on the *Wavesong*, I seem to remember. To answer your question, Frenn, karchholders live in the mountains, ruled over by the Karchlord. He used to have a ruthless army that, years ago, before the Singers negotiated a truce, burned down half the towns along this coast. People don't forget things like that in a hurry. These days, karchholders are usually seen only in small raiding parties, and I'm pretty certain they're now involved in these merlee hunts. As to why, I have my suspicions, but I expect we'll find out more when we get there."

His last words contained dark echoes. But he smiled and gave them both a push toward the *Wavesong*. "You two go aboard and start packing. I have a few things to sort out, but I want to be ready to leave as soon as that manager sends the carriage. Actually, I'm glad he's going to send word ahead of us, because it'll do no harm to have the Karchlord chew his knuckles for a few days. Meanwhile, we'll go visit the lordling and see if we can't persuade him to part with some more suitable transport for the mountains. I have a feeling our friend's fine carriage and well-bred horses won't get us very far on a mountain track, plus the fact it doesn't do to travel by the same method for too long. People get to hear about it, and I'd prefer not to be recognized on the road — Oh, and don't forget your mittens and scarves!" he called as they hurried across the gangplank. "You'll need them where we're going."

"Mittens and scarves?" Rialle said. "He means those little bags for your hands and those fluffy wraps, doesn't he? I don't like them, they make me itch. Where's he going now, anyway?"

"Oh, off interrogating more Mainlanders, I expect," Frenn said casually. "I'm really glad I stowed away. Chissar'll be green when we get back and tell him 'bout everything! I can't wait to see the mountains where these karchholders live, can you? Do you think it's far?"

Rialle looked out to the sea, once more frothing with white-caps now that the *Wavesong* was safe in harbor. "What about the children?" she whispered. "The merlee said they ate children."

But Frenn was jumping on the gangplank to make it bounce, and didn't hear.

*

After the fish-people hunt, Metz's ship got blown off course by the storm. It took five days of fighting their way through high seas to reach Silvertown, and then they almost missed the harbor beacon. According to the lowlanders, a fire was supposed to be kept burning at Silvertown day and night to guide sailors along the Silver Shore. But the day their ship arrived, the beacon had been allowed to burn so low, it was little more than a spark against the shadowy cliffs.

Metz emerged from his cabin in a foul temper and threatened to roast the harbormaster over his own pathetic fire. Meanwhile, the lowlanders unloaded their cargo as fast as they could. Before Kherron had time to protest, he found himself surrounded by buckets of eggs on the quayside.

He thought that after all the trouble they'd gone to get them, the karchholders would be in a hurry to take the eggs to their lord. But the first thing they did when they set foot in town was find a tavern and get drunk. They left Kherron on guard in the barn, with strict instructions to come find them at once if anyone tried to make off with the Karchlord's property. As if anyone in their right mind would. The eggs were getting more rotten by the day. One whiff, and any potential thief would keel over in his tracks.

Kherron made himself a bed in the straw as far away from the buckets as possible, placed his dagger within easy reach, and closed his eyes with a sigh. The ground swayed beneath him, making him feel quite queasy. He'd just have a short nap, then he'd decide what he was going to do next. If these karchholders thought he was going to carry their stinking, slimy eggs all the way to the Karch for them, they had another thing coming.

Just a short nap.

In the end, he slept a lot longer than he'd meant to, and only his pallet-trained ears prevented that sleep from becoming his last. A faint rustle woke him. As he lay rigid, listening for more clues, heavy breathing came from the darkness. He jerked out of the straw and reached for his dagger, but his fingers clutched at nothing. A strip of moonlight, shining through the crack between the big double doors, revealed a huge black shape bending over him.

For a horrible moment, Kherron couldn't breathe at all. Monster, he thought. Sea monster come for revenge.

Then wine fumes wafted into his face as the monster gave a loud hiccup and tripped over Kherron's leg. It crashed face-down in the straw, and hundreds of braids, knotted with bones, splayed around its head like a fan. Metz.

Kherron dived beneath the nearest cart, Cadzi's warning echoing in his ears, as Metz sat up and shook his head. The small eyes fixed on Kherron's hiding place. "No 'scape, boy," he slurred. "I'm goin' to have those pretty fingers of yours for my death-braids. . . . C'mere!"

There was a hiss as the big karchholder drew his sword. He chuckled and started toward the cart.

Kherron backed farther under, humming *Aushan* under his breath. Metz paused to shake his head again. Then his blade suddenly plunged between the spokes of the nearest wheel and buried itself in the straw beside Kherron's left ankle, piercing his boot on the way. Kherron tried to jerk his leg away but it was pinned firmly to the ground.

He kicked frantically, singing *Aushan* for all he was worth, never mind if anyone heard. Metz dropped to one knee and reached under the cart, trying to get a grip on Kherron's other ankle. Desperate, Kherron tried to pull his foot out of the trapped boot, but it was too tight, and there was no time to undo the laces. He twisted his head. His dagger! It was lying under the rear axle, just out of reach.

A final bar of *Aushan* did it. As Metz raised both hands to his ears, Kherron gave the sword a hard kick with his right foot, sending it spinning across the barn. He wriggled to the back of the cart, snatched up the dagger, and ran at the big man. Before Metz could recover from the Song, Kherron gritted his teeth and jammed the point as hard as he could into the big man's side.

The blade grated between two ribs, the shock tingling right up to Kherron's elbow. Blood spurted around the handle, and Metz bellowed. Kherron let go and backed away, appalled at what he'd done.

Yelling curses, Metz heaved upright. His hand flew first to the dagger buried in his side, then to his sword down in the straw. By this time Kherron was on his feet, singing for all he was worth — *Yehn, Yehn, Yehn.* The barn darkened still further. Dry-mouthed with fear, he dodged Metz's clumsy lunge and put his back to the wall.

"Where are you, boy?" the karchholder roared, no sign of the drunken slur now. "Come out, you tricky little khiz-imp! I knew you was a spy all along. Come out where I can see you, and I'll give you a message to take back to your master — one written in your blood!"

Keeping to the shadows, Kherron slipped around the wall toward the doors. They were still open a crack. Metz either didn't have the brains to block his escape or was too badly hurt. Kherron didn't hang around to find out which. Once in the yard, he ran.

Metz crashed through the doors after him. "I'm going to gut you for this, boy!" he bellowed. "Gut you like a fish-man, real slow. Then I'm goin' to take your heart back to the Karch and serve it up on a plate, a big red plate so your blood don't run off. . . ."

The street gates were chained shut for the night, but fear brought strength Kherron hadn't known he possessed. Quick as an eel, he slipped over the high yard wall and fled down the alley. Behind him, growing fainter and fainter, Metz could be heard calling for someone to open "this khiz-devil gate."

Kherron chose turnings at random, heading deeper into the maze of dark alleys. Overhead, ribbons of moonlit sky provided enough light to see where he was going. He tried to run quietly, but his boots echoed alarmingly on the cobbles. Once he rounded a corner and ran straight into a group of boys busy scribbling on a wall. They scattered like flies from a kicked carcass. Kherron caught his breath, took another turn, and ran on.

The houses ended unexpectedly. The harbor stretched in front of him, ships creaking at anchor, their rigging black against the bright gold of the beacon fire. He skidded to a stop and stared in dismay. What an idiot! He must have been running in a circle. He turned back to the shadows, then stopped again, his heart thudding afresh.

With a dagger in his side and a head full of wine, Metz was coming down the waterfront like a tidal wave, sword whirling above his head. His curses had brought a curious audience out of the taverns, blocking any escape Kherron might have made. In the light of the lanterns they carried, the big karchholder's blade bled like a wound in the night.

Kherron backed to the edge of the quay and glanced over his shoulder. The water was deep and black, and he couldn't swim.

He faced Metz again, flesh prickling. His hand groped at the empty space where his dagger had been, and his knees turned weak. His brain wouldn't work.

"Here, Islander!"

There was a rattle at his feet, and something slid across the cobbles and bumped his toes. Kherron looked down. It was a sword, glinting red in the lantern light. As the waterfront came back into focus, he picked out a dark figure near the front of the crowd, straggly braids around his shoulders, one leg stuck out at an angle.

Metz's gaze fastened on the sword. His lips drew back in a snarl. "Go on then, boy!" he said. "Pick it up . . . if you can lift it!" He held his side and roared. Some of the audience laughed too, but not many. They almost seemed to disapprove, but were clearly too afraid to interfere.

Kherron shook his head. Seeing Cadzi had set his brain working again. He remembered who he was.

"I don't want to fight you," he said, giving the words as much soothing *Challa* as he could manage with terror stealing his breath.

Metz laughed again. He took his hand away from his side and spread the fingers. "What's this, then? Paint?"

The crowd began to clap slowly, making Kherron's head throb.

"It was an accident."

"Accident?" Metz took a step closer. "It was no accident, you sneaky little khiz-imp!"

Kherron cast a final desperate glance at Cadzi, then bent and grasped the hilt of the sword. It was heavier than it looked, and he had to use two hands. More out of panic than any belief it would help, he hummed *Yehn*. Metz's eyes narrowed, and he began the slow, menacing stalk of a hunter approaching its prey.

Kherron felt sick. The sword felt all wrong. He lifted it above his head, but this made his arms ache. So he dropped its point to the cobbles and eased his feet backward over a mooring chain stretched across the quay. To trip now would be fatal.

Metz smiled. "Enough of your trickery, spy," he snarled. "Now you die!"

He came fast, alarmingly fast for such a big man. Kherron barely had time to step aside as Metz's blade whistled past his ear. *Yehn,* he sang with more passion than he'd ever put into any Song in his life. *Yehn makes you die. . . .*

The night air hummed. Kherron shut his eyes. Vaguely, he wondered if dying would hurt.

But the next blow never came. Instead, there was a splash, followed by a ragged cheer from the crowd. He opened his eyes in time to see everyone surge forward and peer over the edge.

Kherron looked, too. For a moment he saw nothing but black water lapping the harbor wall. Then an arm floated into view, and little bones popped to the surface, dragging up braids like feathery seaweed. Finally, the back of Metz's head appeared, blood swirling from a scalp wound.

The crowd was silent. Looking up, Kherron spotted Ortiz and Malazi near the front, also staring silently. Then Cadzi called something, and the two karchholders hurried down some nearby steps, seized handfuls of wet tunic, and dragged Metz's body out of the water. They felt his neck, glanced up, and shook their heads.

Cadzi limped across and took the sword from Kherron's numb fingers. "He tripped," he said, giving Kherron the same strange look he'd given him on the ship. "Must've hit his head when he fell. You've the luck of the Khiz, Islander, you know that?"

"He — he's dead?" Kherron whispered, hardly able to believe the *Yehn* had worked.

Cadzi nodded. "So, now we've got a body to lug up to the

Karch, besides all them stinking Half Creature eggs. Just what we need."

"Maybe not," Malazi said.

Ortiz gave him a sharp glance, and Cadzi's eyes narrowed. "You thinkin' what I'm thinkin'?" he said.

Malazi looked out to sea. "I'm thinking that wound in Metz's side would cause a lot of trouble in the Karch, and not only for the lad. I'm thinking it would've been easy to lose a man overboard in these storms, 'specially if that man was looking for fish-people. . . ."

"An' Frazhin's not likely to hear about what happened here tonight," Ortiz put in. He indicated the crowd, who were dispersing with amazing speed now that the excitement had ended in a death.

"I don't know," Cadzi said. "What about the Khiz?"

Kherron began to edge back along the quay, following the stragglers. Behind him, the karchholders were still arguing about what to do with the body. He glanced at the waterfront buildings. If he could get back in the alleys before they remembered him, he should be able to give them the slip.

He forced himself to walk past the moored ships — running would only attract their attention. Then his steps faltered, and all thoughts of escape fled as he recognized the pennant snapping from the top of one of the masts. Even as Cadzi turned his head and said, "Where's the Islander?" Kherron's sweat turned to ice. Portholes dark, hatches closed and locked, a ship he'd never thought to see again floated like a silent guard between him and his goal.

"*Wavesong*," he whispered, and everything suddenly caught up with him at once. His knees gave way, and he had to sit down on a pile of chain. He smiled weakly at Cadzi.

*

In the end, Ortiz and Malazi got rid of Metz's body by dragging it along the harbor arm and dumping it over the wild side, where spray driven in from the Western Sea crashed onto the rocks beneath the wall. Meanwhile, Cadzi helped Kherron back to the tavern where they'd taken rooms, teasing him about fainting at his first sight of blood — as if the fish-people on the ship had been nothing. Kherron kept quiet. Let Cadzi think what he liked. If Singers were in Silvertown, he wanted to be elsewhere. Now that Metz was dead, staying with the karchholders might not be such a bad idea — at least until he was well away from the *Wavesong*.

In the morning, they loaded the eggs into a cart and left town through the North Gate. Kherron rode in the back with Cadzi, while the other two shared the bench seat up front. They seemed reluctant to talk, but it was only after they'd growled at him a few times that Kherron realized why. These big dark-skinned men were nursing hangovers, same as any off-duty orderly. He smiled to himself. Served them right.

A thick silver mist had drifted in from the sea during the night, making it impossible to see what sort of country they were passing through. He knew only that it was flat. As they headed inland, villages passed like ghost towns, all drab wooden huts and mud. Kherron glimpsed the occasional face at a window — but as soon as they caught him looking, the faces vanished.

Toward midday, they entered a forest where huge trees loomed on both sides of the track, then vanished behind them, almost as if the cart was standing still, and the forest was flow-ing past like some strange green river. It was certainly wet enough. Water dripped down Kherron's neck from the overhanging branches, and the pony's hooves squelched. There was also a peculiar silence in the air, which Kherron couldn't place until he realized he could no longer hear the sea.

The karchholders seemed a bit more alert now, looking around them rather than staring miserably at their own knees. He eased forward until he was sitting beside Cadzi. "Why did you throw me your sword last night?" he asked.

"Seemed only fair." Cadzi carried on watching the trees. "You were unarmed, and Metz was goin' to kill you. You saved my life getting me off that Singer rock like you did, so now we're even."

Kherron thought about this. "He'd still have killed me. I, uh, don't know how to use a sword."

Cadzi frowned. "Then we'll have to put that right when we reach the Karch, won't we? Finest training ground in the world. Used to be anyways — Khiz! This leg of mine itches worse than a Half Creature's nest!" He scratched under his bandage, then sighed and looked at Kherron directly for the first time since they'd left Silvertown. "Look, Islander, I didn't even think you might not be able to handle a blade. In the Karch, most boys your age have already added a braid or two to their manhood bone. You did all right."

"Those bones in your hair . . ." Kherron said slowly, sifting through the undercurrents in the karchholder's words. "They're something to do with duels?"

Cadzi laughed and slapped his good thigh, making the other two jump. "You want Metz's finger, is that it? But you got no hair to put it in, Islander!" He threw back his head and laughed at his own joke, then sobered and gave Kherron a narrow-eyed look. "If Metz had killed you, he might have taken yours. But you didn't really kill him, did you? He was drunk, an' he fell in.

Serves him right for pickin' a fight when he could barely stand on his own two feet."

Idiot! Kherron wanted to scream. You know nothing. Nothing!

But he took a deep breath and said, "Did you see the Singer ship in harbor?"

"Could hardly miss it."

Kherron made his voice as casual as possible. "Do you know what Singers are doing in Silvertown?"

This earned him another sharp look. Then Cadzi chuckled. "What of it, Ortiz?" he called. "You hear any Singers abroad last night?"

The karchholder glanced around. "Na. Didn't hear a khiz."

Cadzi was still watching him far too closely for comfort. Kherron changed the subject. "What's this khiz you all keep talking about?"

"Oh, you'll find out soon enough, Islander! Don't worry, if your crazy luck holds, you've nothing to fear, even if old Frazhin decides to test you with it."

There was death in this. Kherron shivered, remembering how back on the ship, Cadzi had called Metz "Frazhin's man." "Who's Frazhin?" he said. "Test me with *what*?"

But Cadzi put a finger to his lips. "You ask far too many questions, Islander. You're making my head hurt. Let me get my rest, or this here leg's never goin' to be fit for the ride up to the Karch."

Kherron frowned. "Why can't you stay in the cart?"

The two up front laughed, but Cadzi waved them quiet. "Don't tease the boy. He couldn't know, could he? It's like this, Islander. This heavy old thing would never make it up the mountain — we'd be over the first precipice, eggs an' pony an' all. So what we got to do soon as we get out of this forest is transfer the eggs into packs and ride up. Besides, it's quicker on ponyback, and with Singers abroad I don't want to be hanging around down here any longer than we have to — to say nothing of the trouble we'll have getting up to the Karch if the snows come early." He looked hard at Kherron a moment, then grinned. "Oh, I get it! You can't ride, either, can you?"

Kherron shook his head.

Another chuckle. "Not to worry. It's three days up to the Karchhold from Vale, where we'll ditch this cart. Steep, rough terrain for the last part, and we won't be hangin' around. You'll learn!"

7
TRUTh

The foothills turned out to be a lot farther, higher, and colder than Rialle had imagined when Toharo first mentioned them back in Silvertown. For the past two days, they'd done nothing but climb into the sky, where the air was brittle enough to make clouds of their breath. In spite of her mittens, Rialle was so stiff and cold by the time they reached the lordling's castle, all she wanted to do was wrap herself in as many cloaks as possible and fall into bed. But the plump and plainly nervous Lord Javelly had other ideas, and the Singer party found themselves as guests of honor at their first Mainland banquet.

If there was one thing Lord Javelly did seem confident about, it was food, and he seemed most anxious to impress the Second Singer. This meant parading dish after dish around the entire hall, before returning them to the kitchens to be carved and served. To fill the wait between courses, a thin man entertained them by blowing into a peculiar arrangement of pipes attached to a bag.

The first time Rialle heard this contraption played, she nearly jumped out of her seat. But Frenn, who'd been poking some unidentified strips of meat around his plate with his finger, grinned. "He's got an animal in that bag, you know," he whispered. "And he's torturing it by blowing air into its ears. Those horrible sounds it's making are its screams. We learned all about it in orderly training."

Rialle stared at the pipes in horror, until Frenn dug her in the ribs with his elbow and winked. "You're so gullible sometimes, Rialle! Of course there's no animal in there, silly! How would they feed it? C'mon, this is getting real boring, and if I eat another bite I'll burst. What do you say we do some investigating of our own?"

Rialle glanced at the end of the hall, where Toharo sat on a raised dais with Lord Javelly, four of the orderlies, and a group of nobles whose robes were trimmed with bright feathers. The lord still seemed nervous. Oversized rings glittered as he ran his pudgy fingers around his collar.

She closed her eyes and was *there*.

". . . Wh-what trade?" Javelly was saying.

Toharo sighed. "Oh, come. You must realize when Singers oversee a treaty, they listen carefully to make sure it's kept. Do you think the Echorium has grown deaf?"

"N-no, Singer! Of course not! But you have to understand the Karchlord put me up to it. I had no choice —"

"It's not too late to make amends." Toharo again. "All I require from you is a promise not to hunt any more Half Creatures. Then I'll leave you with a small trust gift, and we'll be on our way. . . ."

Rialle opened her eyes and gazed longingly at the huge fire

crackling behind the dais. The other two orderlies had vanished somewhere on unfathomable Singer business. "I don't know," she said doubtfully. "Singer Toharo told me to keep my ears open and listen to what the ordinary people are saying."

"You can still listen. This bunch won't be making sense much longer, anyway."

It was probably true. About all she'd picked up so far were silly jokes concerning Lord Javelly's expanding waistline, or some nobleman's plans for this girl or that — which made her blush when she understood them, and left her feeling uncomfortable when she couldn't.

"C'mon!" Frenn said, taking her hand. "Toharo won't mind." He gave her a sly look. "Besides, I think I know where they keep the goods they send up to the Karch. They might have your captured merlee here."

Rialle cast a final look at the dais, where Toharo had just emptied one of his pouches across the table. Bluestones and silver flowed like cool water among all the hot colors, making her long to be back in the Echorium with Frenn and Chissar messing around to get her attention, and Kherron glaring whenever she did better than him in class. Then she remembered Kherron might never glare at anyone again, and Chissar would have no rival for her attentions because Frenn would be in orderly training.

"All right," she said.

No one gave them a second glance as they left the hall. After dragging her down some cobwebby corridors, Frenn put a finger to his lips and opened a door, letting in a blast of cold air. He looked left and right, then quickly pulled her into the moonlight and led her across the courtyard at a run.

Blowing on their hands, they reached another door set in the wall near the gates. Inside, a flight of shadowy steps led into darkness. Frenn took a torch from its bracket and crept down, Rialle following close behind, her heart thumping as shadows loomed around them.

"How do you know they're down here?" she whispered, scenting another of Frenn's jokes. "If Javelly's got the merlee, they'd have to be in water. They can't survive very long on dry land, or their gills shrivel up."

"Quite the expert all of a sudden, aren't you?" Frenn whispered back, giving her a strange look. "There's more ways to discover things than Singer tricks, you know. They teach us a few of our own in orderly training. While you were busy snooping, I was chatting with the serving boys. This here's the back way into the dungeons, the one they use to feed the prisoners — when they bother to feed them at all, that is." He chuckled at the look on her face. "Got you again, didn't I? Now, there should be a hidden door here somewhere. . . . Ah, here it is!"

He leaned on the wall, and a whole section of stone moved. Rialle sucked in her breath, then slammed a hand over her nose as a thick, musty smell wafted out and folded itself about them.

Once through the gap, the smell was about ten times worse. The back of her nose prickled, her eyes began to water, and she doubled over with a huge sneeze.

"Shh!" Frenn hissed. "It's not as bad as all that." But she noticed he had a hand over his nose, too. When her sneezes finally stopped, he whispered, "I think we found them."

Rialle blinked. The darkness ahead of them glittered. Then she realized why. Eyes. Hundreds of round, unblinking eyes, each reflecting a tiny torch flame in its depths.

"Wh-what are they?" she whispered. "They're not merlee."

A soft fluffing of feathers came out of the dark, like muffled sighs. All the echoes in this place were muffled, which was probably just as well, considering how loudly she'd sneezed earlier. The creatures were in cages, Rialle realized, their eyes staring through holes in the mesh. A narrow passage ran between the cages to steps at the far end, leading up. All was dark at the top, the door shut.

"The castle boys use this secret panel to sneak in and collect feathers," Frenn whispered back. "Apparently, the nobles will pay a lot for them. Look at those colors!"

Rialle looked sadly at the blues, scarlets, greens, and golds crushed against the mesh of the cages. Now she knew where Javelly's men had got their fine cloaks. "But what are they?" she whispered again, feeling a stab of pity for the creatures. "Some sort of bird?"

"The serving boys call them quetzal," Frenn said, holding the torch closer to one of the cages. "They're Half Creatures like your merlee, so they're supposed to be protected by that treaty Toharo mentioned."

The quetzal cowered away from the flame, but they'd been so tightly packed in, they couldn't move very far. What Frenn's torch revealed made Rialle feel sick.

The quetzal faces were eerily human, but they had feathers instead of hair and beaks where their noses and mouths should be. Worse still, each beak had been strapped closed. They had arms and hands covered in small fluffy feathers, but they couldn't undo the straps, because their wrists had been roped tightly behind their backs. The nearest quetzal was covered in soft blue down from head to toe. It stood upright like a human, but its legs ended in claws, which shifted uneasily in a white ooze of droppings. A single bright blue tail feather trailed in the mess. Bald patches showed where other feathers had been plucked out.

Frenn pointed to the bleeding stubs behind the creatures' shoulders. "Serving boys said they had to cut their wings off to fit them all in. I thought they were joking, but —" Something unreadable passed across his face.

"Cut off their *wings*?" Rialle stretched a hand through the mesh and touched the blue quetzal's trembling, hot body. "Oh, you poor thing!" Before she realized it, she was humming *Shi*.

Frenn's hand clamped over her mouth. "Shh!" he hissed. "Stop it! Do you want to get us in trouble? You're not supposed to sing, remember?"

Rialle blinked, and two tears rolled down her cheeks. "If they've cut off quetzal wings, what have they done to my poor merlee? We've got to find them, Frenn!" She looked wildly around the dungeon.

"They're not here," Frenn said gently, pulling her away. "We've got to go back and tell Singer Toharo about these. It might take him all night to sort through that fat lord's lies."

Rialle hung back. The cages were suffocating. She didn't know how the poor quetzal could breathe.

From the far end of the dungeon came a scrape, like bolts being drawn back. "Quick, someone's coming!" Frenn dragged her through the secret door and put his shoulder to the panel, cutting off the choking smell. "Phew!" he gasped, leaning against the wall. "That was close."

Rialle looked at the hand that had touched the blue quetzal's plumage. She could still feel its tiny, hot heart beating beneath her fingers.

She made a decision. "You go back and tell Singer Toharo about the quetzal," she whispered. "I'm going to look for the merlee. If they're in the castle, I'll find them."

Frenn frowned. "I don't know, Rialle. . . . I think we'd better stick together. If those creatures are meant for the Karch, there might be karchholders around, and —"

He broke off and stared past her, eyes growing wide.

Rialle whirled, just in time to see a large hand descend on Frenn's shoulder.

"Caught you!" roared a gruff voice. "Stay right there, you little thieves! Don't even think about running."

*

The sentry didn't have a spear, but he was huge. He picked Frenn up by one arm, as if he was no bigger than a First Year, and wrenched the torch from his grasp. Frenn kicked the sentry's shins and struggled to reach the Echorium dagger in his belt. But his captor merely chuckled, cast the torch to the ground, and with a casual flick transferred the weapon to his own pocket. Meanwhile, his gaze pinned Rialle against the wall.

"Might've known there'd be a girl involved," he said, giving her a gap-toothed grin. "Can't resist all the pretty colors, can you? All right, hand over the feathers you stole, an' maybe I won't beat you too hard. Maybe not at all in your case, sweet one." He ran his tongue around his lips in a way that turned Rialle cold inside.

"You touch her, and you'll be sorry!" Frenn yelled. "And we're not thieves, we're on Singer business!" He'd managed to brace his feet against the wall, but was having difficulty freeing his arm. He pulled a face at Rialle and mouthed, "Run, stupid!"

The sentry chuckled. "Oh, *Singer* business, is it now? I doubt that, somehow. But even if you are, that makes you spies, don't it? And you know what Lord Javelly does with spies." Getting tired of his captive's struggles, he twisted Frenn's arm behind his back. The boy's face creased in pain.

Something hard and tight formed in Rialle's stomach. She

raised her chin and stared the sentry in the eye. "Let him go." She tried for some *Aushan*. But as always when she practiced the fear-song, it came out a little weak.

The sentry frowned at her, then laughed out loud. "What'll you give me if I do, sweet one?"

"I said let him *go*!"

Panic must have lent her voice strength because the sentry was clawing at his ears and had released Frenn.

Rialle stared in dismay. But Frenn was quick to take advantage. In a moment, he'd reclaimed his dagger from the man's pocket, grabbed her hand, and was dragging her up the steps and out into the night.

*

By the time they reached the banquet hall, they were both panting and shivering, but for different reasons.

"You were brilliant back there!" Frenn gasped as he pulled her through all the sweaty, wine-breathing guests toward the lord's table. "Old Toharo couldn't have done any better himself."

"I hurt him," she whispered back.

"Big deal. He was going to hurt us."

"Maybe not —"

At this, Frenn turned and pushed her behind one of the thick musty banners that hung from the rafters. "What did you think he was doing to my arm? He would have, all right? You stopped things before they turned nasty, and that's what Singers do. That's why Toharo's here. We learned all about it in orderly training."

"You learned an awful lot in four days, didn't you?" Rialle muttered. But Frenn was already scrambling onto the dais, and didn't hear.

Toharo took one look at them, then told the orderlies to pack away the bluestones, and ushered their whole party from the hall. Lord Javelly, Rialle noted, had chosen a huge pendant as his trust gift, which he fingered as he watched them leave. The Second Singer didn't speak until they'd climbed a spiral stair and entered a small round room. He left the orderlies on guard, pushed Rialle and Frenn inside, and shut the door. He put his hands on his hips and regarded them sternly. "Now then, what have you two been up to? You smell like a farm."

Frenn grinned and bounced on one of the beds, but Rialle couldn't help feeling sorry for the poor, wingless quetzal. While Frenn outlined what they'd seen — he left out the episode with the sentry, she noted — she closed her eyes and thought of dungeons. Dark. Smelly. The horrible, damp press of stone on all sides. If the merlee were in one, there'd be water, too, maybe a tail splashing —

Someone slapped her cheek, jolting her back.

She frowned at the Second Singer. The blow had been a gentle one, but it was enough to distract her from her search. Frenn stopped bouncing and sat on the edge of his bed, suddenly quiet.

"Enough of that, young Singer," Toharo said, frowning at her. "Let me deal with any farlistening from now on. The Karch is no place for adolescent tricks. Are you listening, Frenn? That includes you! I wouldn't be taking you up the mountain at all, but I don't for the life of me know what else I'm supposed to do with you. It'll be more dangerous if I leave you here, and at least if you're with me I'll be able to keep an eye on you both."

"But if the merlee are here, I can find them, I know I can."

"I know where they are," Toharo said.

Rialle stared at him, but Frenn nodded wisely. "Told you he'd find them," he mouthed.

"You know? Then . . . are they all right? Can I see them? Are we going to take them back to the sea?" Her tiredness vanished at the thought of releasing the captives into the warm seas around the Isle. They'd be able to go home to the Echorium, where Frenn wouldn't get into so much trouble, and she wouldn't have to hurt anyone with *Aushan*.

The Second Singer was watching her as if he could hear every thought in her head. He sighed. Then, to her surprise and embarrassment, pressed a hand to the cheek he'd slapped earlier.

"You're very young for this, Rialle. I don't know what Eliya was thinking of, sending you out from the Isle so soon. I think she's growing old and forgetful, which is just one more thing we have to worry about." He sighed again, and began to shake out their mattresses. "Try to get some rest now, both of you. I have a feeling tomorrow's going to be a long day."

*

Rialle dreamed of the merlee, all jumbled up with the First Singer on the Pentangle. In her dream, Eliya's lined face cracked open, and inside was Kherron, his green eyes glittering as he laughed at her shock. "Call yourself a Singer?" he said. "You can't even help your friends when they're in trouble!"

"I helped Frenn," she said.

But Kherron's lips twisted. "Misuse!" he cried. "You misused a Song. You've broken an Echorium Law, and now you must be punished." He called the orderlies, and because he was First Singer now, they came and took Rialle's arms. They dragged her to the stool, while she struggled and begged them not to. But she had no strength, and no sound would come because her moonblood had taken her voice away and locked the Songs in a small, round room inside her head —

She awoke with a gasp to find the hands on her arms didn't

belong to the orderlies in her dream, but to Frenn. He was shaking her.

"Thank the Echoes!" he said when she opened her eyes. "I thought you were going to scream the place down! It's only a dream, Rialle. Shh, silly, before Toharo hears you."

She blinked at the gray light. "What time is it?"

"High time you were up and packed. The others are down at the stables already, saddling the ponies Javelly's lending us. Toharo went off snooping before dawn, but he'll be back soon. C'mon, there's some breakfast on a platter the servants brought up — not bad grub."

They breakfasted on fruit, and were down in the courtyard before sunup, shivering in the freezing air. Clouds hid the peaks, and more clouds rose from the nostrils of Javelly's shaggy little ponies as they clattered through the tunnel under the castle wall. The orderlies had arranged a wooden contraption, like two chairs set back-to-back, across the withers of one of the ponies. Rialle rode on one side of this, while Frenn rode on the other. She had to take a pack as well to balance the weight, and felt sorry for the pony. But when she tried to get down and walk, Toharo ordered her lifted back on again. "Stop being so silly," he told her. "I don't want to lose you over the edge. It's icy, you know." Rialle privately thought they had a lot more chance of falling over the edge on the pony than off it, but said nothing.

The track climbed steeply. Soon they were so high, they entered a cloud. Rialle's stomach did a repeat of its antics aboard the *Wavesong,* and she was glad when Toharo called a halt. The Second Singer dismounted and sang a single pure note. The cloud swallowed the sound.

Rialle held her breath and listened. On the other side of the pony, however, Frenn was fidgeting. It wasn't long before he leaned across and poked her shoulder. "Get down a moment, will you? I want to try something."

She didn't have much choice. His poke had been hard enough to push her off the narrow seat. She gasped as snow trickled inside her boots. It was *cold*.

Frenn crouched to examine the snow at closer quarters. After a moment, he scooped some into his mittened hands, grinned, and tossed the ball straight at her. It hit her on the shoulder and broke in a glittering shower of ice. She let out a cry of surprise, then quickly tossed some snow back. Singer Toharo looked around with a frown.

"Now we're in trouble," Frenn said, still grinning.

But the Second Singer merely sighed. "I wondered how long it'd take you two to work that out," he said. "Stay there and try not to fall into any drifts while I'm gone. I'll be back as soon as I can." With that, he climbed onto the ridge and vanished into the cloud.

While Frenn bent for more missiles, Rialle stared after the Second Singer, absently brushing ice crystals from her braid. The note he'd sung earlier had returned as a whisper on the wind, bringing with it strange echoes.

"I'm going, too," she announced. Before her courage could desert her, she struggled onto the ridge.

At once, a massive silence settled around her. It was as if she were alone in the entire world. Slowly, step by trembling step, she placed her boots in the Second Singer's prints and crept forward. Then the cloud swirled apart, and Singer Toharo was there in front of her, so close her heart banged.

He was looking at something green near his feet.

Crushed in cold prison, can't breathe . . .

"Oh!" Rialle gasped. "Oh, *no*!"

She fell to her knees and scraped away the rest of the snow. Ice glittered beneath. Once, she supposed, it must have been a pool, but now all the water had frozen solid. Trapped inside were two merlee — one male, one female — their hair caught in silver coils, tails glimmering faintly in the snow-light, arms raised, fingers spread as if they'd died trying to push something away. Their eyes stared straight at her, turquoise and beautiful as the far-off sea on a summer's day.

From a great distance, she heard Singer Toharo say, "Don't look, Rialle."

But it was too late. Someone was singing *Shi,* and *Shi* makes you cry. Even the clouds were crying — tears of soft, drifting white that fell gently on her cheeks, where they melted and ran with her own.

"Don't, you silly girl. Don't, it's dangerous." Toharo held her tight, pressing her face to his robes until the Song was muffled. But he didn't sound angry. In fact, there was a strange catch in his voice she'd never heard before. "Come on," he said, gently drawing her away. "I think it's time I spoke to this Karchlord."

Only when they were walking back down the ridge did Rialle realize. The Second Singer of the Echorium, manipulator of lords and maker of treaties, was crying, too.

8
KHIZPRIEST

By the time they reached the Karchhold with the fish-people eggs, Kherron's backside was so sore, he was sure he'd never be able to sit down again. Ponies, he decided on the first day, were worse than rowboats. And the one Cadzi had given him was the worst of the bunch. Even the pack animals were better behaved — which was saying something, because the smell of the eggs made them snort and roll their eyes like Echorium Crazies. To add to his misery, snow had found its way through the hole Metz had made in his boot, turning his left foot into a block of ice. What he wanted more than anything else in the world was a good hot bath and somewhere soft to sleep — preferably on his front. But Cadzi had dragged him up here, into the freezing heart of the mountain, and told him to wait.

Kherron stamped his feet and blew on his hands. At least he wasn't expected to wait sitting down, not that there was any-where *to* sit in this crazy place. Flaring torches set in brackets around the walls made the red rock sweat like blood, and the whole cavern smelled of smoke. Other than that, the Karchhold was a bit like the caves on the Isle of Echoes, all interconnecting passages and concealed entrances. He couldn't wait to explore.

He glanced at the slice of dazzling snow-light where they'd come in. He considered finding his own way to whatever passed as a dormitory in this place, and asking if they had any dry boots. But Cadzi had been fair to him so far. It seemed a bit rude just to make off without a word.

"I'll count to a thousand, and then I'll go," he decided.

Bad move.

Before he reached a hundred, two men emerged from the tunnel. Cadzi was limping badly, as if he'd had to walk a long way, and the other — for a moment, seeing those long loose robes, Kherron's knees turned weak. But the robes were black rather than gray, and decorated with crimson spirals that twisted eerily as the man moved. The newcomer's skin was dark like Cadzi's, but his head had been shaved to leave a single black braid sprouting from the crown, bound at both ends by golden rings. His beard had been trimmed to a point, and he carried a spear of black crystal that glittered like the night sky without a moon.

Even as Kherron was taking a step backward, this spear swung up and pierced the exact center of his forehead. He froze.

"Well?" said the newcomer in a soft, but dangerous, voice. "Aren't you going to introduce us?"

Cadzi swallowed. "Uh — yes, of course, Khizpriest! Islander, this is Frazhin, our Khizpriest. He looks after our souls up here." He glanced at the crystal spear and added, "You'd do well to tell the truth before the Khiz."

Khiz.

A chill rippled through Kherron. He glared at Cadzi. So the karchholder had tricked him, after all. Brought him in here because he'd killed Metz, and now? The Khiz pricked his forehead, and all thoughts fled.

"So-o. You're from the Singer Isle. Not a Singer yourself, by any chance?" Frazhin said, still softly. His voice seemed to vibrate down the spear, right into Kherron's head.

"No!" All the pent-up frustration of his final interview with Eliya came out in that denial, and the Khizpriest chuckled.

"What a shame. But you claim you can be of use to us? You have — what was it again, Cadzi? Gifts?"

Cadzi nodded, his gaze still on the spear. Kherron thought the karchholder seemed tense. He tried to draw his head back from that tiny, burning prick in the center of his forehead, but he couldn't seem to move.

"What gifts do you have, Islander?" Frazhin whispered.

"I . . . I . . . I have inside knowledge," Kherron said, raising his chin. "I was born and bred on the Isle of Echoes, and I can tell you anything you need to know about Singers. You might be surprised by some of the things I know." He managed some *Kashe*, but it wasn't very strong, and — horror of horrors — his voice squeaked.

Frazhin smiled. "Oh, I doubt we'd be very surprised."

Kherron licked his lips. "There was a Singer ship in Silvertown harbor. . . ."

The Khiz pressed harder. "What do you know about that?"

"Nothing! Only that Singers don't leave the Isle unless there's a very good reason, and —" He frantically searched his memory for something, anything that might interest this dark priest. "— and maybe they've heard your Karchlord is ill. You see,

Singers believe they can heal. Usually, people bring their sick to the Isle, but sometimes the Singers send orderlies to collect Crazies from the Isle villages, and — and it's possible they might try to take your Karchlord the same way."

Frazhin let him finish. He stared into his eyes a moment, then thankfully lowered the Khiz. "Did you tell him Azri was sick?" he asked Cadzi.

The karchholder eased his weight off his injured leg. "Uh, I might have let it slip."

"Did you tell him how sick?"

"No — no details, Khizpriest, I swear!"

Frazhin smiled again and turned back to Kherron. "So, Islander. That brings us to the question of how you know so much. Are you a spy?"

"No!" What was wrong with his voice? It was all over the place.

"Oh, don't worry, Islander. I believe you. A spy wouldn't pass the test of the Khiz. Later, I'll have another little test for you. But first, run along with Cadzi and bring me those eggs I hear you were good enough to extract from the merlee for us. The Karchlord's holding a special banquet tonight, and he'll appreciate his favorite delicacy being properly prepared." Frazhin chuckled again, and stroked the Khiz with a scarred hand.

Cadzi took Kherron's elbow and hurried him out. Somehow, his legs carried him out of the cavern. But when they emerged into the snow glare, he had to stop and lean against a rock.

Cadzi gave him a sympathetic look. "Sorry about that, but there's no keepin' things from Frazhin. If I'd smuggled you into the Karchhold and he'd found out, he'd have treated you a lot worse. You know what the Khiz is now, anyway." He grinned. "Don't worry, you did fine. Now all we got to do is hand this load of eggs over to the priests, and we can relax a bit. A banquet, huh? We don't get many of them these days. I wonder what we're supposed to be celebrating?"

Kherron wasn't listening. They were moving again, and the trudge through deep snow to where they'd stabled the ponies in a lower cavern was reminding his body how much it hurt. More snow took the opportunity to melt inside his boot. And now, as if saddle sores, a frozen foot, and a cracking voice weren't enough to worry about, he had a new injury. He rubbed his forehead, half expecting his hand to come away covered in blood, but it stayed clean.

As they went, Cadzi pointed out the various entrances to the Karchhold, most of which Kherron had been too weary to notice on his way up. Some looked like shadows in the snow, others no more than piles of red rock. "That one leads to the Karchlord's levels and the banqueting cavern," Cadzi said. "You only go in there on invitation. Above the cavern we've just come from are the priests' levels. You *never* go up there."

"There are more Khizpriests?" Kherron said in alarm, thinking of all those glittering crystal spears.

But Cadzi chuckled. "Don't panic, Islander! I said priests. There's only ever one Khizpriest."

"But all the others want to be Khizpriest," Kherron said slowly, picking the truth from Cadzi's words. "How do they choose?"

The karchholder gave him a sharp look. "Very clever today, aren't we? A glimpse of the true power up here, and you want it for yourself? Forget it. Priests have short life spans, even shorter than our Karchlord's looks likely to be. Hey, there's a thought! Maybe he's havin' his funeral banquet early, in case he don't last the winter."

Kherron frowned. "What did the Khizpriest call the fish-people? Merlee?"

This earned him another sharp look. "I'd have thought you'd know that, comin' from the Singer Island like you do. That's what Singers call them. Wrote it into some treaty a while back. Fish-men's good enough for the rest of us, though. What's the point in giving things fancy names? Only confuses people."

By this time, they were back in the pony cavern. Cadzi ducked under the rail and caught the arm of a tall, skinny boy who'd been rubbing down the animals they'd ridden to the Karch.

The boy stared curiously at Kherron, who stared back equally curiously — had he really been singing to the ponies? Whistling actually, but it was quite tuneful, and it filled the cavern the way they'd been taught to fill chambers with songs back in the Echorium. Under the boy's hands, Kherron's willful mount of the past three days was quiet as a dopey dolphin, its ears flicking back and forth in obvious pleasure.

"How did you do that?" he said. "That beast hated me."

The tall boy grinned. "You've just got to know their language, that's all. One day I'm going to fight for the Karchlord Azri, and when I do I'm going to need my mount on my side, so I practice every chance I get. These lowland ponies can be a bit funny sometimes, but they're affectionate enough once you earn their trust. Aren't you, my beauty?" He gave Kherron's mount a final pat, then vaulted the rail to land lightly beside Cadzi, who'd taken the easier route out again.

"Need some help, old man?"

Cadzi scowled. "That's enough of your cheek, single-braider! Those packs we brought with us have to go up to the priests' audience cavern. You an' the Islander can take them up between you — give you a chance to get to know each other."

He chuckled and turned to Kherron. "This lanky pony lover's my son, name of Lazim. Always whistling some nonsense or another. You two should get along like an avalanche. Now I got to go sort out Metz's woman. Apparently, she's throwin' a fit in there, wanting to know what happened to his body. These Karch women can get quite violent when they're upset, so you'd be best keepin' out of her way for a while, Islander. If you can manage to drag young Lazim here away from his precious ponies when you've finished, he'll show you where you can get something to eat and do something 'bout that boot." He glanced at Kherron's foot, then gave Lazim's braid a fond tug and limped off through the snow.

The two boys eyed each other. Kherron looked at the swinging braid with its bone fastening and thought of Metz floating in the harbor. "You've killed someone already?" he said.

Lazim flushed. "Oh, that's just my manhood braid. We all get one when we turn fourteen so everyone knows we're not children anymore. This is just a quetzal finger bone — I asked for it specially, because I wouldn't feel right wearing some dead woman's finger. . . . But I'm not afraid!" he added, with a glance at the priests' entrance. "If Lord Azri asks me to kill for him, I'll do it."

"What's a quetzal?" Kherron asked, which seemed more tactful than asking who Lazim was intending to kill.

The boy avoided his eye. "Oh, they're just Half Creatures. Less intelligent than ponies, or so people say. I never seen a live one."

There was something he wasn't telling, strange vibrations in his words. Kherron was too cold and tired to work it out.

"Maybe we'd better get these eggs delivered?" he suggested.

Lazim nodded in relief, strode across, and seized two of the packs. "Right! Keep the priests happy, that's what Father always says. That way they leave us alone."

It took three journeys to ferry the eggs to the priests' cavern. Each time the red rock closed around him, Kherron broke out in a sweat, but the place didn't seem to worry Lazim at all. He chattered the whole time, his long legs making short work of the snow, and didn't seem to care when the tunnels carried his voice deep into the mountain. But then, Kherron supposed he did live here. Maybe it was like the Pentangle in the Echorium. Some people screamed when the orderlies dragged them to the stool, whereas once you understood how the Songs worked, it wasn't so bad. You could even fight them if you knew enough.

"I bet he's powerless without that Khiz-spear of his," he muttered, thinking aloud. He glanced over his shoulder at the dark entrance, now high on the slope behind them.

"What did you say?" Lazim crunched to a stop and blew on his hands. "Brr! Do you think it's getting colder? I'll bet there'll be more snow tonight. Soon we'll need sleighs to get up and down the mountain — you'll like that, Kher! No riding!"

Kherron eased the bangle he'd taken from Rialle off his arm, and slipped it into his pocket. "You go on," he said. "I think I dropped my bracelet in the priests' cavern somewhere. I'll meet you in the stables, all right?"

Lazim frowned at his arm. "But I'm sure you . . ." Then he grinned. "Ah, I get it — the ponies, right? Don't worry, I won't be much longer. Then we'll go grab us something to eat. I'll bet you're starving! Father never was much of a one for feeding on the march. He says in the old days, the Karchlord's army used to ride for weeks without food or sleep. Says we're all growing soft and fat. He's probably right. There hasn't been a decent fight in years."

Kherron smiled as he began to climb back through the snow. He didn't want Lazim to think he was afraid of ponies, but neither did he want any son of Cadzi's to know what he was really up to. He had a feeling that what he was about to do didn't exactly fit with "keeping the priests happy."

*

By the time he'd climbed back to the priests' cavern, the eggs had gone — or at least, they were in the process of going. Wraithlike forms in black and crimson swooped silently upon the packs, gathered them under their robes, and vanished as silently as they had come. Though Kherron crept as close as he dared and strained his eyes through the shadows and smoke, it was impossible to see where the priests were coming from or where they went.

He stood in the middle of the empty cavern, staring around at the hundreds of tunnels in frustration. Then, out of nowhere, Singer Graia's voice whispered in his head. *"Use all your senses. Use your ears."*

How could he have forgotten? Smiling, he closed his eyes.

There. A faint echo trickling down one of the tunnels, like wet seaweed squelching underfoot.

He crept into the tunnel. It was very dark. But as his eyes adjusted, the darkness formed itself into stairs, winding almost vertically in a tight, steep spiral. Kherron eased his feet upward, step by trembling step.

As he climbed, the squelching noises grew louder. Then torchlight flickered ahead. He knelt and peered cautiously around the spiral.

It was another cavern, much smaller than the one below. A dark opening in the opposite wall suggested the stair continued — but between him and the other opening, three priests sat cross-legged around a large basin. Purple steam rose from this basin, filling the cavern with a burnt-hair smell.

Kherron held his nose and eased farther up the spiral for a better view. The priests all looked identical with their bony faces, pointy beards, and shaven heads, but they were obviously the ones he'd spotted below, for the packs waited in a pile on the floor next to a huge golden tureen with ornate handles. Each priest had a small bowl in his lap and wielded a long needle of glittering red metal.

The procedure was this. A priest would take an egg out of one of the packs, drop it into his bowl, dip his needle into the basin, carefully pierce the egg, then add it to the tureen. Every time an egg dropped in to join the others, it gave a small squelch.

Kherron clenched his teeth. The sound reminded him of Metz's ship, when he'd put his hands inside the freshly slain merlee and felt around. The priests worked quickly, but there were thousands of eggs still in the packs, and no hope of getting through the cavern without being seen. He'd have to find another way.

He'd begun to back down the stair, groping his way in the dark, when something cold touched the back of his neck, gentle as the kiss of a snowflake.

Hairs rose all over Kherron's body. For the second time that day, he froze — one foot dangling in space, hands braced against the cold rock. It's nothing, he told himself firmly. No one's there.

"Soo-o," came a hiss in his ear. "If it isn't the Islander, spying." The spear pricked harder. "You told the Khiz you weren't a spy. Explain!"

What an idiot! To get caught by the Khizpriest himself.

"I — I thought someone was harming the eggs, sir!" Kherron's brain fumbled for a decent excuse. "I, uh, heard the packs being carried off, and I didn't want anything to happen to them, not after bringing them so far and going to all the trouble to get them in the first place. So I came to check they were all right."

"You heard my priests moving around?" Frazhin's voice was dangerous, but the Khiz relaxed slightly.

"Um, well, not exactly, sir. More heard the eggs, actually, squelching as they moved them."

"Is that so? You have sharp ears, Islander."

The coldness retreated. Kherron slumped against the wall and put his dangling foot back on the stair. He was shaking like a First Year. What had happened to his voice? No point even thinking about trying to use a Song until it sorted itself out.

He took a deep breath, then another. *Find out how the Khiz works.*

"What are they doing to the eggs, sir?" he asked.

Frazhin chuckled, put a hand on his shoulder, and pushed him back up the stair. "You're polite, Islander, I'll give you that. Go on up and have a look. It must have been hard to see very much from where you were hiding."

Kherron stiffened. "I'm supposed to be meeting Lazim. . . ."

Frazhin's voice hardened. "If the Khizpriest of the Karch wants you, then everyone else takes second place. I'll forgive you this once, since you're new. But from now on, don't refuse me. Understand?"

"Yes," Kherron managed, "sir."

Behind him, in the dark, Frazhin chuckled again. "There aren't many Karch boys who'd dare come up here like you did. Go ahead, they won't bite."

The priests working on the eggs did not look up when the Khizpriest pushed Kherron into the cavern. Frazhin peered over their shoulders, dipped his khiz into the purple smoke, and stirred the contents of the basin.

He gave Kherron a dark smile. "This is the Lord Azri's secret medicine," he said. "Only priests know about it. The karch-holders think merlee eggs are magic, and so does the Lord Azri.

I don't want his faith destroyed. If I hear any rumors about the eggs not being magic after all, I'll know where they started. Understand, Islander?"

Kherron nodded quickly, eyes on the dripping khiz. He understood enough. The Khizpriest had just as much power over people as Eliya did, maybe even more. He'd traveled halfway across the world, and nothing had changed.

*

He spent a miserable afternoon in the smoky cavern with the priests, keeping them supplied with eggs from the packs and transferring the eggs to the tureen once they'd been injected with the purple medicine. The work had a relentless rhythm, as bad as any exercise in tempo his teachers had given him back in the Echorium. Already sore after clinging onto the pony's mane most of the way up the mountain, Kherron's arms trembled with the constant need for minute, careful movements. The Khizpriest had given him a little spoon of red metal for the job, and soon Kherron hated that spoon more than the pony he'd ridden to the Karch, more than the rowboat he and Cadzi had escaped in, more than the First Singer herself.

When Frazhin vanished up the second stair, he remembered why he'd come and tried to draw the priests into conversation. But they ignored him so completely, he decided they must be deaf. Then he dropped an egg with the tiniest plop, and all three glared at him while he fumbled around on the floor with the spoon. They weren't deaf.

By the time he'd added the last egg to the tureen, his stomach told him he'd missed lunch and probably supper as well. He rocked back on his heels in relief and rubbed his arms, wondering where to start looking for Lazim. But before he could escape, the Khizpriest returned, saving him the bother.

The priests rose to their feet in a swirl of crimson and black, put the lid on the tureen, and lifted it between them. It wobbled slightly as they staggered toward the stair, and Kherron watched curiously, wondering what Frazhin would do to them if they dropped it. But of course they didn't drop it. Down they went, as silent as before, guiding the tureen around the narrow spiral so skillfully, it didn't even scrape the rock.

Frazhin observed Kherron's arm rubbing with some amusement. "Tired, Islander?" he said. "Not used to physical work, are you?"

Kherron stiffened. "We don't eat merlee eggs on the Isle. That's the first time I've prepared them."

"No, of course you don't — I was forgetting." Frazhin's smile did not touch his eyes. "And nor does anyone here — only the Lord Azri, remember? So no sneaking one from the pot. That medicine's powerful. If anyone steals the Lord Azri's eggs, I always know."

Kherron bet he did. Not that he had any intention of eating one of the foul slimy things, medicine or no medicine. "I won't, sir," he promised.

Frazhin smiled again and caressed his khiz. "Good. Now then, time for your little test."

"But —"

"You thought that was it?" The smile widened. "You've much to learn about the ways of the Karch, Islander. Follow me."

Kherron followed meekly, down the dark stair, across the audience cavern, and deeper into the mountain. They passed through huge underground vaults where torches flared bright as day, then ducked along low tunnels where the trapped smoke made Kherron cough. When he was hopelessly lost, certain the Khizpriest was going to vanish up some dark stair and leave him here as punishment for spying on the eggs, there came the sound of voices, laughter, and music, a glimmer of torchlight, and — best of all — the mouthwatering scent of meat roasted with herbs.

Kherron's stomach growled, which drew another amused look from his guide. "Hungry, Islander? You've come at the right time. Quiet, now."

They pushed through a curtain and plunged into light and noise, into flame flashing off red metal and gold, into the press of human flesh, into colors worn in eye-clashing combinations with no thought for the songs they sang. The cavern was so high, Kherron looked up expecting to see stars. Instead, he saw clouds of smoke. But there had to be a roof somewhere, because massive pillars of twisted rock plunged out of that smoke to meet the floor, where they'd been carved into circular tables for the karchholders' feast. The chunks removed from the pillars had been fashioned into huge chairs that looked much too heavy to move.

As Kherron blinked around, trying to take all this in at once, the Khizpriest — who'd somehow got behind him again — took hold of his elbow. He steered him to an alcove, where another curtain partially blocked their view of the banquet.

"Look over there," he said, holding the thick material aside. "The central pillar, the table raised above all the others. Tell me what you see."

Kherron stretched his neck to see past all the heads and flashing goblets. He was uncomfortably aware of the Khiz balanced across Frazhin's palm, but the Khizpriest made no attempt to use it — yet. He wondered if Lazim was here somewhere, and if he was mad at him for not turning up. Then Khizpriest, khiz, Lazim, sore backside, frozen foot, aching arms, hunger, thirst, ponies, merlee eggs, even his cracking voice, faded to nothing beside what he saw in the center of the Karchlord's banqueting cavern.

"Singers," he whispered, and a chill shot from the center of his forehead all the way to his toes.

9
QUETZAL

Rialle perched on the edge of her cold stone chair and stared miserably at her plate. Her feet didn't reach the ground, and the wide armrests, carved from the same block as the seat, meant she couldn't even lean over and whisper to Frenn, who sat in another gigantic red stone chair beside her. The orderlies were at the same table, but the way it was cut around the pillar, they all had to sit with their backs to the karchholders, so this didn't make her feel much safer. To make things worse, Singer Toharo was on the opposite side of the table, partially hidden by the pillar in the center. She couldn't ask him anything without getting up and walking all the way around the platform, which he'd specifically forbidden them to do.

"No creeping off this time and poking your noses where you shouldn't," he'd warned them both. "I have important matters to discuss with the Karchlord Azri, and I can't be worrying all the time about what you two are up to. Just sit quietly in your

seats and behave yourselves. No farlistening, Rialle! And whatever you think of the Karchlord, don't let it show. Remember,
we're his guests."

Guests they might be. But the Karchlord wasn't here, and the
Singer party was the object of much whispered speculation.

Rialle's back prickled at the thought of all those eyes staring
at her. She pulled her hood farther forward, pushed a stray blue
hair inside, and sneaked another look at Frenn. He was busy
devouring some slices of white meat with his usual appetite. Her
stomach clenched.

At last he looked up. "All right?" he mouthed.

Rialle shook her head. Her hands were cold. Her feet were
cold. She couldn't face food. And although she was thirsty, the
wine in the red metal goblets was foul. She'd spat her first
mouthful back in disgust. Every time she closed her eyes, she
saw the poor merlee frozen in their pool of ice.

"How can you eat that?" she whispered. "It might be merlee
meat. Or a child!"

Frenn patted her arm. "Don't be silly, Rialle. They have
children of their own here — look. 'Sides, it don't taste at all
fishy. Here —" He took an orange fruit off the edge of his plate,
leaned over, and slipped it onto hers. "If you don't like the meat,
try this. It's quite edible. Better than seaweed salad."

Rialle started to laugh, choked at this reminder of the
Echorium, and slid to the other side of her seat to see what
Toharo was doing.

The Second Singer's hands were clenched on the arms of his
chair. His head twisted from side to side, eyes scanning the
cavern. Every time a servant climbed onto the platform to pour
the disgusting wine or bring a new dish to the table, he stopped
them with a sharp note and asked when Azri was coming. The

servants stammered that the Karchlord wasn't feeling well, he'd come when he was feeling strong enough. They trembled when the Second Singer used *Aushan*, giggled when he changed to *Kashe*, but always the answer was the same. Toharo let them go with increasingly exasperated sighs, drummed his fingers on the stone arms, and went back to searching the many smoky tunnels and alcoves for a sign of their host. After a while, the servants stopped coming to their table.

"Azri's probably trying to decide how dangerous we are," Frenn said through another mouthful of meat. "Bet you anything he's already here, spying on us from behind one of those curtains."

Rialle turned cold. She glanced over her shoulder.

Frenn chuckled. "If I were the Karchlord, I wouldn't come at all. He's broken that treaty Toharo told us about, hasn't he? The one to protect the Half Creatures? Toharo will give him a hard time, you can be sure. . . ." His voice trailed off, and he frowned at something across the cavern.

Rialle twisted in her chair, but all she could see were drunken karchholders. She was just about to risk trying the orange fruit when everyone at the far side of the cavern suddenly began cheering, whistling, and banging their plates with their swords.

A bugle sounded. As the echoes circled the unseen roof, a loud voice called out, "Make way for the Karchlord Azri! Overlord of the Silver Shore, Blessed of the Khiz, Prince Among Men!"

The Second Singer leaned forward in his chair. Something hot and tight lodged itself in Rialle's throat as she fixed her eyes on the tunnel. She wanted to leap up and scream, *Why did you kill the merlee? Why? Why?*

Two young karchholders entered first, each with a single

braid in his hair. Between them, they carried a black banner emblazoned with two red swords crossed above a jagged lightning strike. Next, three shaven-headed men in black-and-crimson robes struggled with a huge golden tureen. Behind them, four older karchholders carried the Karchlord himself on a red metal throne supported by long poles. Almost unnoticed at the back of the procession, a small boy hurried with a pair of gilded crutches.

Rialle stared in confusion. As the procession came closer, it became obvious Azri was no older than Frenn. His thin arms were weighed down by bracelets, his legs covered by a scarlet blanket, his dark hair loose and unadorned. When he lifted a hand to brush something from his eyes, there was such a look of pain on his face, she winced in sympathy.

"Is this some sort of joke?" Frenn whispered. "That can't be the Karchlord, surely?"

"Don't feel sorry for him," Rialle whispered back, hardening her heart. "Remember what he's done. Whatever's wrong with him, I'm sure he deserves it."

The karchholders carried their Karchlord onto the platform and lowered his throne beside Toharo's chair. The tureen was placed beside it within easy reach. One of the shaven-headed men removed the lid, bowed, and backed down the steps. The banner was raised up the central pillar by pulleys, until it swung in the smoke above their heads. The small boy stood quietly behind the throne with the crutches.

Singer Toharo sat back. He said something that floated around the table on a soothing wave of *Challa*. Azri smiled a little and whispered a reply. Without taking his eyes off the Second Singer, he dipped his hand into the tureen, picked out something small and green, and swallowed it. Berries, Rialle supposed, finding it difficult to maintain her hatred for the Karchlord. He was probably too sick to eat anything else.

Frenn fidgeted beside her. "What are they saying? I can't hear."

"I can't hear, either."

Frenn frowned at her tone. "C'mon, Rialle! Are you afraid you'll get into trouble? Toharo didn't mean you couldn't farlisten across the table, for Echoes' sake! Go on, I won't tell."

"I don't feel like it. I've got a headache." It wasn't an excuse. Ever since the banquet had started, a tightness had been growing behind her eyes, just like on the day they went searching for wreckage on the west beach.

Azri, she noted, didn't offer the Second Singer any of his berries. Meanness fitted her mental picture of him, and she felt a bit better about hating him. Toharo, however, didn't seem too upset. He had, in fact, shifted himself farther away from the tureen, as if he didn't like the look of what it contained. The berries did have a strong smell, almost fishy. Rialle wrinkled her nose. What was it Singer Graia had said? *Use all your senses?* The smell seemed strangely familiar, only her brain was too sore to think.

"Wonder what's wrong with the Karchlord's legs," Frenn said.

"I don't care. I hope he dies."

"Rialle!"

"You didn't see those poor merlee." She blinked and took a deep breath. "I hate it here. I wish Toharo would hurry up. I want to go home."

"It *is* a bit cold —" Frenn began, rubbing his hands. Then they both flinched as Toharo jumped to his feet and thumped the table with his fist.

"Half Creatures *do* have feelings, I tell you! Your priests are lying to you."

Toharo's Singer-trained lungs filled the entire cavern with *Aushan*. Rialle had never seen him so angry, not even after she'd swum with the merlee. She cringed. The karchholders at the other tables looked around in alarm, hearing the Song even if they were too far away to hear the words.

Azri paled and seemed to shrink into his throne. The karchholders who'd carried him to the platform crowded around protectively, hands on their swords. Rialle caught her breath. But at Toharo's hum, they froze. Then Azri whispered something, and they backed off.

Toharo, lips pressed tight, sat down. He beckoned one of the orderlies to bring his pouch, and opened it across the wide arm of his chair. Silver shimmered in the torchlight, and the flames made the bluestones ripple like the sea.

"What's he doing?" Frenn said, peering around the pillar. "What are they saying now? Rialle, *please* listen. It might be important." He gave her a sly look. "Maybe they're talking about your merlee. Those you found on the mountain might not be the only ones that got captured."

Rialle looked at him sharply. She hadn't thought of that.

Quickly, she closed her eyes and imagined what it would be like on the other side of the platform, between the Karchlord and the Second Singer. The click of bluestones as Toharo replaced them, Azri's labored breathing . . . a small jerk, and she was *there*.

"They're talking about the treaty," she reported. But she couldn't concentrate with her sore head, and kept losing the sense of it. Azri said something about his sickness. Toharo replied it was his own fault and he should come to the Isle for therapy.

Frenn's eyes lit up when she reported this. "Bet you anything he's too scared," he whispered. "Eliya would give him *Yehn* for what he's done. *Aushan*, at least."

"Shh!" Rialle frowned. Toharo had just said something about merlee and eggs, but she'd missed it. She tried to focus, getting snatches of Toharo and Azri's conversation all mixed up with Frenn's.

Suddenly, the Karchlord convulsed, frothed at the mouth, and began to bang his head against his throne. Rialle jerked back in alarm, her heart thumping. Had she done something to him, trying to farlisten when she wasn't feeling well? But the fit didn't last long, and no one seemed very surprised, least of all the Second Singer. No sooner had the karchholders rushed forward to hold him, than Azri slumped back against his throne, panting heavily. Toharo sat back with an exasperated sigh.

"He's faking it," Frenn said in disgust, scowling at the Karchlord.

"No —" Rialle began.

But she didn't have time to explain the strange feeling she'd picked up from the Karchlord as she jerked away. For at that moment, a second bugle blast echoed through the cavern.

"What now?" Frenn said, twisting in his seat to look.

A strange drumming noise echoed in the rock, growing louder and louder. The karchholders looked around curiously, and Singer Toharo glanced up. Rialle squeezed her hands into fists as a pony and rider galloped out of one of the tunnels, dragging what looked like two bundles of feathers on the ends of long leather leashes. A few people screamed.

"Echoes!" Frenn hissed. "Now he's done it, for sure."

Fluffy hands tied in front of them, two of the quetzal they'd seen in Lord Javelly's dungeon skidded in the wake of the pony, scrabbling at the rock with their claws in a desperate attempt to remain on their feet. The poor things looked as if they'd already been dragged up the mountain on their faces. What was left of their bright plumage dripped melting snow, and their beaks were packed with ice. The blue one Rialle had touched through the mesh of its cage had somehow kept its sole remaining tail feather — but not for much longer. Karch children dared one another to grab this tempting prize as the creatures were dragged past.

Reins in his teeth, the rider galloped his pony right up to the central platform, where he jerked the quetzal forward until they bounced against the edge and collapsed in shivering heaps at the Karchlord's feet. Rialle bit her lip. The blue quetzal's eyes were fixed upon her, pleading silently.

Singer Toharo leaped from his chair and glared down at Azri. "What is the meaning of this?" His face darkened to the color of a thundercloud. His voice would have stopped a storm in its tracks.

Azri opened his eyes. He blinked at the quetzal a moment, then beckoned for his gilded crutches. With the boy's aid, he struggled to his feet and shuffled to the edge of the platform for a better look. A hush fell over the cavern, broken only by the crackling of the torches.

"What are these birds doing in here?" Azri whispered.

"I beg the indulgence of the young Lord Azri, Overlord of the Silver Shore, Blessed of the Khiz, Prince Among Men!" The rider dismounted and made an exaggerated bow. "These are the quetzal I told you about. You remember the feathers my Lord Javelly sent up before the snows for your bed? Well, they came from creatures like these. Now he sends you a mating pair so you might breed them in your Karchhold and sleep in comfort for the rest of your days."

The karchholders muttered uneasily. There were undercurrents in the rider's voice, not terribly polite ones. The rest of your days, he seemed to be saying, won't be many.

Toharo's scowl deepened. "This is a direct violation of the Treaty!" he said to the rider. "I warned your lord only yesterday. Is his memory span so short, he's forgotten our trust gift already?"

The rider smirked. "My Lord Javelly sends his gift to the Karchlord, Singer. If the Lord Azri accepts, the quetzal will no longer be Javelly's property."

"Clever," Frenn muttered. "That sneaky lowland lord's put Azri in a corner. It's called politics. We learned a bit about 'em in orderly training. Watch what Azri says now."

Rialle couldn't have cared less what Azri said, so long as the quetzal weren't hurt anymore. "Singer Toharo will help you," she whispered. "Just hold on a little longer."

Meanwhile, Azri leaned on his crutches and squinted at the quetzal. "Why did you cut their wings off?" he asked. "They can't fly very far in here."

Laughter rippled around the cavern, although it hadn't been a joke. Rialle thought she even detected shades of *Shi* in the words. She frowned at the Karchlord.

Javelly's rider smiled. "Wing feathers aren't soft enough for mattresses, my lord. Besides, wings make them troublesome in public, and they have other talents that might amuse you. Have I your lordship's permission to demonstrate?"

Azri closed his eyes and seemed to think this over. Or maybe he was in more pain than she'd thought, because he swayed a bit on his crutches. Beside him, Toharo tightened his lips. But before either the Karchlord or the Second Singer could say anything else, one of the shadows underneath the platform uncoiled and stepped into the light.

Rialle turned cold all over without knowing why. For the first time since the poor creatures had been dragged into the cavern, she forgot about the quetzal, and remembered Toharo's warning back on the *Wavesong*.

Beside her, Frenn stiffened. "It's one of them creepy black-robes who came in with the Karchlord," he whispered. "The sneak must've been hiding under there the whole time, listening to what we've been saying."

But Rialle saw at once it wasn't one of the men who'd carried the tureen. He might have been dressed the same, but this man was much older, and he had hair — a long black braid, at least, sprouting from the crown of his head. Something dark glittered in his hand. She couldn't quite see what it was, some kind of spear maybe. Where the flames touched it, colored lights danced, now crimson, now purple, now dark blue —

She tore her gaze away. Toharo's head turned sharply, and the two men stared at each other in silence.

Listening, Rialle thought. He was there all the time, listening to us.

The newcomer's black eyes shifted from the Second Singer to the quetzal. He studied the creatures a moment, then asked casually, "Are they good to eat?"

The quetzal moved closer to each other, trembling afresh. They'd obviously understood.

Javelly's rider fiddled with the ends of the leashes and shot a glance at Toharo. "Er, yes, Khizpriest, very good. Not that I'd dare taste meat destined for my lord's table myself, of course! But I understand my lord has asked his cooks to experiment with methods of preparing them. He says to tell the Lord Azri a wine sauce is best. Karch wine, naturally."

Nervous titters rippled around the cavern.

The Khizpriest didn't smile. "Bring one over here."

The rider passed his pony's reins and one of the leashes into nearby hands. He dragged the blue quetzal closer to the Khizpriest. It fought weakly against its leash, looking back over its shoulder at its mate. "This is the female," the rider said, with a sly look at Azri. "If you care to look closely, you'll see where she lays her eggs."

The Khizpriest lifted the quetzal's shivering tail feather with his glittering spear. Her beak was still strapped, even as it had been in Javelly's dungeon, but she managed a muffled squeak and began to struggle anew. The feather finally came loose, trailing from the Khizpriest's dark fingers like blue fire.

Rialle curled her hand, remembering the softness and heat, the feel of that fast-beating heart. Then the quetzal's musky fear-scent reached the platform and she sneezed violently.

The Khizpriest turned his head, and for a horrible, breath-stealing moment stared straight at Rialle. Then his black gaze passed on and stopped at the Karchlord. "I'll have my priests boil this one for you, Lord Azri," he said in the same casual tone as before. "The meat might do you good. As you can see, I've already plucked the creature for the pot." Chuckling, he let the blue tail feather float to the floor.

Rialle looked at the Second Singer in anguish. Why didn't he *do* something?

Azri's hands tightened on his crutches. He seemed to be struggling to get the words out. At last he whispered, "I don't eat Half Creatures."

The Khizpriest's brows came down. "If you want to get well, my lord, you'll listen to one who knows, and send this stranger from the Western Sea back where he belongs. It's obvious he doesn't understand our ways."

"If you cook them, I won't eat them!"

Priest and Karchlord glared at each other. But the argument seemed to exhaust Azri. Afterward, he had to be helped back to his throne by his karchholders, where he sagged, panting again.

Toharo had watched the entire exchange, stroking his chin with one hand, eyes narrow. Truth-listening. At last, to Rialle's relief, he began to hum deep in his throat, and said, "The Treaty specifically forbids consumption of a Half Creature. I admit the eggs are a gray area, but to cook a full-grown quetzal for human consumption would violate the Treaty, and I'd be forced to take action." He turned to the throne. "If you're as anxious as you say you are to restore goodwill between us, Lord Azri, then I'd suggest you return these quetzal, and any others this man brought up the mountain, to the forest where they belong and let them go."

The captives lifted their black eyes to the Singer, a glimmer of hope in their little faces. But Azri pressed a delicate hand to his eyes and stared at the floor, as if he hadn't even heard.

The Khizpriest turned a triumphant gaze on Toharo. "These negotiations have overtired the Karchlord. I suggest you sit down, Singer, and let the Lord Azri finish his meal in peace. I'll deal with the quetzal now."

"You will not!" Toharo's voice was sharp, *Aushan* again. "I haven't heard the Karchlord give you permission to touch these creatures. Or should the Echorium be making treaties with priests now?"

Rialle almost cheered.

Javelly's man didn't know where to look. He cringed under the Second Singer's glare, darted another glance at the Khizpriest, licked his lips, and finally appealed to Azri. "Maybe your honored guests from the Echoing Isle would care for some amusement while you decide what to do, my lord?" he said slyly. "When your priest hears these quetzal, he might change his mind about cooking them."

Azri removed the hand from his eyes and frowned at the rider. He glanced at the Khizpriest, then gave a weak wave of assent. The Khizpriest scowled, but said nothing.

Now only Toharo was left standing on the platform, tall and imposing in his gray robe, with his blue curls tumbling loose down his back. Rialle wondered if he was going to sing to the entire Karchhold. *Give them Aushan,* she willed silently. *Make them all scream.* Then she kicked herself for thinking such a thing. There might be innocent people here, who'd never dream of hurting a Half Creature. About the first thing they learned in the pallets was that a Singer must never misuse a Song. Evidently the Second Singer thought the better of it, too. For after a moment, he shook his head and returned to his seat.

Javelly's rider looked relieved. He glanced around the cavern, then dragged the blue female toward a table where some Karch women were arguing in shrill voices. The Khizpriest followed, sweeping karchholders out of his way with his spear. Azri leaned back against his throne and closed his eyes. Only Toharo remained rigid with disapproval, lips pressed into the tight line Rialle was beginning to know so well.

She watched Javelly's man remove the strap from the blue quetzal's beak and push the terrified creature closer to the argument. The women carried on regardless. Nothing else happened.

"Huh!" Frenn said. "If I were her, I'd peck that creepy priest's eyes out, at least."

"Shh! I'm trying to listen."

Someone near the demonstration was finding it very funny.

Laughter rippled outward from the group. Rialle pushed the pain to the back of her mind and closed her eyes. Hardly a jerk, and she was *there*.

". . . fascinating," the Khizpriest breathed.

It was no good, she had to see as well. Slowly, focusing on the Khizpriest's voice, she opened her eyes. It was strange at first, hearing in one place and seeing from another, but not too bad as long as she kept her head still.

The women gawked over their shoulders and, one by one, fell silent. But the argument continued — first in one shrill voice, then in another. The children at the same table giggled. The blue quetzal turned its unblinking eyes upon them and giggled, too. Those karchholders near enough to see what was going on clapped their hands in delight.

"It's a perfect mimic!" exclaimed the Khizpriest. "Amazing! Javelly was telling the truth, for once."

"It's a perfect mimic!" exclaimed the quetzal. "Amazing!"

Azri's eyes snapped open. He leaned forward and looked from quetzal to Khizpriest and back again. For the first time since he'd been carried into the cavern, he laughed out loud. The blue quetzal fluffed her feathers and copied the Karchlord's high-pitched laugh exactly.

Frenn laughed, too. "Brilliant!" he said. "Do you think they can sing as well?"

Rialle sat very still, a chill creeping up her spine. "I hope not," she whispered, suddenly seeing the danger.

Toharo, his cheeks paler than she'd ever seen them, gathered his robe about him, crossed the platform in two long strides, and gripped the backs of their chairs. "Come on, you two," he whispered. "Quickly. Don't say a word until we're safely away from those creatures, do you hear? I have to get a message to the

Echorium as soon as possible. . . . Echoes! Why didn't we know about this before?"

*

As the quetzal repeated the Khizpriest's words, Kherron's lips twitched.

He'd spent most of the banquet huddled miserably in the alcove where the Khizpriest had left him, peeping around the curtain now and then to check that the Singer wasn't looking his way. But when that quetzal said, "It's a perfect mimic!" in exactly the same tone as Frazhin, and the Khizpriest's cheeks turned purple, even the fear the Singer would hear him wasn't enough to stop his laugh from bursting free.

It was a long time since his voice had been so full of *Kashe* and, even if it was all over the place, the Song made him feel better. He collapsed on the bench in the alcove and pressed his hands to his mouth. What fun he'd have if he could somehow smuggle one of those creatures back to the pallets.

Then Frazhin dragged the curtain aside and jerked the Khiz in his direction. "Quiet!" he said. "No time for that nonsense."

Kherron leaped to his feet, the *Kashe* gone as if it had never been. "I'm sorry, sir! I wasn't laughing at you. Only that quetzal was so funny —"

The curtain fell again, cutting the two of them off from the banquet. The Khiz came up in a glittering arc and pierced Kherron's forehead. He clenched his fists at his sides and swallowed. Now he didn't feel like laughing at all.

"Singers," the Khizpriest whispered. "You said Singers. Plural. I see only one. Explain!"

"I —" Kherron licked his lips. "I only meant they're all from the Echorium. The Singer's the one in the silk robe with the blue hair. The rest look like orderlies to me."

"Are you quite sure? First impressions can be quite revealing."

"Why . . ." He hated the way that icy touch played with his head. Jumbling his thoughts, making his voice squeak. "Why is it so important, sir?"

"Let's just say those silly creatures of Javelly's have given me an idea. I'd heard they did party tricks, but I had no idea how good they were. I want you to take another look. The Singers are leaving now, and they'll have to pass this way. There's a hole in the curtain just here. Look very carefully, Islander, and don't try lying to me. The Khiz will know."

Kherron shuddered. He believed it. As instructed, he put his eye to the hole. Frazhin moved with him, keeping the Khiz just beneath his ear. Kherron slid his eyes sideways and wondered what his chances were of knocking the spear out of the Khiz-priest's hand and dropping it by "accident" on the rocky floor. It looked fragile, though somehow he doubted it'd break as easily as he hoped.

"Pay attention," Frazhin said.

The Singer party was now striding swiftly toward one of the tunnels. Though the curtain concealed him, Kherron couldn't help jerking back as the tall Singer passed so close to the other side, he could have reached out and touched him. That blue hair, the swirling gray robe, the arrogant chin, those eyes fixed straight ahead, a deep frown between them, the subtle aura of power . . . Male Singer, he couldn't help thinking. That could have been me.

"Pay attention!" Frazhin snapped again.

Kherron returned his eye to the hole. There were eight order-lies altogether, all dressed identically in Singer gray. The shortest wore a cloak with the hood pulled up, which seemed a bit strange indoors, even if it was nearly cold enough in here to freeze the sea. Kherron frowned and moved the spy hole for a better look. Then the one in the cloak turned his head to say something to his companion, who was also a little on the short side for an orderly. Kherron jerked back a second time.

Ridiculously long blue hair, moist gray eyes, a voice sweeter than honey . . .

"No," he whispered. "No, it can't be."

He was still reeling with confusion when Frazhin pushed him back against the wall, touched his forehead with the tip of the Khiz, and said, "I see. Very interesting. Very interesting indeed."

*

The Singer party had been assigned a small, damp cave in a disused part of the Karchhold, with only a thin curtain to shield them from the freezing drafts that howled along the tunnels. There were very few torches down here, and the walls glistened with sheets of ice.

Toharo said it was an insult, but Rialle was glad to escape the banquet and the sight of those poor quetzal being tortured. Boil them in wine? How could anyone *do* such a thing? Even Toharo hadn't tried very hard to stop them. Maybe he'd do something after he'd sent his message to the Echorium.

She watched the Second Singer as he exchanged quiet words with the orderlies. Two left the cave to stand guard outside the curtain, while the other four found places on the low stone benches that lined the walls. Frenn passed them goblets of water from a red metal jug that had been waiting in the cave when they got back, and the orderlies drank deeply before wrapping themselves in their cloaks and going to sleep.

Rialle licked her lips as the water sloshed into the goblets a second time. It was a good thing she was thirsty or she couldn't have drunk water that left such an unpleasant metallic aftertaste.

No one complained, though. Even Singer Toharo gulped noisily, then wiped his mouth with his sleeve before setting the empty goblet aside and getting to work.

Rialle knelt on the floor and watched, fascinated, as the Second Singer took a silk-wrapped package out of his robes, laid it on one of the benches, and peeled away the silk to reveal a rough, uncut bluestone about the size of a sea-eagle's egg. Frenn darted out with drinks for the orderlies in the tunnel, then hurried back in to watch as well. He poured the last of the water for himself and scowled into the goblet. "Typical," he muttered. "I do all the work, and there's only half a cup left for me."

"Shh!" Toharo said. "I need absolute silence for this." He cupped his hands around the bluestone and closed his eyes.

Rialle held the shell end of her braid so it wouldn't tinkle. The silence wasn't really absolute, not now that she was listening closely. The torch spat sparks that hissed in the ice coating the wall, there was a chink outside as one of the orderlies set down his goblet, and everyone's breathing suddenly sounded three times as loud as normal. But Toharo straightened his shoulders, filled and cleared his lungs a few times, then brought the bluestone to his lips and began to sing.

The first note was pure as sunlight over the sea, soft as the shadows in the Echorium, as perfectly controlled as any Rialle had heard on the Pentangle. Her heart began to beat faster. It wasn't a Song, as such, but it brought memories so vivid and real, she almost expected to see Eliya in the cavern when she turned her head. She shut her eyes and sighed as Singer Toharo's song transformed the freezing cave into the First Singer's five-sided chamber filled with gentle Isle night noises and a warm salt breeze from the sea. Any moment now,

Chissar would walk in, and he and Frenn would start laughing and joking.

The song faded all too soon, and red rock closed around them once more. The Second Singer shook his head and lowered his hands. "Tired," he muttered, frowning at the bluestone. "Must be tired."

Frenn yawned. "Me, too! I could sleep for a week."

Rialle leaned against the nearest bench and curled her legs under her cloak. "Is that why you gave bluestones to Azri and Javelly?" she asked. "So you can talk to them at a distance? Is that what the merlee meant when they called me stone-singer?"

Toharo came to sit on the bench. He rested a hand on her head and gave a soft hum. *Challa*, shh, *Challa* makes you dream. . . . "Don't worry about that now," he murmured. "You'll learn the use of bluestone all in good time."

"But you *were* speaking to Eliya just now, weren't you?"

"Mmm." Toharo's hand lifted, and he chuckled. "I'll have to watch my job. Some Singers don't pick up anything at all unless they're actually touching the stone."

"Did you tell her about . . ." She frowned, blinking to clear the mist from her eyes. ". . . tell her about the frozen merlee?"

Toharo pulled his robe around him and settled against the wall. He sighed. "Try to get some sleep now, young Singer. I know it isn't very comfortable, but . . ." He yawned. ". . . but at least it's . . . Echoes, but I'm tired!"

There was nothing more from the Second Singer. When Rialle looked around to see why, she couldn't help a giggle. Toharo's chin had fallen forward onto his chest, and he'd fallen asleep sitting up, his blue curls shadowing his face.

"Suppose it must be pretty tiring singing all the way to the Isle from here," she said, turning to Frenn. "How do you think blue-stone works?"

She half expected another lecture. No doubt he'd learned it all in orderly training. But Frenn had curled up against the bench, his head resting on his arms, sound asleep, too.

Rialle giggled again. They'd both have stiff necks when they woke. She looked around for somewhere to lie down, but the orderlies and Toharo between them had taken up all the bench space. Maybe if she folded her cloak and used it for a pillow? She started to fumble with the clasp, but the floor didn't seem nearly as hard as it had when she'd first sat down. It was like . . . a cave full of quetzal feathers, warm and soft, and she was sinking. She gave up on the clasp, curled on the floor next to Frenn, and surrendered to the darkness with a smile.

She might not have been so relaxed had she known the orderlies on duty outside the curtain were both sound asleep, too.

10
CAPTIVE

The Khizpriest was up to something. A First Year would have picked up that much. But as to *what* he was up to . . . try as he might, Kherron couldn't discover a thing.

Crouched in the dark at the back of the pony cavern, he rubbed his forehead and frowned. It had to be something to do with the Khiz. Ever since the Khizpriest's glittering spear had touched him, his voice had been as weak as Gilli's and almost as uncontrollable as Frenn's. If he tried to use a Song to get answers, the karchholders just laughed at him and told him to run along and make himself useful clearing snow from the tunnels with the other boys. He couldn't even find out why the Singers were in the Karch, though after that little show at the banquet, he thought he had a fair idea.

"They weren't looking for me at all," he said. "Ha! They don't even know I'm here."

One of the ponies snorted, and Kherron shifted back a bit. A rail kept the beasts out of this area, presumably because the roof was so low they'd brain themselves if they tossed their heads. He'd have moved the rail and let them get on with it, except it would probably upset Lazim, and Lazim was the only friend he had in this place. Anyway, no one ever came down here now that the blizzards had started, so it made a useful hiding place.

He found a more comfortable position in the straw, took out the quetzal tail feather he'd picked up after the banquet, and ran it thoughtfully through his cold fingers. In the gloom back here, it glowed like bluestone under a full moon. Was there some power in the quetzal plumage? Something the Khizpriest wanted for himself? One of the ponies rolled its eyes at the strange glow, but the feather itself told him nothing. Kherron tickled the straw with it, frustrated.

"C'mon, Lazim," he muttered. "Where are you? It's feeding time, you know."

Even as he spoke, there was a rattle at the cavern mouth, and the ponies crowded around the outer rail, whinnying and nipping one another. One animal squealed, and there was a brief kicking match before Lazim's voice sang out. "Whoa, my beauties, there's plenty for all of you. Stop that now, no need to push. . . ." Almost *Challa,* the words turned into a soft whistling as Lazim ducked under the rail and began to measure grain into the mangers.

Kherron waited until the boy had finished the feeding and started to break the ice on the water trough before he climbed to his feet. "Lazim?" he whispered.

"Who's there?" No *Challa* in that.

"It's me." He hobbled stiffly to the rail. The nearest ponies, seeing him loom suddenly from the shadows, shied.

Lazim cursed. "Get off my toe, you stupid lump of khiz-dung!

That really you, Kher? Khiz, you gave me a fright!" He came to the back of the cavern, elbowing ponies out of the way with a casualness Kherron had to admire. He put his head on one side and gave Kherron an amused look. "What on earth are you doing hiding back here? I thought you hated ponies."

Kherron smiled. "I do, but I hate shoveling snow more, and I needed to ask you something. I knew you'd come down here eventually."

Lazim ducked under the rail, pushing aside curious muzzles. He grimaced. "Someone's got to look after the poor things. It's all very well for Father to bring them up from their pastures. But as soon as it starts snowing, all the multi-braiders disappear inside till spring, and it's left to us single-braiders to keep things working properly." He frowned at Kherron. "What's so important, anyway? It's freezing back here. Why didn't you wait for me in the dorm?"

Kherron scowled. "And have half the Karch listen in? Don't be stupid, Lazim."

The boy's expression turned wary. "So what did you want to talk to me about?"

"I need to know more about your priests. What do they get up to in those secret caverns of theirs? How does the Khiz work? Why is the Khizpriest so interested in the quetzal?"

"You don't ask questions like that in the Karchhold, Kher! Not if you want to live."

"Is he really going to boil them?"

Lazim shrugged. "Who cares? Just so long as nobody tries to boil my ponies." He stroked one of the muzzles, which had huffed at this, almost as if the animal understood. "Don't worry, little one," he murmured in his *Challa*-voice, "you're safe. Only Half Creatures like merlee and quetzal can heal our Karchlord."

"It's not the Half Creatures that heal him, you idiot —"
Kherron broke off, a sudden flare lighting up his head. Echoes!
How could he have been so *stupid*? He'd seen it with his own
eyes, hadn't he? There was Azri, hobbling around like an old
man. And the Khizpriest prepared all the Karchlord's food.

Lazim stared at him, interested now. A pony nibbled his manhood braid, unnoticed. "Go on," he said.

Kherron shook his head. "No time to explain now. I don't
suppose you know where the Singers are staying, do you? I have
to warn them about the Khizpriest." Now that he'd decided
what to do, it was as if he'd gained the top of the Five Thousand
Steps, with the knowledge that any way he chose to go from
here would be easier. The Second Singer might even be grateful enough for his warning to put in a word or two with Eliya
when they got back. He started to duck through the rail, but
Lazim blocked his way.

"No, I don't know. It's a secret. And you don't ask about
secrets in the Karchhold, not if —"

"I know, not if you want to live. But the Singers were at the
banquet the night the blizzard started. Surely they wouldn't try
to get down the mountain in this weather? They must still be
here somewhere. This is important, Lazim!"

He filled his lungs with warm pony smells and tried for a
Song. It was painful, but in the end some *Kashe* squeezed out,
though an octave lower than he'd ever sung it before. He decided
he liked the result. No time to think about it now, though.

"C'mon, Lazim," he said, forcing a smile. "There's always
rumors going around a place like this. You must've heard something."

The boy smiled back. "Oh, I hear a lot. But I keep my mouth
shut."

Kherron rather doubted that. "Come on! You can tell *me*. I'm not about to spread it around, am I? No one would listen to me, anyway. You know they treat me like dirt up here. A pale, soft-handed Islander who hasn't any hair to put a manhood braid in, even if he could lift a sword in the first place." More *Kashe*.

Lazim glanced at the flattened straw where Kherron had been sitting. He chewed his lower lip. "I'm sorry, Kher. Father said not to tell you."

"And I suppose you do everything your father tells you, do you?" The *Kashe* shattered. It was all he could do to keep his hands from the Karch boy's throat.

Lazim made a fist and struck the muzzle nibbling his braid. The pony reared back with a snort of surprise. He shook his head. Slowly, he said, "I suppose it's only fair you should know, since you're from the same island. But if you're thinking of rescuing the Singer, think again. You've met the Khiz when the Khizpriest is in a good mood. Think what it can do when he's angry."

Kherron shuddered, but he had something. *Rescue the Singer*. His heart beat faster. Better and better. All he had to do now was keep his head.

"Lazim," he whispered. "If you know something, please tell me. Are you saying the priests have the Singers up there, as well as the quetzal?"

The boy bit his lip. "I've already said too much."

"I promise I won't tell anyone where I heard it."

"You can promise nothing! Not before the Khiz! You don't understand."

"I do understand." No Song in that, just truth. He took a deep, calming breath. "Lazim, if you tell me about these rumors you've heard, I'll tell you something you might be very interested in concerning your Karchlord's health."

The boy stared at him a moment, then glanced at the munching ponies. He slipped under the rail and beckoned. "In here," he whispered.

Kherron eyed the beasts doubtfully. But it might be worth it to hear what Lazim had to say. With a sigh, he ducked under the rail.

The boy pulled him right into the thickest press of bodies. Swishing tails stung Kherron's eyes, shaggy quarters bumped him. His leaky boots squelched in urine-soaked straw, and he hated to think what else he might be treading in. He breathed through his mouth and stuck close to Lazim.

At last, the boy stopped and glanced around again. They were sandwiched between two of the tallest beasts. Kherron couldn't even see over their withers. Still not satisfied, Lazim leaned down and whispered what he knew in Kherron's ear.

Kherron felt the blood rush to his head and drain away again. He had to grip the nearest mane to keep from falling under the ponies' hooves.

"It's only a rumor, you understand," Lazim said quickly. "I expect they're all still alive up there somewhere. Priests spread rumors like that when they take people, to cover themselves if things go wrong — and there was only one Singer in the delegation, wasn't there? I expect that's where the rumors about the others being dead came from. The priests' levels are so big, they could have the whole of Silvertown up there, and no one would ever know." He squeezed Kherron's arm. "Now it's your turn. What do you know about Lord Azri's health?"

Hating to think what the Khizpriest would do to him if he found out where the information had come from, Kherron told Lazim he suspected the priests were poisoning the merlee eggs.

*

When Rialle woke up, she was lying on the red metal floor of a cage.

At first she thought, This is a dream. She'd dreamed of the locked room in Frenn's head often enough, and of the Songs inside — sometimes just vague blobs of color, other times flaring at the windows, trying to get out. But she'd never dreamed of them quite like this before, nor of herself locked inside with them.

She turned her head, still half asleep, expecting to see Frenn and the orderlies, and Singer Toharo still asleep sitting up on the bench. But the shadows on the other side of the mesh were deep and dark, and her nose tickled.

She sneezed.

She'd never sneezed in a dream before.

She jerked fully awake, heart pounding, and stared at the red metal in terror. The cage was inside a cave, all right, but not the one where she'd fallen asleep. Smoky crimson light came from two torches set on opposite walls, enough to show her the glint of more cages set around hers in a rough circle.

"Frenn!" she screamed, her voice choking in fright. "Frenn! What happened? Where are we?"

She leaped to her feet and rushed to the mesh, counting. One, two, three . . . seven cages, only seven! Someone was missing. Then unblinking black eyes fixed upon her, haloed by crumpled feathers, and she realized the shapes in the other cages weren't fully human. She pressed her hands to her mouth as soft ruffling sounds came from the shadows. "Quetzal," she whispered.

"Quet-zal . . . quet-zal . . . quet-zaalll . . ." The word echoed around and around the cave, growing and fading again, just as the Pentangle had caught and magnified her voice.

She whirled and stared at the shadows in confusion. Then

she realized. The creatures' beaks were no longer strapped. "Oh, Echoes . . ."

"Oh, Echoes . . . Echoes . . ." the quetzal repeated. "Quet-zal, quet-*zaall*."

She pressed her hands even harder to her mouth. What had Singer Toharo said when he led them from the banquet? *Don't say a word until we're safely away from those creatures.* She looked around the cage in fresh horror. The door was locked. All it contained was a bucket in the corner with a badly fitting lid. Obvious what it was for, but the thought she'd be here long enough to have to use it made her tremble all over. Whoever had brought her here had taken her cloak, and the cave was freezing.

But there was worse to come. No sooner had the quetzal fallen silent, than soft footsteps approached out of the shadows, and the old priest from the banquet appeared. He stopped outside her cage and looked in at her. His spear glittered as he pushed it through the mesh.

Rialle took a step backward, her breath coming faster. Her knees turned weak, her head sparkled with stars. If he touched her with that thing, she knew she was going to faint.

But the spear came no closer. "I don't want to hurt you, young Singer," the Khizpriest said gently. "All I ask is that you sing your magic Songs for me. Once should be enough — the quetzal are quick learners. After you've sung, I'll have my priests bring you something nice to eat and drink. I'm sure you must be very hungry. You slept a long time."

He chuckled, and the spear tinkled against the metal of her cage. The quetzal must have liked this sound, for the tinkle came back from all sides, like Isle glass breaking. "It's a perfect mimic!" one finished in the Khizpriest's voice. "Amazing!"

Rialle flinched.

The Khizpriest gave her a dark smile. "See?" he said. "What did I tell you? Quick learners and excellent memories. They put my priests to shame. Now, are you sure you understand what I want you to do?"

Rialle clung onto the mesh, trembling afresh. "I can't," she whispered.

The Khizpriest raised one eyebrow. "I hope you're not going to try telling me you're not a Singer. I have it on good authority, and then there's the hair. I should have realized earlier, that beautiful blue braid you were hiding under your cloak all this time." He lifted the end of her braid with the tip of his spear.

Rialle snatched her hair away with a shudder. She licked dry lips. "What have you done with the others? Where's Singer Toharo? You can't keep us here like this! When the Echorium finds out —"

The spear raised again. "Ah, but they're not going to find out, are they? At least, not until it's too late. Who's going to tell them? You?" His chuckle was like darkness seeping out of the earth.

"What do you mean?" she whispered, her stomach churning.

"I know a lot more about Singers than you think. This little bluestone, for instance?" He reached into his robe and opened his hand.

Rialle's heart sank. "That's Singer Toharo's! Where is he? What have you done to him?"

"I'm sure you're old enough to understand I couldn't risk news of your capture getting back to the Echorium. After all, I need only one Singer to teach my quetzal. You should be glad I chose you."

The *Shi* burst from her, even as it had when she'd seen the merlee frozen in the pool. She slid down the mesh. Her knees cracked on the metal floor. *Yehn*, whispered the Khizpriest's dark voice. *Yehn*, death.

After a horrible lifetime when she thought the darkness would take her, too, she became aware of the Khizpriest watching her, a smile on his face. She raised her tear-streaked face and squeezed her hands into fists, ashamed he should see her like this. Singer Eliya wouldn't have approved.

"Good," he said. "You carry on like this, and we'll get along just fine."

For a moment, Rialle didn't understand what he meant. Then she realized the quetzal were still singing. *Shi*. Though the tears would not stop, she pressed her knuckles to her teeth and swallowed the Song. She shut her eyes tightly. A dream, she willed. Please let it be a dream. Please, please, please.

But when she opened her eyes, the Khizpriest was still there.

"Seems I chose well," he said, his smile broadening. "You have a lovely voice, young Singer. Don't stop on my account." He withdrew his spear and walked away.

Rialle gripped the mesh until it cut into her fingers. "Wait!" she called, her voice ringing around the cave.

He turned in surprise.

She took a deep breath. "I need water if I'm going to sing properly — good, clean water. And I need food as well — fruit and vegetables, not meat. I can't sing unless I keep my strength up. And I — I need that bluestone. Singers can't work without one."

He came back and frowned at her through the mesh. Her heart thudded as he caressed his glittering spear. Then he smiled again. "Water and food, yes. But not the stone, I think. You Singers pride yourselves on sorting truth from lies, but you forget others might have this gift, too." He chuckled, and touched her forehead lightly through the mesh with the sharp tip of the crystal. "I admire your courage, young Singer. But don't try lying to me again." His final words were dangerous, almost *Aushan*. He gave her a narrow-eyed look, then swept out of the cave in a swirl of black and crimson.

Rialle clung onto the mesh until he'd vanished into the dark heart of his domain. Only when she was sure he'd gone did she put her freezing fingers into her mouth. She began to shake violently. *Not a word*, she thought. *Not a word*.

The only sound that passed her lips all night was when her stomach retched up onto the floor of her prison what remained of the sleeping draft they'd all drunk.

*

Kherron could think of two ways to get into the priests' levels. One was to sneak up there and spy on them in the hope one of them would lead him to the captives — not his favorite option, after what had happened last time. The other was this.

He'd been waiting in the audience cavern for what seemed like all day, blowing on his fingers, jogging in circles to keep warm, and running his story through his head until it was word perfect. But in all this time, no one came. He began to get impatient. Didn't the karchholders ever worry for their souls? The cavern got gloomier and gloomier as the blizzard piled more snow outside. If he waited much longer, the drifts would seal the entrance, and he wouldn't be able to get out again. Not a nice thought.

He peered at the dark openings in the walls. Though he couldn't hear anything, he bet they were watching his every move. Just as they'd watched when he'd been waiting for Cadzi to come back — Of course! That was it.

He smiled and said loudly, "I'll count to a thousand — no, make that a hundred, and then I'll go."

As he'd guessed, on the count of ninety-nine, a shaven-headed priest appeared from one of the tunnels. "I want to see the Khizpriest," Kherron declared. The priest nodded, beckoned that he should follow, and silently led the way up one of the spiral stairs.

They must have climbed far past the level of the cave where he'd helped poison the merlee eggs, though it was difficult to tell for sure. The stair twisted so much, he couldn't even be certain they'd gone straight up. Finally, the priest led him along a low tunnel where they both had to duck, and into another cavern.

Kherron caught his breath. The whole place had been polished, and hundreds of Kherrons loomed out at him from the red walls, distorted horribly because the rock wasn't flat. Here he had a huge stomach and tiny head, here a monstrous face with huge eyes and gaping mouth balanced on fragile quetzal-like legs, here he was tall and thin, here squashed into a blob. Kherron grinned, put his fingers into the corners of his mouth, and made a face at the nearest wall. He laughed at the result. Just for a moment, he forgot where he was. It'd be fun to get the others in here, make Gilli scream.

Then the Khizpriest was standing behind him.

He whirled, heart in his throat. It was if Frazhin had stepped out of the reflections. Black eyes studied his face a moment. Then, quite unexpectedly, the Khizpriest laughed, too. "If it isn't the Islander! Come to see your little Singer, have you?" He laughed again.

Little? Toharo was the tallest Singer he knew. Kherron said carefully, "What have you done with him?"

"Her, Islander, her. You do remember, don't you? The pretty one in the cloak who gave you such a funny turn? She's being more stubborn than I anticipated. Maybe you can talk some sense into her."

Kherron swayed. The polished walls started to make him feel sick. For a horrible moment, he wasn't sure where the floor ended and the rock began. His carefully rehearsed story went clean out of his head. "Her?" he whispered. "You mean —?"

Frazhin chuckled. "Why don't I show you? That's what you came up here for, isn't it? To gloat? No love lost between you two, so the Khiz informs me."

Kherron thought fast. He didn't know what he'd been thinking when he saw Rialle in the Karchlord's banqueting cavern, but whatever it was, the Khiz obviously didn't know, either. He curled his lip. "She got me into a lot of trouble once. I have a debt to repay."

The Khizpriest's black brows came down. For a moment, he thought he'd overdone it. But Frazhin shook his head and said, "Sometimes I don't know what to make of you, Islander. All right, follow me. Something tells me this should be interesting."

They entered another maze of tunnels. They didn't use any stairs, but he had the feeling some of the tunnels sloped. He got so involved counting turnoffs and strides and trying to work out where they were in relation to the rest of the Karchhold, he didn't realize they'd arrived until he heard muffled sneezing ahead.

He quickly covered his own nose. Quetzal reek.

Then he saw her.

Her hair was a mess, frizzing out of its braid, and her orderly's clothing rumpled and stained. A jug of water, half drunk, sat just inside the door of her cage. A foul-smelling bucket occupied the opposite corner.

Kherron stared at the cage, all sorts of emotions chasing through him. Locked in a cage like a Half Creature . . . He couldn't think how it had happened. Surely Toharo would have tried to stop them from taking her? Then a chill rippled through him as he remembered Lazim's rumors, and suddenly it didn't matter how many times Rialle had bettered him in class. No one deserved this.

He thought she was too far gone to care. But the moment the Khizpriest stepped into the light, Rialle scrambled to her feet. "I'm not going to sing, however long you keep me in here," she announced in a quavery voice. "So you might as well kill me now and be done with it."

Kherron saw how her words made Frazhin's hand tighten on the Khiz. Heart racing, he stepped past the Khizpriest. "You idiot, Rialle!" he hissed. "Do what he says. Are you trying to make things worse for yourself?"

The gray eyes widened. She stared at him in pure astonishment for ten rapid heartbeats, then let out a little cry and staggered to the far side of her cage, where she clung onto the mesh, her back turned, shoulders shaking.

Kherron walked slowly around the cage, acutely aware of the Khizpriest watching his every move. When he was facing Rialle again, he lunged forward and gripped her fingers hard. She tried to pull away, but his hands had muscled up during the ride to the Karch, and it was easy enough to hold her. She glared at him through the mesh.

"Why are you doing this?" she whispered bitterly. "Do you hate the Echorium that much? Singer Toharo would never have found you if you'd stayed hidden. He thought you'd drowned! It was your own fault for running away in the first place, and now the Second Singer's missing, and I don't know where Frenn is." She choked. The gray eyes brimmed with tears.

Kherron looked over her head, through the double layer of mesh. Frazhin, of course, was listening to every word. "Do what the Khizpriest says!" he said loudly, pushing his face close to hers and squeezing her fingers hard. "Do you hear!"

She glared at him again, as he'd known she would. When he was certain she was looking at his lips, he mouthed in a pallet-whisper, *"I'll get you out. Trust me."* He let go of her fingers, straightened, and sneered down at her. "You're pathetic!" he added with as much venom as he could muster. For good measure, he spat into her blue hair — and though he'd been waiting for years for a chance to do exactly that, he didn't enjoy it. Not one bit.

"Pathetic!" echoed the quetzal, giving him a bit of a jolt. "Pathetic, pathetic!"

Huddled on the floor of her disgusting cage, Rialle shuddered. He'd been afraid she wouldn't understand. But she had the sense not to look up.

*

The priests might enjoy keeping prisoners, but it soon became obvious they didn't like getting their hands dirty looking after them. So after that little test, Kherron got the job of feeding the prisoners, and later — when he was trusted with the keys — cleaning out their cages. It was disgusting work. The quetzal messed worse than ponies, and pecked his fingers if he got too close. And though Rialle was cleaner, the less said about carrying her slop bucket outside to bury its contents in the snow, the better.

Kherron made sure he complained all the time so the Khizpriest wouldn't suspect. But whenever he fed Rialle, he seized the opportunity to exchange a few hurried pallet-whispers. Since part of his job was supposed to be to persuade her to sing, he punctuated these with loud threats for the benefit of the silent priests waiting at the entrance. Rialle played her part a lot better than he would have, had their positions been reversed. Sometimes she acted the righteous Singer, other times getting quite upset and bursting into tears. Kherron suspected not all these were faked. He felt sorry for her and knew the longer she stayed in the cage the more chance there was the Khizpriest would lose patience and try a more direct method of persuasion, but he couldn't risk leaving the door unlocked as she wanted him to. Where would she go? The blizzards still raged, filling the Karchhold with drifts of blue ice. If she ran off and hid in the lower caverns, the priests were bound to find her eventually. Then he'd be in trouble, too, and their one chance of getting out of here would be gone.

"When it stops snowing," he told her, time after time. "Then we'll escape."

She gripped his hands hard. "Frenn and the others? You'll get them out, too?"

"I'll try," Kherron promised.

But no matter how much he snooped, he could find no sign of Singer Toharo or the others. It looked very much as if Lazim's rumors might be true, but he was afraid that if he told Rialle, the news would destroy what little strength she had left. She looked very pale and ill, and she hardly ate a thing as it was.

The day the wind finally stopped howling through the tunnels, she flung herself at him and started telling him some nonsense about bluestone, and how she might be able to contact Eliya for help if he'd only bring her the stone the Khizpriest had stolen from Toharo, or the necklace Singer Toharo had given to the Karchlord at the banquet. Kherron eased her off, sat her down gently against the mesh, and went to get the slop bucket. Rialle's whimpers did funny things to his insides, and he forgot to spit on her as he left. He suspected she was turning into a Crazy. He didn't blame her. He knew he would, stuck in that cage.

He did the business with the bucket and carried it back up, thinking hard. He'd have to do something soon. The only question was, what? The blizzard might have eased off, but the snow it had left behind was so deep it came up to his chest in places. He couldn't imagine going anywhere very fast in this, even in the new boots Cadzi had found for him. What had Lazim mentioned? Sleighs? He was thinking so hard, he didn't notice he wasn't alone in the tunnel until the Khiz hissed out of the shadows and pinned him against the wall.

Kherron swallowed his heart and quickly banished all thoughts of escape from his head.

But the Khizpriest had other things on his mind. "This is taking too long, Islander! The blizzard's stopped. You promised me you'd have her singing before now."

What could he say that wouldn't be a lie? "Give me a few more days, sir. I've been making good progress."

A frown. "I'm not so sure. Something's giving her strength, hope even. What I can't work out is where she's getting it from — certainly not from you!" The Khizpriest chuckled, then gave Kherron another jab with the Khiz. "Tell me about Singer powers, Islander. How do they use them, exactly?"

"I, um, don't know, sir. I'm no Singer."

"So you said before. But you told Cadzi you'd had this Song treatment. How did they give it to you?"

With feeling, Kherron described the Pentangle, the Singers standing on the five points, and the spinning stool in the center. "They give people a special potion beforehand," he said. "I don't know how it's made." Which was the truth, because no amount of bribery would get the orderlies to talk about how they mixed the Song-potion. For once, Kherron was glad he didn't know something. The recipe would have marked him as an insider, for sure.

"Do the Songs work without this potion?" the Khizpriest asked.

Kherron said sort of, and tried not to think of Metz falling into Silvertown harbor.

"And what about the spinning? How does that help?"

Kherron shook his head. "I don't know."

Frazhin sighed and lowered the Khiz. "We'll have to forget the potion and the spinning, anyway. Five points? Javelly sent seven breeding pairs, so if I take five ships, put a pair of quetzal on each, and keep the Singer with me, that still leaves a few to play with. Good! Your little Singer must be quite attached to her cage-mates by now. I think it's time we found out how much she cares for them."

Kherron cleared his throat. "Ah . . . sir?"

A frown. "What is it now?"

He took a deep breath. "Can I ask what you plan to do with the Songs?"

Frazhin laughed. "Haven't you worked that one out yet, Islander? When your little Singer has taught the quetzal all she knows, I'm going to take the lot of them to the Echoing Isle and let them sing to their hearts' content. Then my priests will be able to go in and finish off these Singers without the help of the Karchlord's pathetic army, and none of us will be bothered with such things as Singer delegations and treaties ever again." He chuckled. "That please you, Islander?"

Kherron smiled weakly. Even though the Khiz had released him, he knew he couldn't risk a spoken reply.

*

Rialle heard the entire thing, sitting in her cage with her knees drawn up to her chest. To her dismay, she didn't know what to make of it.

As soon as she'd woken after that awful first night in the cage, she had begun a methodical search of the Karchhold, far-listening for any hint of Frenn and the others. It wasn't easy. Not only didn't she know where the other prisoners were being kept, which meant she couldn't focus on their surroundings, but every time she thought of Frenn's blue eyes, lopsided grin, and stupid jokes, she lost all concentration and jerked back to the cage, trembling. Following Kherron around was simpler, since she only had to stay with him when he left the cavern. She'd felt certain he was on her side, yet now he seemed to be helping the Khizpriest. . . . Or was he? Truth-listening over a distance was impossible. She could only go on his actions, and he hadn't made much of an effort to find Toharo's party. Maybe he didn't want to find them. Or maybe there was another reason.

"Frenn isn't dead," she whispered fiercely. "He isn't!"

"Frenn isn't dead, he isn't!" mimicked the blue female, who seemed more attentive to her voice than the others.

Rialle stared at the fluffy blue fingers gripping the mesh of the cage nearest the entrance, and turned cold as she remembered what she'd just overheard. If the Khizpriest threatened the quetzal, she didn't know what she'd do.

"If I could only talk to you," she whispered. But apart from repeating her own words and embarrassing fits of tears, all any of the quetzal ever did was hoot and whistle softly — though sometimes the blue female stared at her so intently, Rialle was sure she was trying to tell her something. She clenched her teeth in frustration. If she could sing to the creatures as she'd sung to the merlee, she might be able to make them understand the danger of mimicking her. Except that was exactly what the Khizpriest wanted.

This was getting her nowhere.

She pushed the quetzal firmly to the back of her mind, took deep breaths, and settled herself against the mesh for another session of farlistening. The only trouble was, she couldn't concentrate on the endless caverns of smoky red rock. As they did more and more often lately, her thoughts drifted to the distant sea.

Stone-singer?

Curl of a rainbow tail. Strong green hands pulling her through sunlit waves.

. . . be warm and safe in the shoal.

Rialle smiled. "Merlee," she whispered.

Stone-singer come swim. Safe now. Hunting stop.

Their songs were faint as the distant waves and contained echoes of sadness. She knew now that many had been lost to the hunters the day she swam with them, including their shoalfather, and that she'd been lucky to escape capture herself. But no more nets had come since and they were happy now.

"I wish I *could* swim with you," she said. "But it's not over yet." Then she reminded them they must be careful, because the hunters might come again. In return, the merlee reminded her of the world outside the cage, giving her the strength to hold on, because one day she might get out.

"Who are you talking to, young Singer?"

There was a sudden roaring in her ears, and the gentle seasongs were replaced by alarmed quetzal hoots, her warm dream by the cold kiss of the Khizpriest's spear.

Though she'd expected him to come, Rialle stiffened. "No one," she said, still slightly disoriented.

The Khizpriest's eyes narrowed. "Never mind. I've got an interesting problem for you. Watch."

Rialle's heart sank as he crossed to one of the quetzal cages and jabbed his spear through the mesh. The trapped quetzal scrambled away from the crystal, whistling wildly, but there was no escape. Almost gently, the Khizpriest stroked the glittering tip down the nearest creature's breast.

"I understand they're fragile little things," he said. "Let's say I kill one a day until you sing for me — and because I know how much you'll miss them, I'll leave the bodies in here to remind you. Soon as you start singing, I stop killing. Fair?" He drew back his arm.

Rialle leaped to her feet. "No!" she gasped.

The Khizpriest smiled and withdrew the spear. "So you do care for them. How sweet." He lifted a dark eyebrow. "Well? I'm waiting."

Rialle licked her dry lips. "I need more water, and some time to warm up my voice. It's been a while since I sang, and I have to do my breathing exercises." All true, but mostly she needed to talk to Kherron. He'd *have* to let her out now.

The Khizpriest gave her a narrow stare. "You've got until dawn," he said in the end. "If the quetzal aren't singing by then, the blue one dies." With that, he swept out of the cavern.

Rialle sagged against the mesh. She was tired after farlistening all the way to the Western Sea, but sleep would have to wait. She closed her eyes and concentrated, forming a mental picture of Kherron's most recent surroundings. He'd gone from the priests' levels, and she wasted several sunsteps searching for him in all his usual haunts. The dormitory, the cooks' levels, the pony cavern . . . She almost gave up at this point, in the hope he'd come with her breakfast before the Khizpriest came to murder the quetzal. But there was one place she hadn't tried.

Teeth clenched, she thought of the Karchlord's levels. The smallest of jerks, and she was *there*.

Azri spent most of his time asleep, so she expected to hear his servants again, whispering about stupid things — the sort of whispers that went around the pallets, but seemed a whole world away from the red cage and the terror she lived with every day. But tonight, Azri was definitely awake, and it seemed she was only just in time.

"So you're the Islander?" Azri said in his scratchy voice. "I've heard a lot about you. You're the one who told my loyal friends here about the poison in the merlee eggs, aren't you?"

"Yes, sir, I did."

Kherron's voice had that new depth she'd noticed lately. What was he up to now?

She listened uneasily.

"I didn't know whether to believe you at first," Azri went on. "When I stopped eating them, my headaches got a lot worse, and the fits came more often. But then I found I could stay awake longer, and I started to remember things. Yesterday I walked all the way around my bedchamber without my crutches. My men tell me poison can work this way — take away the pain but make me sick at the same time." He paused.

Rialle held her breath. There was a tension in the Karchlord's cavern, the sort of silence you got on the Pentangle just before a Song. Kherron wouldn't be there alone. How many people were with him? She thought she heard a man cough, the sound muffled as if it had been caught in a hand.

"And now my loyal friends tell me you've more information for me. They also tell me you know a way to heal my fits that doesn't involve a long voyage to the Singer island. Is this true?"

"Yes, sir."

"I'd like to hear this way."

Several people in the Karchlord's cavern exhaled. There was a rustle, as if they'd all relaxed slightly. A few scrapes — weapons? No, they were sitting down, dragging chairs across the rocky floor. Flames crackled in a brazier, and she heard a servant empty coals into it with a rattle. They kept their Karchlord warm enough. Sometimes Rialle could draw comfort from the sound of the fire alone, but this time she grew colder and colder as she listened.

"Sir," Kherron said. "As you now know, your Khizpriest is holding a Singer captive in the priests' levels. He's also got the quetzal that Lord Javelly sent you. Remember what happened at your banquet? Well, I think I've found out what he's up to. I think he plans to use the Singer to teach the quetzal the Songs of Power, and then he's going to use the Songs to destroy the Isle. So far, she hasn't sung for him, so they're still here. Your Khizpriest's plan might work if you don't get the Singer out of there soon, but it gave me an idea, too." He lowered his voice. "All we need to do, sir, is to sneak you up there long enough for the Singer to give you a session of therapy. Usually, you'd need at least five Singers, but with the quetzal mimicking her voice, I'm certain the Songs will work for you here just as well as they work in the Echorium."

Rialle stopped listening at this point, put her arms around herself, and shivered hard. "No, Kherron," she whispered. "No, no, no."

11
KARCHLORD

They brought the Karchlord to her that very night, a pair of grim-faced karchholders carrying him on a seat made from their clasped arms. Kherron put his finger to his lips and quietly unlocked the cage. He placed a velvet cushion on the floor so Azri wouldn't have to sit on the cold metal. Then the karchholders lowered their lord inside the cage and left in a hurry, casting nervous glances at Rialle as they went. If the whole thing hadn't been so deadly serious, she would have laughed. How could grown men with bones in their hair possibly be afraid of her?

Kherron, seeing her expression, hurried across and grabbed her hands. Coward, Rialle thought bitterly. You could have warned me. If I hadn't farlistened, I wouldn't have known this was coming at all. But she held her tongue because the Karchlord was watching them. Sitting there on his cushion in his loose bed robe with his head resting against the bars, he seemed very young.

"I know what you're thinking," Kherron said in a pallet-whisper. "But we've worked it all out. Azri didn't know what his priests were doing. They've been poisoning him for years to keep him weak. Now he's stopped eating the poison, his body's getting stronger, but he still has fits. If you cure him, he's promised to take us back to the Isle and ask Eliya's advice about the Khizpriest. All you have to do is sing him therapy."

She shook her head. "You know I can't sing up here, Kherron. That's just what the Khizpriest wants."

If Kherron squeezed her hands much harder, he was going to break her fingers. His eyes glittered green in the gloom, bright as quetzal plumage. "It's your only chance, Rialle! It's not as if we're asking you to sing *Aushan* or *Yehn*, for echoes' sake! What's the matter? Don't you want to get out of here?"

She stared at the floor. "You know I do." Now more than ever — but could she trust Kherron?

"Then sing!"

"I can't."

"Why not? Is it because of me? What I said to you outside Eliya's chamber? I'm sorry, all right? Forget me. Do it for yourself. Do it for Frenn! Once Azri's better and the karchholders start searching this place, we're sure to find him."

She shook her head miserably.

"Azri, then! You don't like him because he ate your merlee's eggs, is that it? It wasn't his fault. The Khizpriest told him they'd cure him."

Merlee eggs . . . those little green berries! So that was what her nose had been trying to tell her at the banquet. She glared at the Karchlord, any sympathy she'd been feeling replaced by fresh hatred.

Kherron's voice lowered. "C'mon, Rialle . . . there's no other way. Don't you think I haven't been racking my brains since I saw you in here? Stop being so stubborn! We're not in the pallets now, you know. This is real life."

She closed her eyes for control, opened them again, and pointed a trembling finger at Azri. "Don't tell *me* about real life! He killed my merlee! Froze them to death in a tiny little pool on his horrible mountain. Don't try to deny it, Karchlord! I saw them."

"Shh, Rialle!" Kherron glanced nervously over his shoulder. "You'll wake the priests. And you mustn't talk to the Karchlord like that."

But Azri roused himself and said softly, "No, let her be. She's got a right to be upset." He turned to Rialle. "Singer, I never meant any harm. I believed the merlee eggs would cure me, so I arranged for a breeding pair to be brought up to the Karch so my men wouldn't have to hunt and kill so many. I thought maybe if we could breed them in captivity, then I'd have a supply of eggs nearby, and we wouldn't even need to kill the females because we could collect the eggs just after they were laid. I didn't know the poor things froze to death. No one told me. The eggs just kept coming, and I kept eating them. And I swear I didn't know old Frazhin had you up here like this, or I'd have done something sooner. He told me all the Singers had left. I'd no reason to disbelieve him. Please don't cry, Singer. If you don't want to heal me, I'll understand. I'll do what I can to get you released, anyway, and I'll send some of my men to make sure you get home safely."

Truth.

Rialle hung her head, suddenly ashamed, thinking of the fit she'd witnessed at the banquet. What would it be like to live like that, never knowing when you might start frothing at the mouth? And Azri was so young to be in charge of a whole Karchhold, no wonder his priests took advantage of him.

"I'm sorry," she whispered.

Kherron smiled at her. "So you'll do it?"

Rialle bit her lip and looked at the open door of her cage. She wanted nothing more than to dart out of that gap, flee through the tunnels, and race down the mountainside under the wide open sky until she reached the sea. She'd swim and swim and swim until she reached the merlee, then they'd dive to the bottom of the Western Sea, so deep no one would ever find them again. She trembled and looked at the quetzal. They gave soft, curious hoots.

"You'll let the quetzal come with us, too?" she said.

Azri nodded. "I promise."

"And Singer Toharo and Frenn and the others?"

"If they're still here, yes, of course."

Rialle took a deep breath and turned back to Kherron. "I'll try," she said. "But it might not work. This isn't the Pentangle, and I'm only a novice."

"Don't be silly, Rialle!" Kherron said firmly, surprising her. "You're by far the best Singer in our class. You always were." While she stared at him, openmouthed, he left the cage and vanished down the tunnel.

Rialle let out her breath and shook her head. It must have cost Kherron a lot to admit that before a witness. She wiped her face on her sleeve and considered Azri. Without his jewelry, he didn't look much like a powerful lord. "You're supposed to have a potion to help you relax."

"I've had some wine," Azri said. "I feel quite sleepy."

"And you're supposed to spin. I don't suppose you can twist yourself around?" She glanced at his legs, embarrassed. "No, don't worry, just sit still. I'm going to sing what we call *Challa*. Try to relax. You might have some dreams. I don't know if it'll work without the Pentangle, but I'll do my best for you, Lord. I promise."

Azri murmured, "Thank you, Singer. I won't forget this." But Rialle didn't feel at all worthy of a Karchlord's thanks as she chose a position between two of the quetzal cages at the back of the cave. She completed a short breathing exercise, looked into the eyes of the blue female, then filled her lungs with the musky air. The last thought that crossed her mind before she opened her mouth was: *Don't sneeze. Whatever else you do, don't sneeze.*

*

As soon as he heard the Song, Kherron saw the one big flaw in his plan.

Rialle was singing carefully to fill the cave and no more. It was about the first thing novices learned, so they wouldn't waste their talents needlessly. But the quetzal had no such training, and it was their voices that reached the tunnel where Kherron stood guard with Ortiz and Malazi. The two karchholders glanced around, wide-eyed, and took their hands from their swords to cover their ears. Kherron ran back to the cave, pinching himself to stay awake. *Challa, Challa* makes you dream.

The first thing he saw was Azri, sound asleep in the central cage with a smile on his lips. He glimpsed Rialle in the shadows near the back of the cave, eyes closed, the end of her braid clutched tightly in one small fist. But it was the quetzal who gave him a jolt. All fourteen of the stupid creatures were clinging onto the mesh with their little fluffy fingers, wing stubs lifted, beaks wide open, bodies trembling in delight as they echoed the *Challa,* louder and louder, no control at all. The whole Karch must be able to hear them, never mind the priests.

Kherron filled his lungs. "Stop!" he yelled.

The *Challa* continued, dislodging splinters of ice from the roof.

He rushed to Azri's side and slapped the Karchlord's cheeks. "Change Songs, Rialle!" he shouted, using his voice to destroy the *Challa*. "Give him *Kashe*, quick! Wake him up! He can't help us if he's asleep."

Too late.

There was a short scuffle in the tunnel. Then Ortiz and Malazi were dragged into the cave, each struggling in the grasp of four shaven-headed priests. Behind them strode the Khizpriest, carrying his khiz before him like a lance. More priests waited outside, blocking any escape.

Kherron dropped his hand to his dagger, but didn't draw it. The karchholders had already been disarmed, and there were too many priests to fight alone. Rialle had stopped singing at last. She was staring at the Khizpriest as if she thought he was about to run her through with the Khiz, which, Kherron thought, he might yet do. One by one, the quetzal fell silent. Azri slept on, oblivious.

Frazhin cast a glance around the cave. His gaze stopped at the sleeping Karchlord. He chuckled. "Interesting," he said. "All the little birds together."

He turned to his priests. "All right, that'll do nicely. No point leaving them here to get up to any more tricks. It's stopped snowing, and there's a good moon tonight. Take the Singer and the Half Creatures to the sleighs. We'll leave immediately."

More priests piled into the cave, bringing leather thongs. Working their way around the cages, they strapped the quetzals' beaks, bound their little wrists, and dragged them out in a flurry of flying feathers and scrabbling claws. The Song seemed to have excited the creatures, and more than one priest got his fingers pecked before he managed to fasten the strap.

Meanwhile, Frazhin kept his khiz leveled at Rialle. "Thank you, young Singer. Your loyalties are misplaced, but the result's the same. Lovely voice."

Rialle pressed her hands to her mouth in horror.

The Khizpriest smiled at Kherron. "Well done, Islander. I'd have preferred it if you'd told me about your little plan first, but it seems to have worked out quite nicely in the end. I presume that was the Dream-Song she sang, since the Prince Among Men still appears to be breathing?"

When Kherron opened his mouth to protest, Frazhin waved the Khiz in his direction. "Not to worry, it'll suit our purpose just fine."

Rialle's gaze shifted from the Khizpriest to Kherron. Her eyes widened, full of the betrayal she must have seen. Kherron quickly shook his head, but she launched herself across the cave and beat her fists against the outside of the mesh, making him glad he was in the cage with Azri. "I should never have listened to you!" she screamed. "Singer Toharo warned me! He said even *Challa* can be a weapon in the wrong hands. Even *Challa*!"

Kherron pressed his face close to hers. "It would have been all right if you'd sung *Kashe*," he hissed.

For a moment, she seemed to forget the priests and the Khiz. Her eyes flashed. "It wouldn't have worked, stupid! Don't you know anything? Always blowing off theory, weren't you? There was a woman in the Echorium who had fits like Azri, and she had to have —"

She gasped as two priests seized her arms, pulled her away from the cage, and began to wind a rope around her wrists. "No!" she screamed. "Kherron! Do something! Don't let him —"

"Give her the sleeping potion," the Khizpriest ordered. "I don't have time for this."

Rialle struggled wildly, lashing out with her feet and twisting her head from side to side, but a third priest seized her braid, pinched her nose, and forced a flask between her lips. Her expression as she swallowed made Kherron wince. Then the priest let go of her hair, and her forehead rattled against the mesh. Whatever they'd given her must have been strong. Her eyelids were already drooping. But she was trying to say something.

He put his ear to the mesh.

"*Challa* first, then *Kashe*, repeat three times . . ."

The priests lifted her between them. One stuffed a cloth into her mouth and tied it behind her head. As they carried her out, she stared at Kherron until her glazed eyes closed. That glimpse of gray beneath her lashes was like a glimpse of the sea.

Kherron shivered.

The Khizpriest signaled that the priests should take the karchholders out as well. When they were alone, he shook his head at Kherron. "Intentionally or not, Islander, you've done me a service. So I'm going to let you live." His tone hardened. "But if you're still here when I return, I'll have you frozen alive in the glacier like those merlee creatures the Karchlord tried to breed. Understand?"

Somehow, Kherron managed a nod.

Frazhin's dark gaze fell on Azri, and his lips curled. "I'll send down for the Karchlord's throne. You'd better stay here and watch over him in case he wakes up. I think you're going to have some explaining to do when I tell the men how you kidnapped their sick young lord, brought him up here, and put him in a cage. Good luck, Islander. You're going to need it this time." Chuckling, he vanished down the tunnel after his priests.

Kherron felt sick. The mesh cast square shadows across the Karchlord's face. The doors of the empty cages squeaked in an icy draft. He hadn't realized this place was so cold.

He knelt beside Azri and tried to put himself in his boots, tried to imagine what a Karchlord prone to fits would do when he woke up to find the cure hadn't worked, and it was too late to stop his priests from destroying the Isle.

More out of desperation than anything else, he started humming *Kashe*. Maybe if he could wake Azri before the karchholders came with the throne, he and Ortiz and Malazi might have a chance of getting out of this alive. The way the Song vibrated powerfully in the rock surprised him. Another shower of ice hissed down. Kherron touched his lips, hardly daring to hope.

Maybe it wasn't too late.

*

It was a tense group that carried the sleeping Karchlord back to his bed. Ortiz and Malazi had managed to convince the men who came running up with the throne that they'd meant Azri no harm, but with Azri still asleep, suspicion hung in the Karchlord's hot, smoky bedchamber like a storm about to break. Only when Cadzi was summoned, with Lazim helping his lame father up all the winding stairs, did they agree to listen to Kherron. The pale Island boy who'd found out about the poison in the eggs deserved a hearing, at least.

So Kherron outlined his plan to complete the Karchlord's cure, using just four quetzal with himself as the fifth Singer. He laced his voice with as many subtle Songs as he could, but to his surprise no one questioned his ability to sing. They seemed a lot more worried about whether the Songs would harm their young lord. Finally, though, Ortiz and Malazi volunteered to take a sleigh down the mountain to collect the quetzal Kherron needed from Lord Javelly's castle, and the meeting broke up. Kherron supposed the fact that Azri kept smiling in his sleep must have helped persuade them, but he'd have given up his chance to sing on the Pentangle to swap places with the Karchlord that night.

By the time he and Lazim left the Karchlord's bedchamber, it was late morning, and he was shaking like a First Year.

"Why on earth didn't you tell anyone you were a Singer?" Lazim said as they waded through the fresh, dazzling snow toward the pony cavern. "Father always said you had the luck of the Khiz. Now we know why!"

"I had my reasons," Kherron muttered. They seemed so pathetic now.

Lazim shook his head. "I know if I was a Singer, I'd be proud of it. I wouldn't skulk around pretending to be some common fisherman's son and lying to people all the time. What I can't work out was how on earth you managed to lie to the Khiz. No one ever has before."

Kherron scowled. "I never lied. Frazhin just didn't ask the right questions. Anyway, I'm not a Singer yet. I'm still a novice."

"Don't see what difference it makes if you've had the training."

"It's all to do with growing up, Lazim. You wouldn't understand."

The boy stopped. Around them, the mountains glittered like vast piles of salt, their sharp edges softened by the recent snow. The sky was an intense blue, as if someone had tipped a whole vat of Singer hair dye up there. Far below, the entire world lay under a thin layer of mist. It was all so bright after the Karchlord's cavern, Kherron had to squint. He was getting a headache.

"Something's wrong, isn't it?" Lazim said, putting a hand on his arm. "You can do it, can't you? You're not just making up another lie to save your skin? Because if you are, it's best to tell Lord Azri now —"

"Course I can do it! I wouldn't be so stupid as to say I was a Singer if I wasn't, would I? It's just . . . oh, forget it." He shrugged Lazim off, but the boy refused to let it alone.

"It's like killing your first man, isn't it?" he said gently. "We all get a manhood braid to show we've done the training, but we still don't know if we can actually *do* it until the time comes. I lied to you before, Kher. I'm real scared. But there's no shame in being afraid, Father says. He says the ones who are afraid underneath make the best warriors, because they think while they fight instead of just blundering in."

Kherron stared at the young karchholder. "Singing's not the same at all! There's no one trying to kill you back, is there?" But secretly, he felt a glow of pride. Cadzi hadn't laughed at him when he'd said he could complete the cure himself if he had some more quetzal to work with. Even the dark-faced karch-holders who'd been ready to murder him when they found him in that cage with Azri had shrunk back a little and looked at him differently.

"C'mon," he said, embarrassed. "Aren't we supposed to be counting ponies?"

Lazim laughed. "I'll count, Kher. You wait outside. They always know when someone's nervous, and if they start milling around we'll be here all day."

Kherron needed no further excuse. He hooked his elbows over the outer rail and leaned back to soak up the sun, while Lazim moved through the cavern, murmuring and whistling in his musical way, pausing here and there to pick up a foot or rub an ear.

They were supposed to be checking that there were enough ponies left to haul the Karchlord's army on sleighs down the north side of the mountain as far as some secret stronghold at the edge of the forest, where Cadzi said there should be enough horses to transport the men to the coast. Lord Javelly was supposed to be arranging for ships to meet them at Silvertown, ready to take them to the Isle — *if* the army got there in time, *if* the horses were still there, *if* Javelly sent the quetzal, *if* Kherron could manage to complete Azri's cure. . . . So much could go wrong, and he was thinking so hard about what to do when it did, he took a lot longer than he should have to notice Lazim's whistling had stopped.

He turned in alarm. The ponies were churning about and snorting near the back of the cavern. "Lazim? You all right in there?" He leaned over the rail and peered into the gloom.

Suddenly, the ponies at the far side of the pen shied, and two struggling bodies flew through. The shorter, stocky one jammed the taller, lanky one up against the rails and set a dagger to his throat. Kherron stumbled back into the snow, one hand groping for his own dagger.

"Don't do it," hissed a familiar voice. "Or I'll kill him, I swear!"

Kherron froze, forgetting to breathe. But he wasn't seeing things — he'd recognize those fists anywhere. "Frenn!" he exclaimed. "Where have you *been*? We thought you were dead!"

"That's obvious," Frenn said. "But I been keepin' an eye on you, Kherron, ever since I got out of that cave and learned you were up here. An' I don't like what I see."

It was a wonder he could see anything. One side of Frenn's head was black with congealed blood, his clothes were torn, his left arm hung limply, his features drooped on that side of his face, and he was propping himself against the rail as if his left leg wouldn't support him. How he'd managed to overpower the Karch-trained boy in such a state, Kherron had no idea.

He said, "You shouldn't be walking around like that."

Dark, haunted eyes turned on him. "Cut the false concern, Kherron. Just tell me where she is."

"You mean Rialle?"

"Course I mean Rialle! What have you done with her? You always were tricky, Kherron, but I never believed you'd stoop to this. If you've hurt her, I'll kill you the slowest way I can think of."

Lazim made a move then, trying to sidle along the rail. Frenn jammed his good elbow into his groin. Lazim doubled over with a groan.

"Don't be an idiot, Frenn!" Kherron said. "We're not your enemies. We've been working for weeks, trying to get her out."

"Expect me to believe that? You've always hated her for bein' a better singer than you, but you've really done it this time."

"She's on her way back to the Isle."

That threw him. His eyes narrowed. He didn't notice when Lazim began to sidle again. The Karch boy pursed his lips, gave a soft whistle, and a shaggy black head bumped Frenn's back, knocking him off balance. In less than a heartbeat, their positions were reversed.

Frenn's eyes clouded. "Go on then," he hissed. "Finish me off! But one day Eliya's going to find out what you've done here, and when she does you'll have the *Yehn* you deserve. Traitor!" He spat at Kherron. It missed by an arm's length.

Kherron shook his head. If Frenn had spoken to him like that in the pallets, he'd have made sure the boy tripped near the top of the Five Thousand Steps, but, as he'd told Rialle, they weren't in the pallets now. He signaled that Lazim should ease off, which the young karchholder did warily. "You'd better tell him, Lazim," he said. "Because he's obviously not going to listen to me."

Lazim explained the plan to his prisoner in the same quiet, calm tone he used on the ponies. Frenn didn't listen at first. He was too busy glaring at Kherron. Then, gradually, he relaxed and a frown flickered across the good half of his face.

"It's all true," Kherron said. "And when Azri's healed, I'm going back to the Isle of my own accord. Eliya has to know what happened here."

Frenn's eyes narrowed. "You always were a fool, Kherron. You goin' to tell her how you put the Second Singer to sleep an' left us all to die in that cave, are you? Or maybe you're planning to blame it all on Rialle?" He laughed without a trace of *Kashe*. "Think Eliya's going to believe you?"

Kherron turned cold inside. "The others really are dead, then?"

"Oh, don't play all innocent with me! Course they're dead! You would be, too, if half the mountain collapsed on your head. I crawled around in there for days lookin' for Rialle, and I found them all. They were broken up like that wreck Graia had us all lookin' for. Singer Toharo, everyone —" He choked. "Echoes, Kherron, how could you do it?"

Though all the signs had pointed to it, Frenn's confirmation of the deaths chilled Kherron like wind from the glacier.

There was an uncomfortable silence. Then Lazim said softly, "They must have wanted it to look like an accident, in case another Singer comes to investigate the deaths."

Kherron winced at the thought of all that rock falling on sleeping men. "Maybe it *was* an accident," he said, but he didn't believe his own words, and wasn't surprised when Frenn snorted.

"And I suppose that sleeping draft they left us was an accident, too, was it?"

Kherron stared at the dizzy white slopes. Singer Toharo dead? He hadn't realized how much he'd been hoping they'd find the others, and that the Second Singer would step in and complete Azri's therapy. Now they were truly alone. He hated to think what would happen if his best wasn't good enough this time.

He took a deep breath. "So it's up to us now. Frenn, if Lazim lets you go, do you promise to help us?"

Frenn scowled. "Soon as this bully lets go of me, I'm goin' after Rialle."

Kherron frowned. "In your state? Don't be an idiot. You wouldn't last a sunstep on your own out there."

Frenn's eyes clouded. "At least I'll be trying, not hangin' around up here trying to cure some half-crazy Karchlord with a voice that might crack at any moment."

It was an effort, but Kherron ignored the taunt. "And a lot of good it'll do Rialle if you freeze to death on the way down the mountain! *Think*, Frenn! Rialle will be fine until the priests reach the Isle. They need her to make the quetzal sing, so they'll look after her. Meanwhile, we've got no choice but to work with the Karchlord. We have to think of the Echorium. There's more at stake than a single life."

"Just the sort of thing I'd expect you to say! Sacrifice Rialle for the good of the Echorium. Ha! Since when have *you* cared about the Echorium? Last I heard, you were runnin' away like some homesick First Year —"

Kherron grabbed Frenn's shoulders and shook him until his teeth rattled. "You're an orderly now, remember? You serve the

Echorium, too. Think of Chissar and the others. Hundreds of lives are at risk. Or do you think the priests will spare the novices when they're done with the Singers? Either you help us, or I'll stick you back in that cave and knock the rest of the roof down myself!"

Frenn's face darkened, and his good fist shot out and punched Kherron in the nose. Blood dripped scarlet into the snow.

It might have degenerated into something ugly if Lazim hadn't stepped between them and knocked them both flat on their backs. Manhood braid flying against the peaks, he glared down at them. "We're all on the same side, remember? This is helping no one, least of all your Singer friend. Now, both of you get up, tug braids or whatever you do on that island of yours, and let's talk about how we're going to catch the Khizpriest before he reaches the Echoing Isle."

Frenn's scowl didn't fade. He sat up and rubbed his limp arm with his good hand. "She won't sing, you know. She won't let that old priest use her against the Echorium."

Kherron exchanged a glance with Lazim. "She doesn't have to sing," he explained gently. "The quetzal have amazing memories. Soon as they hear a voice, they remember everything it's taught them in the past. All the Khizpriest has to do is persuade Rialle to make some sound to start them off. A scream would do."

"Why, you —"

Frenn heaved himself up, but Lazim knocked him down again.

Kherron pressed a handful of snow to his throbbing nose. "Do you think I like it any more than you do? Now come on, Frenn, be sensible. Rialle's smart and she's brave. She'll do everything she can to delay him. We might still be in time to save her."

"We'd better be, or your life won't be worth livin'!"

Kherron smiled, knowing he'd won. "You'd better let Lazim find someone to take a look at those wounds," he said calmly. "You look like a limp seaweed salad."

Frenn's glower deepened. But the subtle *Kashe* Kherron had used wasn't all wasted. After a moment the young orderly's lips twitched into a smile, and he pointed to a dark dot slowly making its way up the mountainside toward them. "Time to see if your boast is good," he said.

Kherron's heart gave an extra thump.

Lazim climbed on the rail, squinted at the sleigh a moment, then grinned. "It's the quetzal, Kher! Khiz, have you two crazy Islanders been fighting that long?"

*

Rialle's dream was full of a strange hissing noise. Silk, hissing at the windows in the fourth-floor dormitory. Something awful had just happened, but she couldn't remember what, because Eliya had sent her for *Challa.*

She opened her eyes, and immediately wished she hadn't. The world was flying overhead — enormous blue sky, spiky branches, dazzling white snow — all a blur. Her pallet was hissing along on a cloud, so fast she didn't dare move in case she fell off. Then something hard and cold struck her on the cheek, shattering the dream in a spray of ice. Just the sort of thing Kherron would do, toss a missile through the door of the girls' dormitory. . . .

She tried to get up to close the door, but straps across her chest and legs held her down. She was wrapped tightly in a fur. Thongs bit into her wrists, and her ankles were tied. Her mouth was full of something soft. A wave of terror almost carried her back into the dark as she recognized the flying chunks to be ice, kicked up by a pony's hooves. The pony was galloping, pulling the thing she was lying on, and a figure in a hooded cloak sat in front of her urging the animal on. She must have made some noise, for the driver turned to smile at her, then turned back and cracked his whip. The sleigh jolted, and the hissing increased.

Rialle shut her eyes tightly. It was all flooding back now. Kherron, the Karchlord, the *Challa*, the quetzal mimicking her voice, the Khizpriest finding them before they'd finished and dragging her away.

Think. She must think.

Though the man driving was just an ordinary priest, the gag meant she couldn't use her voice to influence him. She must save her strength for when he took it out, then maybe she could persuade him to untie her. What would Singer Toharo use? *Aushan,* definitely. And if she could manage it, maybe a bit of *Shi* as well to make him pity her.

But when they stopped, and the driver finally snatched the gag out of her mouth, her stomach heaved, making singing impossible. He watched in amusement while she twisted her head and retched into the snow. Then, when she lay back, gasping and shaking, feeling so wretched all she wanted to do was curl up and die, he smiled again. Behind his bald head, dark branches pierced stars set in purple velvet. There was a sharp scent, the crackle of flames, golden spots at the edges of her vision, like flowers in the snow — or maybe they were in her head?

Unable to stop shivering, she licked her cracked lips. "Water," she managed. "Please."

The priest walked away.

Rialle's eyes filled with tears. She closed them in shame. When she opened them, the Khizpriest was gazing down at her. She lay very still, though her heart hammered.

He touched his horrible spear to her forehead. It felt like a snowball, melting behind her eyes. Then he nodded. This time, the priest brought the water, and even cradled her head in his arm while she drank. Rialle gulped without thinking. Only when the Khizpriest's smile blurred, and it was too late to spit it out, did she realize the water was yet another sleeping potion.

*

Under Cadzi's supervision, Ortiz and Malazi arranged the new quetzal in their cages on four points of the star around Azri's bed, while Kherron went to stand on the fifth. He took a deep breath. This was it.

He'd measured out the Pentangle as best he could, scratching the lines into the rock with a sharp stone. His hands shook as he worked, and only Frenn's "Get on with it, Kherron! Anyone would think you were scared!" had got him this far.

He glanced at the quetzal. The creatures were staring at him with their black eyes in a most unsettling manner, almost as if they knew he was nervous — but that was ridiculous. They were only Half Creatures, less intelligent than ponies, hadn't Lazim said? That must make them very stupid indeed. They'd been watered and fed on arrival, and Lazim had rubbed some pony-ointment into the stubs of their wings and the bald patches around their wrists and tails. "Make them feel better, so they can concentrate on singing," he'd told Kherron with a quick smile. It seemed to be working. The creatures' plumage had lost its tattered appearance and begun to ripple with inner lights — blue, scarlet, gold — making him wonder what they looked like in the wild.

He snatched his gaze away. This wouldn't do. He glanced one last time at the Karchlord, still sleeping soundly with a smile on his face, then closed his eyes.

Breathe. Relax. Forget Frenn's glower. Forget everything except *Kashe,* and then *Challa.*

He opened his mouth and let the first note build until it filled the Karchlord's bedchamber. The four quetzal ruffled their feathers in delight. Then they, too, began to sing.

It was too early to tell whether the Song was working. Kherron had watched enough Echorium therapies to know patients often looked worse before they got better. He only hoped Frenn would have the sense to stay out of the Pentangle until he'd finished. The *Kashe* got a bit out of control, thanks to the overenthusiastic quetzal. He heard someone behind him chuckle, but resisted the urge to turn his head.

Azri had woken up now, yet made no move to get out of bed. He smiled at the smoke above his head, as if it contained things no one else could see. Quite possible, Kherron thought, remembering his own experience of the Songs. When the Karchlord giggled like a First Year and reached both arms toward the smoke, Kherron took the risk and changed to *Challa.* Azri's eyelids drooped, and he settled back into his pillows with a contented sigh.

Kherron kept singing until his legs threatened to give way beneath him, then let the *Challa* drift gently away. On the other four points, the quetzal gave soft, satisfied hoots, before drawing one leg into their belly plumage and going to sleep standing up. Kherron staggered from his own point, pushed past Frenn, and curled up with a groan on one of the Karchlord's fur rugs.

Rialle hadn't told him how long he should let the Karchlord sleep between Songs. Maybe she didn't know. Kherron began to wish he'd paid more attention in class, but he was much too tired to worry about it now. "Wake me up when you've fed the quetzal," he said, and promptly fell asleep.

*

Rialle's second waking was worse. The hissing and sliding had been replaced by jolting and swaying, and the sky was hidden by red canvas. This time vomit sucked back up her nose before the priest could remove the gag, and she choked. But he wasn't about to let her die, and thumped her on the back until she spluttered. When he let her lie down again, her whole body felt bruised. He tried to feed her some fruit. She retched it right back up again. The sleeping potion, when it came, was a mercy. She wanted to sleep forever.

*

It hardly seemed any time at all since Kherron had shut his eyes before Frenn was shaking him awake.

"C'mon, Kherron!" the injured boy said, scowling. "Get on with it!"

"Go 'way," he muttered.

Frenn kicked him in the ribs with his good foot. "It's time!" he said. "Get up, you lazy pile of seaweed. If you don't sing now, all Rialle's hard work will be wasted."

What about *my* hard work? Kherron thought, pressing a hand to his ribs with a wince. But one look at Frenn's face warned him this wouldn't be a good time to argue. He sighed, swallowed the water Lazim brought across, and stumbled back to the fifth point of the pentangle.

Kashe makes you laugh. . . . *Challa* makes you dream. . . .

*

Rialle woke once more in the wagon, thinking she was back in the pallets and had been punished for un-Singerlike behavior — losing her temper and yelling at Kherron. There was something he'd said to her, about getting her out. But she didn't want to leave the Echorium. She struggled and began to scream through the gag, until a harsh voice told her to stop it, or he'd kill one of her little friends. Rialle lay still, terrified he meant Frenn.

*

As the final notes of the third and final *Kashe* died away, Kherron took a deep breath and looked at the Karchlord's bed.

Azri was sitting on the edge, very still, staring at the floor. He was still smiling, which was encouraging. If Rialle was right, the Karchlord was as cured as he was ever going to be.

He cleared his throat, hardly daring to ask. "Sir? How do you feel?"

The quetzal, hearing his voice again, turned their black eyes upon him and hooted softly.

Azri's head came up, and the bluestone necklace around his throat cast cool light across his face. While Kherron had been asleep, the karchholders must have washed and dressed their lord. In place of the bed robe, he wore a simple tunic of black wool worked with a border of red, over plain black leggings. His hair floated around his head in a dark, fluffy cloud. Red metal bracelets clasped both wrists, and his boots waited by the bed. Now Ortiz tiptoed closer, a shiny red sword in a black leather scabbard resting across his arms. He stopped at a respectful distance and peered into Azri's face.

Azri winked at Kherron. Then he reached for the boots, tugged them on, and drew himself to his full height. "What are you all staring at?" he said in a strong, clear voice. "Give me that sword! We have no time to waste. Harness up the ponies and assemble the men in the snowbowl. I want to talk to them before we leave."

12
CHASE

The Karch went to war at sunrise, when the highest peaks blushed pink against a clear sky. Their breath filled the snowbowl with icy clouds, and there was an air of excitement equal to any Echorium outing. Men who'd spent years drunk and idle in the smoky tunnels rewove their death-braids and wore the finger bones of their enemies with new pride. Some had added quetzal feathers, which trailed glowing colors as the sleighs plunged down a frozen river course into a crevasse of purple shadows.

"The River Rush," Lazim informed Kherron and Frenn. "In spring, all this side of the mountain's a raging torrent choked with avalanche debris, and we have to use the trail you came up by. We should gain time on the Khizpriest, going this way."

They changed to horses late that afternoon, when the snow gave way to slush and icy puddles, and soon afterward left the river to head south along the edge of the forest. It was a little-traveled track, easy enough for horses, though not quite as easy for the wagon they'd picked up at the stronghold to transport the quetzal. On their way to the coast, Azri was determined to set the creatures free in the densest part of the forest, south of the Vale to Greenwood path, where they'd be safe.

Crazy, Kherron thought, as the wheels bounced over yet another rut, jolting him into the air. But, according to Lazim, taking the eastern route to Vale would be quicker than following the road along the River Rush to the coast, where they'd meet a lot more traffic. So he held his tongue and consoled himself with the knowledge that the stupid creatures would be gone soon. The presence of the wagon at least meant he didn't have to ride, though by the end of the first day, he wasn't sure volunteering to keep an eye on the quetzal had been such a good idea after all. Since he'd sung Azri's therapy, they hadn't stopped staring at him with those round black eyes like holes in their heads. Looking at them too long made him dizzy, and their smell hadn't improved one bit. Also, traveling in the wagon meant he saw little of Frenn and Lazim, who rode farther back in the column with the single-braiders. Lazim seemed to be trying to teach Frenn how to control his mount with one hand. Frenn wasn't doing too badly, as far as Kherron could see, though when they stopped to make their first camp, the young orderly had a lot of mud on his back.

Azri himself rode a gentle black gelding at the head of his army, while Ortiz and Malazi hovered like mothers on either side, ready to catch the young Karchlord's reins if he had another fit or fell off. Two buglers went ahead with the crossed-sword banner, and every time they passed a settlement, or even a single lopsided hut, they blew a wild, strong note that the quetzal mimicked until it echoed in the mountains, making Kherron afraid the whole Karch would come sliding down on their heads.

"Make way for the Karchlord Azri!" the buglers called as the notes faded away. "Overlord of the Silver Shore, Blessed of the Khiz, Prince Among Men!"

"Make way for the Karchlord Azri! . . ." echoed the quetzal, causing much mirth among the men.

In this way, they made good time, and toward the end of the second day found themselves on the Vale to Greenwood path through the forest. The very same path Kherron had traveled in the opposite direction with Cadzi, which seemed a lifetime ago.

*

He jumped down from the wagon in relief, untied the flaps, and started throwing back the canvas. The whole column had reined in, and horses chewed their bits while their riders stared nervously at the trees, particularly those to the left of the trail, where the forest was untracked and dense. It was very quiet. Evening sunlight dappled the trail with gold, but mysterious shadows lurked between the huge trunks all around. Still in their cages, the quetzal cocked their heads at the trees and let out an eerie crooning sound that got right into Kherron's head.

He banged the mesh with his fist. "Stop that," he hissed. "We're letting you go now. Stupid things."

At last Azri turned his eyes from the trees. He smiled at Kherron. "Doesn't it smell nice in here? I never realized anywhere could be so green."

"The leaves never fall here, my Lord," said the karchholder who'd been driving the wagon. "Men say this is an enchanted place. With respect, my Lord, we shouldn't linger. There are tales of travelers never seen again."

"I doubt we'll lose an army of six hundred men," Azri said with a laugh. "Well, Islander, what do you think? Should we let them go here, or carry the cages farther in?"

Don't know why you're asking me, Kherron thought. But he smiled and said, "I should think here will do fine, sir."

Azri watched, still smiling, as Kherron and the wagon driver unlocked the cage doors. The nearest karchholders eased their horses back slightly. But the quetzal just crouched there, crooning.

Azri frowned. "What's wrong with them? Why don't they go?"

"I don't know, my lord," said the wagon driver. "Maybe it's their wings. After all, they can't fly anymore —"

He broke off as the leaves to the left of the trail began to rustle. Horses whinnied nervously. Then someone shouted a warning, and Azri's gelding reared as a huge, winged shadow came gliding silently out of the forest to land beside the wagon. Those nearby ducked and drew their swords in a hiss of red sparks, and the caged quetzal broke into excited hoots and whistles. But the newcomer did not attack. Instead, it folded its impressive wings around its body and settled in a patch of sunshine. It then proceeded to comb the long feathers with its fingers, smoothing them around its shoulders like a thin man crouched under a feathered cloak several sizes too big for him. Its tail flowed back down the trail, a luminous green-and-gold river. After studying the men and horses at the front of the army, it turned its black eyes on the captives and let out a long series of whistles. The captives replied in kind, and the wild quetzal shook its wings in an angry shimmer of gold.

Kherron shaded his eyes, trying to look calmer than he felt. Azri's horse was back on four legs now, thankfully with the Karchlord still aboard. Ortiz and Malazi were looking for something to fight. Whispers passed back down the column. "Wings are huge . . . look out . . . may be more of 'em . . . those claws look sharp. . . ."

Kherron cleared his throat. "Ah, I think we should —"

At the sound of his voice, all five quetzal turned and fixed their black eyes upon him. The crooning started up again, making his head hurt.

-join-army-stone-singer-tell-

Kherron stood very still, all the little hairs on the back of his neck prickling. Then the wild quetzal shook its cloak of golden wings, and a sweet, musky smell wafted over him.

"Oh, no," he whispered, suddenly understanding where the words had come from. "No, you don't."

"What's wrong, Islander?" Azri demanded, with another glance at the trees. "Is it going to attack? Can't you make it understand I'm letting its friends go?"

"I don't know why you think I'm a quetzal expert all of a sudden," Kherron snapped, forgetting who he was talking to. "Do I look like a bird? Can you see my feathers?" He lifted his arms in imitation of the wild quetzal, and spun in a circle.

Ortiz and Malazi, already jumpy, swung their swords around. Kherron ducked, his heart banging. Stupid — to survive the Khiz, only to be cut down because he couldn't control his tongue. But Azri held up a hand, and the swords lowered.

-join-army-stone-singer-TELL!

This time, the words pierced like a needle. The quetzal's golden plumage shimmered with green lightning, too bright to look at. Kherron clutched his head with a soft moan.

Then a familiar voice behind him said, "Tell them, Kherron. 'Cause if you don't, I will."

He let go of his head and whirled around to find himself looking up at Frenn, who'd somehow persuaded his pony to approach the wild creature. "You can hear them, too?" he asked in surprise.

"Don't be stupid — you know I'm no good at hearin' birds. But I seen Rialle when she heard the merlee that first time, an' you look just the same as she did. All pale and twisted and scared."

Kherron scowled. "I'm not afraid of Half Creatures."

Frenn gave him a sly look and turned to Azri. "My lord, the quetzal are tellin' Kherron something. I think you should ask him what it is."

"Why, you sneaky little —"

Lazim kicked his pony between them, put one hand on Frenn's reins and a foot on Kherron's shoulder. "Don't you two ever stop?" he hissed. "At this rate, all we'll find when we get to that island of yours is a lump of cracked rock."

Kherron considered lying. After all, he seemed to be the only one who could hear what the quetzal were saying. Then he looked at the wild one, its golden wings spread now against the dark trees, black eyes fixed on him, fluffy fingers twitching as if it longed to fasten them around someone's neck — and changed his mind.

He sighed. "They want to come, too," he said. "I think they want to rescue their friends. Don't blame me."

Before the wild creature could start trying to talk to him again, he turned and pushed his way to the front of the column. He didn't look back, though gasps and exclamations told him what was happening behind. It was no great surprise when the sky above the trail darkened, and quetzal feathers began to settle like brightly colored snowflakes in the horses' manes.

*

It was difficult to hide six hundred men accompanied by almost fifty glowing airborne quetzal, and as soon as they left the forest the word spread. People from the lowland towns and villages lined the road, and Azri's army soon collected a tail of curious followers. By the time they entered Silvertown on the third evening, having made up almost a day on the Khizpriest, the column had swelled so much that the stragglers were only just passing through the North Gate when Azri and his crossed-sword banner reached the harbor.

Here, too, word had traveled ahead, and the narrow streets with their deep shadows were packed with people trying to get a glimpse of the Karchlord. After what had happened last time Kherron was here, the crowds made him nervous. He gripped his mount's reins so hard, the beast began to sidle and snort, knocking his knees against sharp corners. He gave it an angry kick in the ribs, which only made it worse.

"Relax," Lazim muttered beside him. "That's the whole trouble with you, Kher. You're always fighting things. You were doing just fine before."

This wasn't quite true. Although he'd made some progress since abandoning the wagon at Greenwood had forced him to take a mount, he still wasn't nearly as good a rider as Frenn, who only had one working arm and one leg to control his pony with. But he forced a grin and unclenched his fists. At least he'd be able to get off soon.

The ships Lord Javelly had promised the Karchlord were waiting in the harbor as arranged, even if they looked ready to sink at the slightest swell. They were covered in barnacles, their sails were faded and patched, and their hulls showed lines of slime-draped holes, too evenly spaced to be accidental, just above the waterline. At least, Kherron hoped they were above the waterline. He began to have second thoughts about the whole thing, but it seemed nothing could diminish the spirit of the Karchlord's army. They clattered through the streets in a gleam of red metal and colorful death-braids fluttering with feathers, while overhead, the wild quetzal glowed like fiery ribbons in the sunset as they glided over the roofs to perch along the gutters and walls lining the waterfront.

Azri urged his gelding onto the quay, its hooves striking sparks from the cobbles. When he reached the end, he reined to a stop and swung his mount to face the crowds packed onto the other side of the harbor. Those who couldn't find space in the streets had crammed themselves onto balconies or hung out of upper-story windows. The buglers blew, and Ortiz's voice rang across the red water. "Silence for the Karchlord Azri, Overlord of the Silver Shore, Blessed of the Khiz, Prince Among Men!"

After the wild quetzal had repeated this announcement from the rooftops, a hush fell over the town. The crossed-sword banner snapped in the evening breeze, the ancient ships creaked, and waves slapped the harbor wall as the young Karchlord stood in his stirrups and raised his right hand.

"I know I've neglected you," he began, and a murmur of surprise rose from the assembly. "I've been very sick, but thanks to the Singers I'm recovering, and I've come to realize the Khiz is badly served by its priests. Taking advantage of my illness, my priests have set sail for the Singer island in order to destroy the Echorium. This cannot be allowed to happen, so I'm going after them. I can't tell you what the outcome of this battle will be. But whatever happens, I promise you this. Never again will the Karch raid your homes and terrorize your families!" Excited whispers greeted this, but died away when Azri raised his hand. "I'm aware many of these horses weren't paid for. Any of you with a valid claim against my men will be paid in full before we leave."

He flopped back in the saddle. From his vantage point, Kherron could see how the speech had cost the young Karchlord. He paled, swayed, and had to hold on to the mane. But the people of Silvertown, those who'd followed the army through the lowlands, the army itself, and even those karchholders about to lose their property to pay for stolen horses, were too busy cheering to notice this moment of weakness.

"Long live the Karchlord Azri!" they shouted. "Long live Azri! Azri! Azri!"

"Long live Azri!" shouted the quetzal, lifting their glowing wings.

Women threw flowers into the air until the sunset rained petals. All along the waterfront, inns opened their doors and announced the ale was free until the Karchlord's armada set sail. And almost unnoticed in all the excitement, a gang of boys darted down the alleys, where they began scrubbing at certain embarrassing slogans scrawled on the walls.

*

As the sun set over Silvertown, and darkness crept across the Western Sea, Rialle woke again. This time, she knew exactly where she was. The slap of waves against wood, the creak of timbers, the queasy roll beneath her — she was on a ship, surrounded by the songs of the sea.

Stone-singer! Stone-singer!

The songs were calling her, like First Years clamoring for more soup. She pressed her hands to her ears, then froze.

Hands moved. Not tied anymore.

She was lying facedown in damp straw, moldy by the taste of it. She spat in disgust and lifted her head. A musky, heavy smell warned quetzal were near. She sat up, rubbing her wrists, pushed her filthy braid over her shoulder, and looked around.

Their new prison was gloomy, but squares of gray light coming through a small metal grille overhead showed they were in a hold. In the shadows, the quetzal crouched as small as possible, claws spread against the roll of the ship, little fingers clinging to cracks in the timbers, trembling. Frightened of the sea songs.

"Don't be frightened," Rialle whispered. "Our friends are near."

She looked for the blue female, but she wasn't among the captives. A pang of sorrow changed to hope as Rialle counted them. Eight of the quetzal were missing. Did that mean the Khizpriest had left them behind?

She knew she had to think, but her head was so fuzzy. Soon the Khizpriest would reach the Isle, and she must find some way of stopping him.

A little shakily, she climbed to her feet and explored the hold. The grating seemed the only way out. She stood on tiptoe and stretched — no good, she couldn't reach it. She looked around for something to stand on. Apart from the quetzal, there was nothing except the straw. Wrinkling her nose, she gathered this into a soggy heap beneath the grating, climbed on top, and jumped as high as she could. On the third attempt, her fingers caught in the metal. She clung on, kicking air, long enough to see the chain securing the hatch to the deck. She dropped back into the straw with a sigh, and closed her eyes.

There was no need to farlisten. This time, the merlee had come to her.

Stone-singer? We make storm when ships come. But we make good wind for you! We do right?

They were so pleased with themselves.

"Not this time," she told them. "You don't understand."

Stone-singer want storm? Puzzlement. *Children safe now, hunting stop, we play in shoal.*

Rialle took a deep breath. It was so simple. All she had to do to prevent this ship from reaching the Isle was tell the merlee the Khizpriest was coming for their children. They might try to rescue her when the ship went down, as they'd tried to do when she swam with them before. But the quetzal . . . she looked sadly at the raw stubs where their wings had been so brutally cut off. Once their feathers got wet, they wouldn't have a chance.

How close were they? She thought hard of the Khizpriest. His glittering spear — her mind shied away, and a chill rippled down the backs of her legs. This wouldn't do. She shuddered, thought of the spear again — and was *there*.

He wasn't far. The same ship, but overhead, on deck. A flapping noise in the background, maybe sails. He was talking to the captain.

"Can't you make this ship go any faster?" hissed the dark voice she knew so well.

"We're trying our best, sir priest! But the wind's changed. The currents are always tricky around here. Some say there's magic in the waters around the Isle —"

"I didn't ask for excuses. Any faster, yes or no?"

"N-no, sir priest." The captain sounded scared. Rialle wondered if the Khizpriest was using his spear on him. The captain began to stutter out an explanation. "It wouldn't be a good idea to get separated from the others, sir priest. Ships disappear in these parts for no reason at all. People say the Singers sink them. They can tell who's on board, and if they don't want you to get to the Isle, they don't let you."

"Nonsense!" hissed the Khizpriest. "Ships don't just disappear."

"They do! I know a man whose brother saw one vanish with his own eyes."

The Khizpriest grunted. "Back in Silvertown, you told me you weren't afraid of anything. Singer magic's not nearly as strong as they'd like you to believe. Besides, we've got one of them to help us."

The captain drew a sharp breath. "Th-that girl you've got in the hold?"

"Exactly."

The captain gave a low moan. "I knew it! I knew she was a Singer, first time I saw her! A Singer on my ship! Oh, what'll become of us?"

"Pull yourself together!" the Khizpriest snapped. "You concentrate on the wind, and let me worry about the magic."

"She'll sing us all to death!"

"I can control her."

"No one can control Singers!"

A low chuckle. "The Khiz can. Now, I want no more talk of — quiet!" There was a short silence, followed by a whisper that made Rialle's hair stand on end. *"Someone's listening to us."*

"N-no, sir priest. None of my men would dare —"

"Quiet, I said."

Rialle jerked away. She stared at the hatch, terrified the Khizpriest's spear would come poking through the grating. But the deck overhead stayed empty. She relaxed slightly. Now what had she been going to do? So hard to think. . . .

Stone-singer? Your head's all misty!

She sat up with a start, a glimmer of hope pushing through the aftereffects of the Khizpriest's potion. Maybe there was still a way they could all get out of this alive.

"Clever merlee!" she whispered. "Now listen carefully, this is what I want you to do. . . ."

*

Seven days out from Silvertown, mist settled over the Karchlord's armada like a thick white fur. The sails hung limp, dripping mournfully onto the deck, and all the rigging sagged. Kherron stared in despair at the ghostly shapes of the other ships. The water, what they could see of it, was like gray glass. The wild quetzal huddled miserably on deck, wings wrapped tightly around them, tails trailing in the puddles, heads sunk into their shoulders until only their black eyes peeped out. Beads of moisture shivered on their plumage, the only blobs of color in this eerie white world. It was just like being back in the blizzard, only wetter.

Kherron pulled his sodden cloak closer and walked across to where Azri, Ortiz, and Malazi were consulting with the captain in the shelter of the mainmast.

"There's always the oars, my lord," the captain was saying. "Far as I know they're still down there, though no one's used them since Singers stopped the slave trade. Most of these old ships went to the breakers. The newer models your priests took are lighter and faster, but they're dependent on the wind. There's a slim chance we might catch them if this freak weather holds, but I don't know. . . . Truth of it is, free men don't make good rowers, my lord."

"My karchholders will," Azri said with pride, and immediately sent Malazi below to find out if the oars could be got working again. There was a sparkle in his eye Kherron hadn't seen before. The young Karchlord was enjoying this, he realized.

Kherron gave the shivering quetzal a stern look. "Stay there and keep out of trouble," he warned them. Then he followed Malazi down the ladder to see what was happening.

The oar housings were rusty, the benches for the rowers half rotten, the hold ankle-deep in water, and many of the oars themselves had badly splintered handles. But the willing karch-holders worked like Crazies, and were soon exercising their muscles in two sweating ranks to the beat of a large drum, while single-braiders kept the place dry by bailing out the water with buckets. As the ship creaked forward again, the men cheered.

Kherron shook his head. The drummer was a bit off, and the pound-pound-pound made his head hurt. He hurried back on deck before someone noticed he wasn't doing anything and tried to give him an oar. While he'd been below, the word had obviously been passed to the other ships. Soon more drums joined the Karchlord's, and the armada slid through the mist like a flock of strange seabirds with stiff paddling wings.

They journeyed through that eerie mist for days, the karch-holders rowing in shifts, and Lazim used up most of the pony-ointment he'd brought along, treating blisters. But in spite of their bleeding hands, the men wouldn't hear of taking a rest. As soon as they'd eaten and had a short nap, they were back at the oars again. The captain shook his head as he watched, and Kherron overheard him mutter to the Karchlord, "Slaves never worked so hard under the whip." Azri just smiled.

It seemed they'd never see sun or stars again. But on the third morning when Kherron went up on deck, there was a subtle change. Between the strokes of the oar-drums, a faint melody teased the edges of his hearing. He shivered.

The quetzal had heard it, too. They lifted their heads to stare at the mist, and softly echoed the melody. Then the one who had spoken to Kherron in the forest gave a sudden whistle and shook out its golden wings in a glitter of spray. In a moment, it was up in the rigging, fingers and claws hooked around the ropes as it stared intently out to sea.

The men on deck roused themselves, pointed at the creature, and began to loosen their swords in their scabbards. Kherron looked up, too, only to find those black eyes were now staring straight at him. He stiffened. But this time there was just one word, soft as the brush of a feather inside his head.

-close-

*

A strange pounding teased the edges of Rialle's hearing, like the thump of her heart. She wasn't sure when it had started, but now she couldn't stop listening for it. There were other noises too. The gentle slap of waves, faint creaks, labored breathing.

"Get up, young Singer. I know you're awake."

The crash of the grating hitting wood directly overhead jerked her back. She stiffened as two shaven-headed priests dropped into the hold and grabbed her arms. Mist curled through the open hatch. The quetzal fluffed their feathers and scrabbled backward, claws slipping on the damp timbers. She shook her head, still disoriented. Even though she'd stopped farlistening, the pounding was still there. Maybe it *was* her heart?

The priests' fingers dug painfully into her bruises as they dragged her beneath the hatch. She looked up. The Khizpriest was on deck, dark and angry, staring down. "They're hurting me," she said, trying for some *Shi*. "I can't sing if I'm in pain."

It didn't work. His spear came through the opening and touched the top of her head. There was an explosion of stars, and her legs gave way. The priests jerked her up again.

"Thought so," the Khizpriest said. "You know something about this mist, don't you? Don't bother lying. The Khiz will know."

Rialle raised her eyes to meet his dark gaze. "It's the merlee," she said defiantly. "I asked them to make the mist. I can just as easily ask them to sing up a storm and sink this ship, so you might as well turn around now, because I'm not going to let you hurt the Singers."

Her heart thumped as the Khizpriest laughed. "Oh, very brave all of a sudden, aren't we? You really expect me to believe you'll sacrifice yourself and your little fluffy friends here to save the Echorium?"

Rialle closed her eyes. The spear was still touching her hair, making it crackle the way it did when she combed it too hard.

"Yes," she whispered. "If I have to, I will."

The spear retreated, and the Khizpriest hissed like an angry snake. "Little fool! Bind her so she can't move! Bind those quetzal creatures, too, in case they try to free her. No food and no water — and no sleeping potion this time, either. She can suffer all she likes until we get to the Isle." His voice lowered, creeping under her skin. "And if you want to get there any quicker, my young *brave* Singer, then you know what to do. Just tell those merlee friends of yours to lift this mist and —"

His head jerked up and he frowned at something across the deck.

"What's going on?" he snapped.

"Oar-ships in the mist, sir priest," came the captain's worried voice. "Gaining on us fast!"

Shouts and running feet echoed above. The priests in the hold looked up in alarm.

Other ships!

Whatever else happened, Rialle knew she couldn't let them bind and gag her now, or the ships would sail on past without ever knowing she was here. She wrenched herself free, kicked one of the priests on the shin, and brought the rope around to slap the other across the eyes. They staggered back as she hummed *Aushan*. The quetzal needed little encouragement. In a flurry of tattered feathers, they leaped on the priests, held them down with their little hands, and began to tear at their flesh with beaks and claws. Between bites, they echoed her *Aushan*.

Rialle made a wild leap for the hatch but the Khizpriest's spear cracked across her knuckles. The grating clanged shut and she fell back into the straw with a moan.

Amused eyes peered down at her. "You stay right there, my little Singer! I'll soon take care of this pathetic army of the Karchlord's, and then I'll be back. You might like to use the time to guess how I'm going to punish you for letting your pets kill my priests." He chinked his spear across the metal and left Rialle sucking her sore knuckles, but with fresh hope.

"Kherron must have done it," she whispered to the still agitated quetzal. "He must have actually done something right for a change."

13

BATTLE

The Karchlord's armada came upon the becalmed ships suddenly. One moment, everything was thick, featureless white. The next, a dark floating skeleton with rags for sails loomed so close, the lookout on Azri's ship, which was leading the others by several lengths, yelled in alarm. "'Ware ship to starboard! 'Ware priests!"

Karchholders rushed to the side, drawing their swords. The oar-drums beat faster. As the oar-ships sped through the mist, intent on their quarry, the spray they raised glittered with rainbows.

Kherron blinked, afraid the quetzal had messed with his head. Then a karchholder pointed to the water and yelled, "Fish!"

"Sea monsters!" shouted another. "Thousands of 'em!"

Men hung over the rail and began stabbing at the rainbow tails.

Kherron roused himself. "Stop!" he shouted with Singer-trained lungs. "They're only merlee. They can't hurt you."

He looked around for the Karchlord. Azri was standing in the bows, one thin hand clenched on the hilt of his new sword, glaring at the ship they were speeding toward as if he could sink it with a mere look. Ortiz and Malazi stood on each side of him, wary, their weapons already out. As the gap between the two ships closed, eager karchholders leaped across, screaming battle cries. "For the glory of the Karchlord Azri! For the Overlord of the Silver Shore! For the Prince Among Men!" Some fell in the water. Others gained the slippery deck and struggled with dark-robed priests, who seemed to be armed with knotted thongs, which they used to whip swords out of men's hands, then to strangle their opponents.

Azri swept the deck with an intent gaze. He turned to Ortiz and Malazi, looking disappointed. "The Khizpriest's not on board. He must be on one of the other ships. . . . Where's the rest of my armada? I can't see a thing in this mist — Khiz! Look out!"

The priests had given up the fight in favor of setting their own robes alight and jumping onto the Karchlord's ship. Sparks streamed behind them as they ran across the deck toward the hatches. The flames kept the karchholders back, and soon the sails and ancient wooden ladders began to burn. The mist filled with the smell of roasting flesh.

Kherron staggered away from the heat and flung up his hands to shield his face. The smoke stole his breath, and the fire was spreading with alarming speed.

But just as he was wondering whether it'd be better to burn or drown, a rough voice yelled, "Water! Get movin', you khiz-lazy single-braiders, form a chain! Get over the side there, Lazim! *Run!*" It was Cadzi, dragging his stiff leg through the flames, buckets swinging from his hands. Under his lashing tongue, boys who'd recently gained their manhood braids passed buckets of seawater hand to hand and threw them at the burning sails.

Kherron ran to join the end of the chain, seized a bucket from a single-braider he didn't know, and threw its contents into the flames. They hissed and smoked, and the single-braider gave him a sooty grin. But the fire had a good hold, and it quickly became obvious they were fighting a losing battle. Kherron looked around desperately, then ducked in alarm as the green-and-gold quetzal swooped over his head and snatched the empty bucket right out of his hand. Other quetzal followed its lead, and soon the half creatures were flying over the rail, scooping up water to douse the flames from the air. The single-braiders cheered, joined by a second cheer from the men.

The priests' ship was sinking. For a moment, Kherron couldn't see why. Then he realized the merlee were pulling it apart with their strong fingers, timber by timber, and smashing the weakened wood with their tails. The quetzal dropped the buckets and swooped over the wreckage, hooting excitedly. There was a brief flurry of bright feathers as they dived. Then four of the creatures lifted from the sea, wings beating like crazy, long tails trailing in the waves.

-stone-singer-help-

The words were urgent, piercing Kherron's head as they had in the forest. He clenched his fists and went to the side to see what they wanted. Lazim was already there, pointing at something the creatures were dragging through the water.

"Look, Kher! Aren't those the Khizpriest's quetzal?"

Sure enough, the quetzal had rescued two of their friends, and were bringing the soggy mats of feathers toward the Karchlord's ship with obvious intent. Kherron sighed and swung a leg over the rail. "I suppose we'd better help them," he said, "or I'll never hear the last of it."

As he and Lazim hauled the half-drowned creatures up on deck, Azri ordered the oars manned again, and the ship began to pick up speed once more.

They steered toward the sound of the invisible battle, which came from all sides in a confusion of clashing metal, pounding oar-drums, breaking timbers, shouts, screams, karchholders yelling "Azri! Azri! Azri!", and quetzal repeating all this until it was impossible to tell where the noises originated. It was a lot harder to find the enemy than Kherron would have thought. Occasionally, the mist would thin, and they'd catch a glimpse of two ships locked together with fierce hand-to-hand fighting on deck, red swords flashing among black-and-crimson robes. They saw three more oar-ships on fire, golden ghosts in the mist — beautiful from a distance, yet Kherron's stomach clenched as he watched the masts fall in showers of orange sparks and remembered their own lucky escape. Whenever they saw another priest ship, the quetzal swooped across, hooting and whistling. But they failed to return with any more rescued captives. Kherron breathed a sigh of relief, which turned to guilt when he realized this meant the creatures had probably drowned.

A lot of bodies were floating past — both priests and karchholders. As their ship nudged its way through the wreckage, he stood at the rail, watching with morbid curiosity as the oars pushed aside corpses like mats of seaweed. When he caught himself searching for one with long blue hair, he set his jaw and walked quickly back to the mast, where Lazim was treating the rescued quetzal with the remaining pony-ointment.

The boy glanced up and met his gaze a moment, then looked away. "I know," he said softly, rubbing ointment into the rope burns around a delicate blue-feathered wrist. "It's not exactly what I expected, either. Don't worry, I'm sure we'll find the Khizpriest soon. He can't have got far in this."

The return of the wild quetzal saved Kherron from a reply. He ducked as a wing tip swept past his ear. When he straightened, the green-and-gold quetzal was perched on the deck, not three paces away, staring at him.

He braced himself. "What is it this time?"

-we-find-you-follow-stone-singer-tell!

The creature took off again and hovered above the bows, looking back, beckoning urgently with its little hands. Lazim glanced at it, then at Kherron. He returned to his task with a smile.

Kherron gritted his teeth, but hurried to where the Karchlord was discussing losses with the captain, and dutifully passed on the message. Azri's mouth twitched into a small, wintry smile. He ordered Malazi below to tell the drummer to increase the tempo, then strode to the bows, gripped the rail with both slender hands, and stared straight ahead as the captain steered a course after their quetzal guide.

The noise of the battle faded as they picked up speed, and the mist at last began to break up. Through the drifting white ribbons, a fifth priest ship slowly took form. A weird vibration in the air sent ripples up and down Kherron's spine, and his forehead began to burn. He held onto the mast and gritted his teeth, trying to see what the dark figure on the poop deck was up to.

By now, every karchholder on deck was at the rail, staring, too. For the Khizpriest was pointing his khiz at the sails. And although there was no wind, those sails were filled with an eerie, unnatural force.

Kherron shivered.

"Faster!" Azri cried. "The coward's running away!"

"No," Kherron said, a new chill creeping through him. "He's heading for the Isle."

*

The ship was moving again, water bubbling and slapping around the hold. The quetzal lifted their wing stubs and let out nervous little hoots as they stared at the walls of their prison. The dead priests' bodies were beginning to smell. Rialle edged farther away, hugged her knees to her chest, and closed her eyes.

"Merlee?" she whispered in a dry voice. "What's happening?"

No one had come with food or water since the grating had clanged shut. She'd never been so thirsty. The quetzal had eaten the priests' eyes and livers, but Rialle knew she'd have to be a lot more desperate before she ate human meat. Men were fighting, she knew that much. There had been screams when she had tried farlistening. Also, that strange beat was still in the air — pound-pound-pound — which meant the oar-ships couldn't be far away.

"Merlee?" she whispered again. She could only think they must have panicked and forgotten her, even as they had when the hunters came while she was swimming with them.

Then the quetzal gave a shrill whistle of warning, and the grating crashed open a second time. She scrambled to her feet, trying to get enough moisture into her mouth for a Song. But this time the Khizpriest was taking no chances. Priests flowed like a black-and-crimson river into the hold, seized her and the quetzal, bound their wrists to stop them from struggling, and hauled them all up through the hatch onto the deck.

Rialle blinked at the mist, hope returning. She'd been wrong — the merlee had done a good job. There wasn't the merest breath of wind. Yet the sails were alive. At first, she couldn't think why. Then she saw the Khizpriest on the raised deck at the stern, sweat streaming down his cheeks, face purple with effort, waving his spear at the straining canvas. She guessed at once what he was doing. He was using his power to blow the ship along.

As the priests dragged her closer, she made up her mind to try to knock his spear overboard, but they didn't take her up the ladder. The Khizpriest came to the edge and looked down at her. The gleam in his eyes chilled her. He'd killed the captain — the body lay at his feet, a bloody hole in its forehead. She wondered if he was going to kill her, too, but he pointed his spear across the deck. "See that?" he said. Rialle thought he meant the dead man. But one of the priests seized her braid and twisted her head around.

She blinked. At first she could see nothing. Then an island took shape in the mist, appearing and disappearing again as the thick white ribbons drifted around it. She recognized the slate roofs of Eastpoint on top of the cliff, and her heart gave an extra thud.

The Khizpriest's lip curled. "See? Your pathetic little trick with the mist failed. I have other ways of powering my ship — and of encouraging reluctant Singers. Give her the potion."

A priest held a flask to her lips. Rialle knocked it away with her bound hands and kicked out desperately. She mustn't fall asleep again, not now! But there were too many of them. They dragged her head back, pinched her nose, and held her jaw until she swallowed.

"Don't worry," the Khizpriest said with a chuckle, coming down from the poop deck. "It's not the sleeping potion, not this time. I want you awake to sing."

Rialle licked her lips, tasting the truth in his words. "More," she whispered. The priests looked at the Khizpriest, who gave a dark smile and nodded. They let her finish the flask.

Coldness lay heavy in her stomach. The thong hurt her wrists, which still hadn't recovered from the journey to the coast. But she had liquid in her mouth and Songs in her head.

The glittering spear came closer and lifted her chin. "Now then," whispered the Khizpriest. "Let the quetzal hear your pretty little voice, and then we'll see if we can't drop them off on these rocks. The Karchlord thinks he's beaten me, sinking my ships, but you'll notice I kept enough of your little pets to cover emergencies such as this. Five points, isn't it? Have to split a pair of them up — what a shame." He put his spear between the nearest pair of quetzal and pushed them apart. They snapped angrily at it, but leaped back with little squeaks when their beaks connected with the crystal. The Khizpriest chuckled.

Rialle took a deep breath. Put the quetzal on the reef? Was he crazy? "Rail," she whispered. "Let me . . . hold onto . . . the rail."

It might not have been the sleeping potion, but there had been something horrible in that flask. Her entire body felt numb. It was all she could do to breathe.

"Merlee?" she whispered. "Are you ready?"

Stone-singer, they called. *Stone-singer. Be safe in the shoal.*

"You'll sing one way or the other," the Khizpriest said, lifting her braid with the tip of his spear.

The shells had gone, she noted with the vagueness of a *Challa* dream, and the end was unraveling itself. Like the inside of her head.

"Why not make things easy on yourself?" whispered the Khizpriest. "Serve me well, and I'll let you live. Soon you'll be the only Singer left in the whole world. Together we'll rule the land and the sea and everything that lives and breathes."

He stepped back. A shadow passed overhead, and the quetzal hooted. Rialle put them out of her thoughts and filled her lungs with damp, salty air.

"A storm, merlee!" she cried. "Sing up a storm now!" She used *Aushan* for good measure, and the quetzal threw back their heads and mimicked the fear-song with just as much enthusiasm as they'd sung *Challa* in the cave.

At an angry hiss from their Khizpriest, the priests rushed forward to silence her, but this time she didn't hesitate to use the full force of the Song.

Aushan makes you scream. . . .

*

Kherron clapped his hands to his ears as a sudden squall filled the sails. The deck heaved beneath his feet. He lost his balance and bruised his shoulder against the mast.

"What is it?" Azri demanded. "What's that awful noise?"

"It's Rialle! She's singing the fear-song! And the quetzal are making it worse!"

He'd know that voice anywhere. He had to admire her skill, but what did the little idiot think she was doing? The crew had shinned up the rigging to do something to the sails to take advantage of the wind, but thanks to Rialle they had to keep stopping to cover their ears. The karchholders looked around for an enemy, then drew their swords and leaped into the water anyway, yelling, "Azri! Azri! Azri!"

"Wait!" Azri shouted. "Wait till we're closer!" But there was no stopping them. Death-braids tossed by the waves, they struck out for the still-distant ship with their swords in their teeth.

"Faster!" Azri called down to the drummer. "Faster!"

As their ship closed on the Khizpriest's, the few men left on deck gathered in the bow, leaning forward, eager to fight. They didn't notice a pair of priests slip over the stern rail, lengths of knotted thonging in their hands, intent on the Karchlord. But one of the priests tripped over a rope, and the tiny scrape alerted Kherron.

"Look out!" he cried, launching himself across the deck. Without stopping to think, he plunged his dagger into the first priest's breast, and whirled to face the other with *Yehn* on his lips. The second priest covered his ears, and a single-braider slit his throat from behind. It was Lazim. The boy grinned at Kherron, knelt, and severed the priest's little finger. "My first!" he said, holding up the grisly trophy. "That wasn't so hard, not really. . . ." He started to thread the finger into his hair, then doubled over and retched onto the deck. Grimacing, Kherron retrieved his dagger and wiped it clean.

By now, the wild quetzal were making swoops across the deck of the Khizpriest's ship where the priests were desperately trying to strap their captives' beaks. In the midst of all this, Rialle stood small and defiant at the rail, long blue hair flying loose in the storm, face raised to the sky, singing for all she was worth.

The priests were kept busy fending off the furious quetzal attack. But the karchholders in the water were having a bad time of it. As the mist cleared, so the sea rose in glittering green hills, and the sky darkened. Weighed down by their swords, boots, and thick woolen clothing, men began to drown.

Frenn appeared on deck and rushed to the bow, shouting something Kherron didn't catch. Only Lazim's tight grip on his tunic stopped the injured boy from flinging himself straight over the side. The wind blew the Karchlord's ship in circles, oars snapped with the force of the waves, the deck tipped first one way then another, and walls of spray lashed them until they could barely see their enemy, let alone fight. It was all the captain could do to keep them off the reef.

In all the confusion, Kherron lost sight of the Khizpriest's ship. When he next spotted it, the smaller vessel had turned around and, still powered by that unnatural wind, was speeding in a straight line for the northeastern horizon, closely pursued by shrieking, *Aushan*-singing quetzal.

*

Storm waves crashed over the rail, drenching Rialle, but she kept singing. The priests had managed to silence most of the quetzal, but seemed unable to touch her while she sang the fear-song. They couldn't prevent themselves from clawing at their ears. If she so much as missed a quaver, however, they came at her again.

"Silence!" the Khizpriest yelled from the poop deck where he'd gone back to powering the ship with his spear. "If you don't stop singing right now, I'll have your fluffy pets thrown overboard."

He wouldn't. He needed them.

There was a terrified hoot, followed by a splash.

She missed another note and the Khizpriest jerked his spear. Four of the priests regained their feet and closed in on her. One of them was holding the foul gag she'd worn on the way to the coast, and the others had more thongs.

Rialle braced her numb hands against the rail and sang with more passion than she'd ever sung in her life. *Aushan, Aushan* makes you scream. . . .

Another splash. Another.

Tears rolled down her cheeks for the poor quetzal. But it was working. They'd turned around. The spray was lashing her other cheek now. Every note she sang took them farther from the Isle and the merlee.

Then the sails flapped and the deck shuddered beneath her feet. She heard the Khizpriest jump down from the poop deck. She stiffened. His spear touched the back of her neck — an icy kiss.

"Stop that right now, or you're next," he hissed in her ear.

Her skin prickled from scalp to toe. She sang louder. The spear jabbed harder. "Stop it, you little fool! Do you want to die?"

Rialle closed her eyes, took a deep breath, and changed songs. *Yehn. Yehn* makes you die. . . .

The Khizpriest hissed like a snake, and something thumped hard in the middle of her back. She opened her eyes. Sea and sky whirled sickeningly, but she didn't realize she was falling until the icy water closed over her head. The shock of it was more powerful than the Khizpriest's potion in her body. Her hands convulsed against their bonds. There was a confusion of bubbles. She opened her mouth to scream. Cold lips covered hers. Salt filled her mouth. She remembered nothing more.

*

The Karchlord's crew lowered sail and used the oars in an attempt to defy the wind. But it was clearly a hopeless gesture. Finally, Azri ordered them to break off the chase and start picking up the men. One by one, exhausted karchholders were hauled back on board and rested the tips of their swords on the deck, death-braids dripping, looking rather ashamed of themselves. Though the storm was still tossing them about, it seemed very quiet. It took Kherron a moment to realize why.

The *Aushan* had stopped.

"He's getting away," Ortiz growled.

"He threw his quetzal overboard. No wonder the wild ones

are so angry. Look!" Malazi pointed to the soggy mats of feathers floating past the ship. Unable to fly without their wings and with their little wrists bound, the creatures must have drowned very quickly.

Kherron stared after the fleeing ship, trying to think. The merlee had vanished, and the storm was blowing itself out as suddenly as it had started. On the eastern horizon, two oarships could be seen, limping under half-sail toward the Isle. There was no sign of any other survivors.

It was Frenn who put all their fears into words. Lazim had finally managed to pull the injured boy away from the rail. But now he broke free and stumbled lopsidedly across the deck to seize Kherron's arm. "Where's Rialle?" He stared at the drowned quetzal in horror and turned on the Karchlord. "Where *is* she? Why don't you go after her? We've got the oars!"

Azri shook his head. "The men are too tired. I'm sorry." He swayed, and Ortiz and Malazi rushed forward to catch him, scowling at Frenn.

"I'm sure she's all right, Frenn," Kherron said gently. "When we get to the Isle, Eliya will send someone after the Khizpriest. He won't hurt someone he can still use."

Frenn's face darkened. He rushed at the line of dripping karchholders and struck their chests with his good fist. "Get down there and row!" he shouted. "Go after her!"

They moved their swords out of the way and fended him off gently. Frenn staggered back, shot Kherron a final furious look, and stumbled down the ladder into the hold. After a moment, a single oar on the port side began to lift and splash uselessly into the sea. The men exchanged glances but no one laughed.

Azri pushed himself upright and fingered his bluestone necklace.

"Steer a course for the Isle harbor," he told the captain. "We've stopped him, that's the main thing. Most of the priests are dead. We'll deal with Frazhin later. The important thing now is to make our peace with the Singers."

He raised his eyes to the building that crowned the Isle, and everyone looked up. High above the cliffs, lit by a sudden shaft of sun breaking through the clouds, the Echorium glowed like a rare blue jewel against the brightening sky.

14
SONG POWER

The army that assembled at the bottom of the Five Thousand Steps was a very different army from the one that had left the Karch two weeks before. The dark faces were grimmer, the eyes warier. Men whose trust rested in red metal had seen magic at work, and lost comrades to forces they didn't understand. Now they were in the Singers' domain, and it was time to find out if all the rumors were true.

The young Karchlord stood ten steps up, surveying his men. He'd washed his dark hair and carefully added a single braid. Singer Toharo's trust gift shone blue around his throat. The crossed-sword banner snapped behind him in the last of the storm. Though he hadn't slain any of the priests personally, the fact that he'd led his men to victory entitled him to braid the rest of his hair and claim the smallest finger bones of the dead, but Azri had refused, saying he'd wear bones when he earned them, not before.

It was a popular move. His men gained the bones they deserved and, at the same time, respected their Karchlord more.

The priests had been defeated, but at high cost. Of the nine oar-ships that had set sail from Silvertown, only three had limped into the Isle's harbor. Of the six hundred men who left the Karch, only a little more than a hundred and fifty stood at the bottom of the Steps, looking up at their Karchlord and the bluestone building beyond.

Kherron knew what they were thinking when they looked up, because he was thinking exactly the same thing. What sort of welcome would the First Singer give men who'd brought their battle to the very shores of the Isle? More to the point, what sort of welcome would she give him? The very thought of what he'd said to her at their last meeting made him wince.

He twisted the red bracelet on his arm and wished there'd been time for a hot bath, rather than a sticky one in cold sea-water. As he did so, he became aware of someone looking at him. He glanced along the beach and saw Lazim's head poking above the single-braiders, the second braid worn proudly now. But the Karch boy wasn't looking his way. Leaning on his arm was a very weary-looking Frenn, and it was Frenn's gaze, icy with hatred, that was making his skin prickle. Kherron sighed and returned his attention to Azri.

"Karchholders!" the Karchlord said, his voice carrying clearly on the wind. "All of you who've fought at my side, whether alive or dead, deserve a reward. When we return to the Karch, there'll be gold and horses for the living, and the women who lost their men will receive their due portion. But today I'm going to dig the first tunnels for a new and more prosperous Karch. I'm going to make peace with the Singers."

A great cheer rose from the men. "Long live the Karchlord Azri! Overlord of the Silver Shore! Prince Among Men!"

As the echoes died away, the army began the long, slow climb. Kherron let the grim-faced multi-braiders go past and waited until Lazim and Frenn caught up. "What happened to *Blessed of the Khiz*?" he whispered.

Frenn scowled and ignored him, but Lazim's lips twitched into a smile. "I have a feeling the Karch is finished with priests."

"And the Khizpriest?"

"Those quetzal looked pretty angry to me. If they leave enough of him to recognize, the Karchlord will soon catch him on the way home — Steady, Islander! This isn't a race, you know." He caught Frenn's arm as the injured boy missed a step and fell to his knees.

Kherron tried to help as well but received a glower in return. "Don't touch me!" Frenn heaved himself to his feet, regained his balance, and scraped his way up the next three steps unaided, teeth clenched with effort.

"Frenn —" Kherron began.

But Lazim put a hand on his arm and shook his head.

"Leave him, Kher. He's more stubborn than Father sometimes. He's tired and hurting and upset, a bit like a pony that's been treated badly. He'll come around. You just have to give him time." He clapped Kherron on the shoulder to show he wasn't taking sides, then hurried to catch Frenn, his long legs taking the steps two at a time.

Kherron shook his head and lifted his gaze to the Echorium. From the highest tower, ribbons of cloud flew like a pennant, gold and pink where they caught the sun. His stomach clenched. Even after all he'd been through, the very thought of stepping into the First Singer's chamber turned his knees weak.

*

They were welcomed at the gates by solemn orderlies, who divided the karchholders into groups of five, made them leave their weapons in a secure chamber by the door, and escorted them away into the blue labyrinth. Azri watched them go with a tight expression. But when Ortiz dropped his hand to his sword and told the orderlies the Karchlord needed an escort of his own men, Azri touched his arm.

"We come in peace, remember?" he said softly. "Put your sword with the others. If they try to hurt me, you'll know where to find it."

When it came to Kherron's turn, the orderlies indicated his dagger. He handed it over without a word. He expected to feel naked, but was surprised how little difference losing the blade made. He pushed his shoulders back and looked the orderly in the eye. "Where do I go, then?"

The orderly's lip curled. "Wait over there and keep quiet. The First Singer wants to see you. She's not at all pleased about losing Singer Toharo. No doubt she'll want a full explanation."

Kherron did as he was told. *Stay calm*, he thought. *Don't fight them; that's what she expects you to do.*

There was some sort of argument going on around Azri. He edged closer to hear.

"Is this really necessary?" Malazi was saying. "You heard the Karchlord! He's come in peace."

"Then he has no need of a weapon, has he?" said the orderly in the midst of the group, holding out his hand for the Karchlord's sword. The others watched warily.

Azri took Ortiz and Malazi aside and spoke quietly to them for a moment. With all the excitement in the hall, Kherron missed what was said but, afterward, the two karchholders joined one of the groups waiting to be escorted away, glancing over their shoulders as they went.

"You must forgive my men," Azri said as he unbuckled the black scabbard and laid it on top of his folded banner. "They think I'm going to throw another fit. I told them I've never felt better, but not to worry because I'm in the right place if I do." He smiled.

Kherron glanced at the corridor down which Frenn and Lazim had disappeared. He tugged an orderly's sleeve. "What's going to happen to Frenn?" he asked.

The orderly gave him a strange look. "He'll be prepared for therapy, of course."

"But a rock fell on his head! He's not a Crazy —" He only realized what he'd said when Azri frowned at him. "I mean, Songs won't help his injuries, will they?" For the first time, he began to hope for the boy.

"The First Singer will be the judge of that," said the orderly. "This way please, Karchlord. You, too, Kherron."

The farther they went along the blue, echoing corridors, the more nervous Kherron became. The familiar winding stairs, the silk curtains billowing at the windows, the soft slap of Singer sandals on stone. Here, his boots and Azri's, made for Karch snows, seemed clumsy and much too loud. He caught himself tiptoeing and deliberately stamped louder. I have nothing to be ashamed of, he told himself firmly. I'm coming back of my own free will.

The orderly stopped at the end of the corridor that led to Eliya's chamber. He looked at Kherron, and for the first time his face showed some emotion. "She wants to see you first. If the Karchlord would care to come this way and wait, I'll have some refreshments brought up."

Azri frowned slightly at what could easily be interpreted as an insult, but followed their escort through a nearby door without protest. The door swung shut with a soft thud, and Kherron was left alone in the corridor.

He stared at the wall under the fourth window. This was where he'd frightened Rialle when he'd come back from the cave. He touched the red bracelet, ran his fingers through his short hair, then took a deep breath and knocked once.

"Come in, Kherron."

He entered, shoulders stiffening from long habit, and stopped in confusion.

The First Singer of the Echorium lay on her pallet, propped on cushions. Her hair, freshly dyed, stuck to the silklike sickly blue feathers. As he hesitated, she waved a sticklike hand. "Shut the door. The draft makes my bones ache."

He noticed the curtain was nailed firmly across her window. With the door shut, the chamber was dim. A single lantern shaded by blue silk flickered in the corner farthest from the pallet.

"I hope you'll understand if I don't get up," Eliya went on. "Keeping track of you two has been quite exhausting." She'd lost none of her command of the Songs. *Kashe* sprinkled her words.

Keeping track sounded rather worrying. But Kherron, encouraged by the *Kashe*, asked, "Us two? You mean you know where Rialle is?"

The *Kashe* faded. "Unfortunately, no. I lost touch with her during the storm. I'll try farlistening for her again later. But I didn't summon you here to discuss Rialle. What I want to know is why *you* came back."

She closed her eyes. Truth-listening.

Kherron licked his lips. Thick blue silence filled the five-sided chamber. Why *had* he come back?

"I . . . ah, realized what important work Singers do. And after the Khizpriest killed Singer Toharo, I . . . I was afraid."

There. He'd said it.

Eliya stared at him so long, he thought she'd fallen asleep with her eyes open. Then she indicated the cushions piled around the walls. "Sit down, Kherron."

He sat warily.

"The punishment for running away is *Yehn*. Do you know what *Yehn* does?"

A chill rippled down the backs of his legs, making him glad he was sitting down. "Kills people, Singer," he whispered.

She gave a dry chuckle. "Not exactly — though some of our enemies claim it's worse. We use the full *Yehn* only in extreme cases when we need to make sure someone can't threaten us — ever again. Not many Singers can manage a really effective *Yehn*. It closes doors in the head — doors which let memory out and experiences in. The Song we give Final Years when they become orderlies or start their training in the Birthing House is similar, but not nearly as drastic. What it does is lock their own Songs away, locks one door, if you like. *Yehn* closes *all* doors and locks them forever. Do you understand now?"

Kherron stared at the frail, blue-haired woman lying on her pallet. It would be so easy to leap across the chamber and snap her neck. He hid his clenched fists under the cushions. "And are you going to punish me?" he asked.

His heart banged, but Eliya chuckled again. "Oh, I think you've been punishing yourself long enough, don't you? You've grown up, Kherron — rather fast, it seems. You've learned things. The hard way, but you've learned." She grew serious again. "Tell me more about this Khizpriest. He has something he controls people with?"

"The Khiz," Kherron said, shuddering. His skin burned at the mere thought.

"Ah yes, the Khiz." Eliya's eyes narrowed. "Tell me everything you know about it. Everything, Kherron."

Kherron touched the center of his forehead and told her.

When he'd done, finishing with the unnatural wind that had enabled the Khizpriest to escape, Eliya sighed and leaned back in the cushions. "Yes," she said. "Yes, I think it'll work. Soon we're going to give this Khizpriest, and a few others, *Yehn*. From what you've told me, that khiz of his acts as an amplifier rather like our very own bluestone. Some sort of crystal, you say? I'd love to know where they found it." At Kherron's blank look, she smiled. "You don't know about bluestone yet, do you? I haven't time to explain now, but you'll be learning soon enough. All things considered, I think it's probably best if you don't return to the pallets. There's an empty chamber in the Singers' wing on the third floor. Get an orderly to show you the way, and ask him to bring you some hair dye. You're to dye your hair blue — what's left of it. Eat nothing, drink plain water only. Try to get some rest tonight. At first light, spend a sunstep breathing and half a sunstep humming. Then report to the Pentangle."

Kherron's heart missed three beats. The chamber spun. Any moment now, he was going to embarrass himself and faint. "You're going to let me sing on the *Pentangle*?" he whispered. Then he had a horrible thought. "*Yehn* . . . you want *me* to sing *Yehn* to the Khizpriest?"

Another chuckle. "One step at a time, young Singer. You can't climb the Five Thousand Steps in a single stride, remember. Leave the *Yehn* to those of us who have experience of such matters." She gave him a thin smile. "You'll sing *Challa* tomorrow. We have a patient in desperate need."

Kherron couldn't hide his grin. His whole being filled with a bright golden light. Now he knew what made the karchholders cheer so loudly after the battle.

The First Singer lay back. "On your way out, send the Karchlord in here. I'm anxious to meet this young man who comes with an army to make peace."

*

Kherron stayed in his new chamber just long enough to let the orderly who'd brought the bowl of blue dye get back down the stairs. Then he changed his boots for sandals and crept back up to the First Singer's chamber.

The door was shut, and soft murmurs came from within. He put an ear to the wood and closed his eyes.

". . . suppose it does belong to you," Azri was saying. He sounded disappointed.

There came a soft clicking sound, and a rustle of silk — someone moving in the cushions. Then Eliya's voice. "Thank you, Karchlord. I'm glad we've had this chance to talk. This is the second time someone a quarter of my age has surprised me today. It's good to know I can still be surprised." She chuckled.

Azri said, "I promise the first thing I do when I get home will be to go through the priests' levels and clean them out. And if any of my men are caught hunting Half Creatures in the future, I'll make sure they're sent straight to the Isle for rehabilitation."

"Thank you, Karchlord. Sometimes it's hard, I know, and we have to do things we don't like. But that's a lesson every ruler has to learn. Don't worry, I have a feeling you'll do just fine."

There was another rustle, then Azri again. "Will I be allowed to watch the Song?"

Eliya sighed gently. "No, Karchlord, I'm afraid not. I'm sure you understand we must protect our secrets."

It sounded as if the interview was over. Kherron backed away from the door, puzzled. What Song were they were talking about? It couldn't be the Khizpriest's *Yehn,* since they hadn't caught him yet. His own coming *Challa*? But Azri already knew about *Challa*. He'd had it himself.

He was about to turn and duck down the stair when someone ran up behind him, almost silent on sandaled feet. He whirled in time to catch a fist before it connected with his ear, but the blizzard of white silk and blue hair still slammed him into the wall.

"You sneak! You *liar*! What did you tell Eliya to trick her into letting you sing? Huh?"

Kherron blinked at his assailant. He'd become so used to seeing swarthy, dark-skinned karchholders, the boy threatening him seemed very pale and young. He reminded himself muscles weren't everything and swallowed an urge to laugh. "Chissar?"

"Thought you could get away with it, did you? Now that she's so frail and weak? I've seen the state Frenn's in. Tried to kill him like you killed the Second Singer, huh? Think you're going to finish the job? Well, I'm going to tell her the truth!"

Eliya? Weak? Kherron's laugh almost burst free. "Chissar, stop it, she'll hear us." The novice was struggling to hit him again, but he didn't stand a chance against Kherron's new muscles. "I didn't lie to her, stupid," he hissed. "You know no one can lie to the First Singer and get away with it. And Frenn's injuries were nothing to do with me."

"Ha! Tell me another one. What about Rialle, then? How come you're the one who comes back covered in glory, and she's still out there somewhere? Afraid she'd tell on you, huh? What did you do to her?"

Kherron sighed. "Nothing."

"She's dead, isn't she? Everyone's saying it. And now you'll probably kill Frenn, too!" Chissar's eyes sparked. But he glanced at Eliya's door and lowered his voice. "Go on then, sing. It's what you've always wanted, isn't it? But you'd better sing note perfect, Kherron, do you hear? If you even so much as miss a quaver, I'll thump you so hard in that lying mouth of yours, you'll never sing another note."

Kherron's stomach gave an uncomfortable flutter. "What are you talking about?"

Chissar's lips curled. "Oh, didn't she tell you? You're such a salad-brain sometimes, Kherron. Haven't you worked it out yet?"

Kherron was still struggling with this when the door at the end of the corridor opened, and Azri came out. Chissar stepped back. "I got to go. She wants to see me. Remember — note perfect!" He smoothed his tunic and gave the Karchlord a curious look as he passed, but Azri seemed deep in thought and hardly noticed the novice.

Kherron pressed himself into the shadows. He thought about asking the Karchlord what he and the First Singer had been talking about, but the look on Azri's face stopped him.

Azri seemed different, somehow. But it was only after he'd gone that Kherron realized why. The bluestone necklace had been missing from the Karchlord's throat.

*

Orderlies moved quietly around the Pentangle, changing the silk shades of the lanterns from lavender to midnight blue. The shadows deepened as they worked, until the entire chamber was dark as a moonless night. When the five Singers came in and took up their positions on the points, the orderlies left in a hurry, and closed and locked the big double doors. Only Singers would be allowed to witness this Song.

The First Singer shuffled painfully to the stool, leaned on her stick, and unwrapped a rough uncut bluestone the size and shape of a human skull. She placed the bluestone carefully upon the stool, secured it with thongs, then flicked it with her fingernail and began to hum. A low vibration began in the Pentangle, taken up by the other four Singers, the floor, the walls, the domed roof, until the entire Echorium thrummed to that single, threatening note.

On their way down the Five Thousand Steps to catch the midnight tide, the Karchlord's men paused to look over their shoulders with wide eyes. Azri fingered his throat and swayed a little as the Song poured down the Steps. Ortiz and Malazi rushed forward to catch his arms, but the *Yehn* passed them by, and he held up a hand with a tight little smile.

In the Birthing House, babies and small children woke and began to cry. Their nurses gathered them close and hushed them, staring at the windows in fear as something dark stirred behind the locked doors in their heads.

The Song passed into the black waves that lapped the shores of the Isle, and was carried far across the sea, where a flock of airborne quetzal caught echoes on the wind. They beat their wings with new energy and mimicked the Song perfectly.

On board his ship, the Khizpriest looked up with a frown. He was exhausted from blowing the ship so far north against the wind, yet he was sure he could hear singing in the air, almost like the voice of the little Singer who'd dared to defy him. It was only his imagination, though — the sea would have taken care of her long ago. He smiled to think of her terror as she slipped under the surface, half paralyzed by the potion she'd drunk, hands bound so she couldn't swim. He hoped she'd lived long enough to regret her defiance. A shame he hadn't had time to teach her a proper lesson with the Khiz, but — What *was* that sound? Even the Khiz was at it now, tingling in the strangest way.

The Song reached the Mainland, where townspeople and villagers stirred uneasily in their sleep. It passed through Silvertown like dark water, touching the greed-filled dreams of a certain carriage manager, and whispering through the night until it reached Lord Javelly's castle in the foothills of the Karch, where the lordling feasted on quetzal meat, laughing at the gullibility of the young Karchlord who'd set sail for the Singer island in leaky old oar-ships to chase his interfering priests. Good riddance to the lot of them. With any luck, they'd all drown, and he'd have some peace. He fingered his bluestone pendant with a smile, thinking of the Singer he'd conned it out of for nothing but a promise he'd already broken. Strange, it was making a peculiar sound.

Yehn. Death of deepest midnight shade.

*

Dawn had broken over the Echorium before the final echoes of *Yehn* died away. Kherron hadn't slept a wink, and thankfully pulled his curtain aside to let in the light. One good thing, though. The sleepless night had given him time to think about what Chissar had said, so now he was prepared. It *was* rather obvious when you thought about it.

He bathed in the basin of steaming water brought up to his chamber by an orderly, and smiled as he slipped the formal robe of gray silk over his head. Sick or not, it seemed Eliya was as crafty as ever.

"Send me to heal Frenn," he whispered. "So everyone will see I'm sorry for what I did and want to make things right — is that it?"

The bluestone walls stayed silent, and Kherron chuckled. He only hoped Frenn would see things the same way.

The Song went better than he expected. It was actually much easier to have four human Singers on the other four points. Quetzal only mimicked, Singers worked with you. A little disappointing Eliya didn't come to congratulate him afterward, but then she was probably still busy sorting things out after the Karchlord's departure. In fact, the entire Echorium was unusually quiet all day — no hums, no shrill voices from the novices' dining hall, no giggles from the dormitories. Perhaps they were still mourning Singer Toharo. Kherron returned to his chamber and spent the afternoon rearranging the furniture to make the room his own.

At supper time, his stomach growling with lack of food, he took the red bracelet from the top of his clothing chest and looked at it thoughtfully for a moment. Then he smiled and slipped it into his pocket. Time to see if Frenn was awake.

He was so busy working out what he was going to say to stop Frenn from thumping him on sight, he didn't notice at first that the door of the cell where they'd left the injured boy to sleep off his *Challa* was swinging in a slight draft. Kherron's heart missed a beat, and he broke into a run.

The cell was empty.

*

He stared at the bare pallet in confusion and more than a little fear. What if his voice hadn't survived after all? Eliya's illness might have affected her judgment. What if she'd been wrong to let him sing, and he'd done Frenn some real harm?

"He's gone down to the beach," said a voice behind him.

He whirled. Chissar stood in the corridor, frowning slightly, as if he couldn't quite make up his mind about something.

"How is he?" Kherron said carefully.

"All right, I suppose. If you count having only one arm and one and a half legs as normal."

"He shouldn't be out. He should be resting."

Chissar scowled. "Try telling that to Frenn! He said he heard Rialle calling him in his dreams. Begged me to let him out, so I got the key off the orderlies."

"You fool! He's in the middle of therapy! This'll set him back days, you know that."

Chissar shook his head. "He was screwing himself up a lot worse in there. A little walk in the fresh air won't do him any harm."

"*Little* walk? Down the Five Thousand Steps in his state? He's probably fallen and broken his stupid thick neck by now." He couldn't believe Chissar would put his friend in such danger.

"He had help," Chissar said, a strange look in his eye.

"Help? Who?"

"One of the Karchlord's boys stayed. Tall, skinny, two braids in his hair? Said he wanted to live in the Echorium now. No idea why — he's much too old to train as a Singer."

"That's Lazim." The pleasure brought on by this news turned to something darker. "But Frenn doesn't realize how important it is that he rests between Songs, and neither does Lazim. I'd better go find them."

He made to push past the novice, but Chissar blocked his way and cleared his throat. "Ah, Kherron, I just wanted to say . . . what I mean is, I was wrong about you. Eliya's letting me sing soon, and she said you tried to help Rialle. Apparently, Singers do this thing called farlistening, and —"

"I've got to hurry, Chissar. Look, we'll talk later, huh?"

"There's something else you should know."

"What?"

The boy glanced up and down the corridor before leaning close and saying in a pallet-whisper, "Eliya's dying. Everyone's saying there'll be a new First Singer in the Echorium by morning."

*

Kherron shook his head as he raced down the Five Thousand Steps, taking them two at a time. He tucked the long Singer robe into the leggings he'd slipped on underneath. Forget decorum, he didn't want to trip and fall. His thoughts raced almost as fast as his legs.

Eliya dying? No wonder the place was so quiet. He tried to guess who would take over. Then he spotted Lazim and Frenn picking their way around the rocks on the west beach, the injured orderly unmistakable with his lopsided gait.

The tide was out. Wet sand, the colors of the setting sun, gleamed around them, dazzling Kherron. They'd gone a long way. He dropped over the edge with ten steps still to go, landed on the beach in a spray of blue-speckled sand, caught his balance, and raced after them.

When he was close enough, he filled his lungs, cupped his hands to his mouth, and shouted with a mild dose of *Aushan,* "Wait!"

Lazim's head turned. He said something to Frenn, who pulled at his arm and stumbled faster, refusing to look back. Kherron sighed and ran on.

It didn't take him long to catch them. Though he seemed in less pain, Frenn still couldn't move very fast, and he cornered the pair in a shady inlet where the cliff rose like a purple waterfall at their backs.

Frenn pushed himself from Lazim's arm. His left hand hung limply at his side, and his eyes were wary. "Don't try to stop me,

Kherron," he said. "I'm finished as an orderly, I know that. The least I can do is find Rialle — and don't try tellin' me I didn't hear her, 'cause I did! She had the trick of it, before — and this afternoon, after my *Challa*, I suddenly knew how to do it." His lips curled. "Your singing must've done something useful to my head, after all."

"Frenn, you should be resting —" The return of that glower told him a lecture probably wouldn't do a whole lot of good just now. He sighed again. "Let me help, then. Three pairs of eyes are better than two, and it'll be dark soon."

Frenn frowned. "You're a Singer now. You shouldn't be grubbin' around on the beach with orderlies."

"I feel responsible."

"I should think you do!" Frenn spat the words. "If it hadn't been for you, none of us would be in this mess."

Lazim had been keeping well out of it, but now he said gently, "Frenn, that's not quite true. You can't blame Kherron for what the Khizpriest did to you. From what I understand, you came to the Karch on a separate mission, anyway, and if Kherron hadn't been there and seen the priests putting poison in the merlee eggs, we'd probably all be dead by now."

"There, you see! Now you don't believe me, either! Stop talkin' about Rialle as if she's already dead! She isn't. I *heard* her."

"Calm down, we believe you." Lazim eased himself under Frenn's limp left arm and gave Kherron a warning glance. "That's why we're here, isn't it? C'mon, we're wasting time. We haven't tried the caves around the headland yet."

They searched until the light bled from the sky, checking behind every rock and in every cave, under every overturned dinghy and chunk of wrecked timber, in every pile of seaweed on the entire south coast of the Isle. Frenn looked ready to collapse, and twice Kherron started to say he ought to go back to the Echorium, but bit his lip. There was no chance they'd find Rialle, of course — not unless they came across her body washed up with the other wreckage. Frenn had obviously mistaken a *Challa* dream for reality, that was all. But he could see there'd be no convincing Frenn unless he was allowed to find out for himself.

It grew harder and harder to see what they were doing, and the dark lumps on the sand began to take on weird shapes. That coil of weed looked just like Rialle's long blue braid. That piece of driftwood, just like a girl's still body.

When the first stars came out, Kherron gave up and sat on a rock to shake the sand from his sandals. He could see Frenn and Lazim still searching the tide-line, faint silhouettes bent against the brighter sea. But it was hopeless, anyone could see that. She wasn't here, alive or dead.

-coming-wait-

He frowned and rubbed his forehead. Then he lifted his head and gazed out to sea, his heart beating faster.

-wait-

There it was again.

-wait-coming-

He stood on the rock for a better view. A handful of colored stars showed out beyond the reef, a faint glimmer in the water beneath. Kherron broke into a smile. Who'd have thought he'd be pleased to see the stupid creatures again?

"Quetzal!" he shouted, pointing. "Merlee, too, I think."

The other two rushed to the water's edge and stared as that rippling rainbow school negotiated the eastern arm of the reef. There was a song in the air, wild and mournful like the sea. It took Kherron a moment to realize this was the merlee singing, with the quetzal mimicking them.

Frenn stumbled into the surf. "It's her!" he said. "I know it is. It's Rialle!"

Kherron's stomach tightened as the quetzal swooped over-head to land on the cliff, glowing ribbons of color against the darkening sky. They pointed to the sea.

-stone-singer-come-

He squinted at the waves. As the school came closer, he saw the merlee were indeed dragging a human girl. Surf tossed her hair, and in the dusk her skin was pale as Karch snow.

Frenn and Lazim splashed in to their waists and carried Rialle out. They laid her in the sand and knelt on either side of her still form.

Kherron walked over slowly, almost afraid to ask. Rialle's wet hair plastered her shoulders and small breasts. Her eyes were shut. Dark lashes curled above bruised cheeks. He swallowed. "Is she —?"

Frenn looked up, and some of the old brightness flashed in his eyes. "She's alive, Kherron! Thank the Echoes — she's alive!"

15
ECHOES

The Echorium sang farewell to First Singer Eliya and Second
Singer Toharo three days later at low tide.

For the occasion, everyone was allowed down to the west
beach — orderlies, nurses and their young charges from the
Birthing House, all the novices, even those who should have
been resting between Songs, like Rialle and Frenn. They assembled on the sand in solemn ranks, while the Singers made a line
of rippling gray silk along the shore, stretching from the bottom
of the Five Thousand Steps as far as the cave where Kherron
had found Cadzi. They'd put Eliya's body in a small boat without oars or sail, which Singer Graia pushed into the shallows
while the Echorium anthem rang out across the Western Sea. In
the absence of Toharo's body, a raft towed behind the boat carried some of the Second Singer's most treasured possessions,
souvenirs from his travels, which would be taken by the sea in
his stead.

Rialle cast a worried glance at Frenn. But he must have been feeling as weak as she was, for this time he made no attempt to lead the Final Years in the pallet-ditty. She concentrated on mouthing the words, which was about all she could manage at the moment. The walk down the Steps seemed to have stolen her breath, and proper singing was out of the question, anyway — strictly forbidden until her therapy was over. Climbing back up was going to be torture but she wouldn't have missed today for the world.

"They're coming," she whispered, recognizing the pressure inside her head.

She smiled. Singer Graia had finally explained it. Apparently, people like Frenn, who were deaf to Half Creatures, didn't suffer headaches when they were close. Graia had also said she'd grow out of the headaches eventually, which presumably meant she'd also "grow out" of hearing Half Creatures. It was a relief to find she wasn't quite grown up yet.

As the last notes of the anthem trickled away, five merlee came for the boat — three large males and two females, their hair trailing silver in the foam. The sun glinted from their tails, haloing Eliya in rainbows as they slowly drew her body out to sea. The whole assembly seemed to be holding its breath. The younger novices fidgeted excitedly and pointed to the creatures, wide-eyed, but not one of them dared break rank and rush to the water's edge.

Rialle stared after the boat, something in her eye. According to Frenn, the merlee had brought her out of the sea, just as they were taking Eliya away today. She believed him. Even Frenn wouldn't joke about something like that. What made her sad was she didn't remember a thing about it. Everything from the moment the water closed over her head to the night she woke

up on a pallet in the Echorium was a blank. Frenn had told her
the Khizpriest was finished, his khiz shattered like glass, his body
torn to bits by the wild quetzal, and that singing his *Yehn* from
such a distance was what had taken the rest of Eliya's strength.
Apparently, as soon as a new Second Singer was appointed, a delegation would be sent out to check on the success of the *Yehn* and
deal with any survivors — but all Rialle had been able to do while
Frenn was telling her the gory details was to stare at his face.

Alive, she kept thinking. Frenn's alive!

Ashamed to be thinking of herself when she ought to be worrying about Frenn, she slipped a hand under her braid to wipe
away the tear. Then she realized everyone else on the beach was
crying, too. It was Singer Graia's fault. She was humming *Shi*,
and the quetzal, perched along the top of the cliff, were mimicking the Song perfectly.

Shi makes you cry. . . .

Singer Graia waited waist-deep in the sea until the boat and
its trailing raft had dwindled to a speck on the horizon. Then
she turned to the sobbing, sniffling assembly and clapped her
hands in the air. "ENOUGH!" Her powerful voice carried to
every ear. "The First Singer doesn't want you to be sad. It's a
lovely day. No one has duty until sunset. Enjoy yourselves!" To
reinforce this, she sang a few bars of merry *Kashe*.

The novices cheered and the ranks broke into noisy, chattering groups. For the rest of the day, no one would mind if Singers
gossiped with women from the Birthing House, if trainee orderlies ran riot with white-clad novices, if First Years shrieked and
rolled in the sand — which, of course, they promptly did.

Frenn agreed they should start back up the Steps at once, so
they wouldn't have to rush. They didn't talk much, needing all
their breath for the climb, but every twenty steps or so Frenn

gave her an encouraging grin. Rialle longed to slip her hand into his but didn't dare. The afternoon sun reflecting off the blue-stone was so warm and bright after the Khizpriest's horrible cave, it was rather like a *Challa* dream. . . . She was afraid if she pushed it too far, she might wake up and find herself back in the cage.

When they were about halfway up, other people began to pass them. The white-clad novices gave her and Frenn curious glances, making Rialle wonder what tales were going around the pallets at the moment. She returned their stares, knowing she had nothing to be ashamed of. Then Chissar caught up, and he and Frenn began to argue about who'd cried most at the funeral. Unable to understand how Frenn had enough breath left to argue, Rialle stopped for another rest, and her eye fell on a slender figure in formal gray silk climbing a few steps below them. The *Challa* dream evaporated. "Kherron," she whispered, the back of her neck prickling.

Frenn and Chissar immediately broke off their argument to come and stand beside her. The new Singer seemed to be concentrating on not tripping over his long robe. But as they all watched, the green eyes raised. He hesitated.

Rialle bit her lip. She'd heard all the stories, of course, of what he'd been up to since she last saw him in the Khizpriest's cave. But she'd been given a cell in the treatment levels while she recovered, and this was the first time they'd been close enough to talk. Aware she was staring, she blushed and looked away.

"You don't have to speak to him if you don't want to," Frenn said. "He's a Singer now, remember."

But it was too late. Kherron had already climbed the remaining steps, and now his hand was on her arm. "Rialle . . ."

She looked at the hand in confusion. It was meticulously

clean now that he was back in the Echorium, but two of the nails were broken, and she could feel calluses on the palm. "Singers aren't supposed to touch novices like that," she said.

Kherron let go as if she'd burned him. "Sorry, I just wanted to —" He glanced at Frenn's scowl and Chissar's narrow eyes, then pulled something from his pocket and held it out. "I just wanted to return this," he said quickly. "I really am sorry."

Rialle smiled. It was the red bracelet Frenn had found on the beach a lifetime ago. It glinted as she closed her fingers over it. She squeezed the metal tightly.

"Kherron, I . . ."

But he was already hurrying up the Steps to catch the lanky karchholder who'd stayed behind when the Karchlord's ship sailed. As he passed the puffing Gilli, who was climbing with a toddler from the Birthing House in her arms, he gave her a quick peck on the cheek. The other young nurses giggled, and a few people whistled and made pointed comments about half-bred Singers. Gilli blushed and covered her face with her hands, but when Kherron had gone her cheeks dimpled.

Chissar stared after the green-eyed Singer in astonishment. "What do you make of that, then?"

"It's them quetzal," Frenn said with a laugh. "I reckon they must've changed something in his head."

Rialle clutched the bracelet tighter and looked out to sea. Any moment now, she was going to burst into tears all over again. A lot of people were still crying — there was no shame in it. But she couldn't keep on like this every time she thought of what had happened.

"Rialle? What's wrong?"

She blinked. Both boys were staring at her as if she might fall off the side of the Steps at any moment and vanish into the sea.

Frenn's eyes betrayed his concern, but his good hand reached for her braid and held onto the end. "Don't worry!" he said brightly. "I've got you!"

She swallowed the lump in her throat and squeezed the bracelet harder still. It all came out in a rush. Everything she'd been trying to say since she woke up to find Frenn sitting beside her pallet. "I thought you were dead, Frenn! All that time when the Khizpriest had me in his cage . . . all that time." She choked, unable to go on.

"Oh, silly . . . come 'ere."

Suddenly, Frenn's arms were around her, and the warm salty smell of him wrapped her like a cloak. She pressed her face into his goat hair tunic, not caring who saw, and he stroked her hair with a gentleness she hadn't thought him capable of. Chissar tactfully climbed a few steps ahead, whistling softly.

Rialle relaxed, enjoying the stroking and wondering how long she could get away with it. Then she realized what Frenn had just done. She stiffened and pushed him back.

"Frenn! Your arm!"

He released her and frowned at his right arm. "What's wrong with it?"

"Not that one." She couldn't help a giggle. "The other one."

His gaze slid sideways to the hand he'd been using to stroke her hair. Very slowly, he opened his large fingers, then closed them again. His blue eyes lit up, and his crooked face broke into a grin. "I can feel the fingers! But how?"

"Doors!" Rialle said, her tiredness vanishing as she understood. "It's the doors in your head, opening again. If the Songs can shut them, they can open them, too!"

She threw the red bracelet into the air, where it flashed and sparkled in the sun like the sudden song in her heart.

OTHER TITLES FROM KATHERINE ROBERTS

Spellfall

When Natalie finds a glimmering candy wrapper floating in a parking-lot puddle, she simply cannot resist picking it up. Suddenly, out of nowhere, an ominous, yellow-eyed man appears and informs her that it's a spell. Soon a bewitching tale of kidnapping and sorcery unfolds.

Available now in paperback.

CRYSTAL MASK

The Second Book in the Echorium Sequence

Twenty years after the events described in SONG QUEST, enemies of the Echorium are again growing strong and a new danger threatens the Half Creatures and the Singers who are pledged to defend them.

Available now!

Following is the first chapter from the second exciting *Echorium Sequence* adventure: **THE CRYSTAL MASK**

The
— Echorium Sequence —
volume 2
CRYSTAL MASK
chapter 1: NIGHTMARE

Shaiala crouched on a moonlit ledge beneath a sky dizzy with stars. The unruly mountain wind stirred her hair, which was long and black and heavy with lumps of purple mud. Below, lurked the shadowy folds of the canyons that had swallowed her friends. She was shouting a warning. She shouted until her throat was as sore as her bleeding feet. But the wind stole her words and whirled them away.

What frightened her was the endless file of Two Hoofs running silently along the trail below. The men wore dusty black robes and had crimson-and-black striped scarves wrapped tightly around their faces so that only their eyes showed. At their hips, curved blades glittered in the moonlight. The small blue centaurs, their human torsos clad in mare's-tail tunics, their ears drooping around pale human faces, and their horse bodies patchy with the last of their fluffy foal coats, hadn't seen the danger. So far from the herd, separated from one another by the steep-walled canyons and exhausted after a night of cracking rocks, they were pathetically vulnerable.

A group of Two Hoofs drove a lilac filly, so pale she was almost white, down the canyon toward its narrow end. The filly stumbled along, her coat streaked with sweat, not even trying to kick her way to freedom. In one delicate hand, she clutched a small green stone still glowing from the heart of the rock.

"Use it!" Shaiala shouted. "Use it, Kamara Silvermane! Fight!"

But the Two Hoofs pinned the filly against the cliff. One of them prized the herdstone out of her hand and tossed it away. Kamara Silvermane reared up. But before she could strike, a Two Hoof blade slashed at her legs. The filly screamed and dropped back to earth, blue centaur blood dripping from one fetlock. The blade at her throat kept her quiet as the Two Hoofs fixed rope hobbles to her forelegs. Then they drove her through a crack in the canyon wall, out of sight.

Shaiala's heart twisted for her friend, but the nightmare wasn't over yet. The Two Hoofs had spotted Kamara Silvermane first because her coat shone fatally in the moonlight, but they soon flushed out the other foals. First the lighter blues, then the purples, and finally the blacks. All were driven into corners, where their herdstones were taken away and hobbles applied. Few put up much of a fight, though a tall, dark colt called Rafiz Longshadow scored a kick that shattered a Two Hoof skull before they got the hobbles on him.

By the time she'd scrambled down to the canyon floor, all her friends had been driven through the crevice. She ran through after them. The sight beyond brought her to a halt. Nearly a hundred exhausted and frightened centaur foals shivered in the natural trap formed by the inner canyon, hobbled and taunted by Two Hoofs. Yet more Two Hoofs were tying the centaurs' small wrists behind them and linking their necks with loops of rope. Most of the foals looked too shocked even to realize what was happening to them. Kamara Silvermane and Rafiz Longshadow had been separated and were trying to move closer together. The Two Hoofs prodded them apart.

"No!" Shaiala screamed, seeing fresh blood on the filly's coat. "Not hurt they! They my friends!"

The men swung around, crimson-and-black scarves billowing loose about their necks. The alarm on their faces turned to amusement when they saw she was alone.

Even in her dream, Shaiala's entire body ached. It seemed as if she'd been shouting and running all night. All she wanted to do was crawl into a corner and sleep. But she launched herself into the air and let fly with one foot at the nearest Two Hoof. It was a kick she'd learned from the centaurs, called a Snake because it would kill an attacking grass serpent before the creature had a chance to bite. Her heel caught the Two Hoof on the back of the thigh. She heard a satisfying crack. Before he'd started screaming, Shaiala had landed and whirled to face the next.

Three more came at her, the laughter dying on their lips as they realized she'd broken their friend's leg. A sideways Dragonfly kick took care of another. Sobbing with a mixture of fury and fear, she spun on her heel and cracked an exposed knee with a well-aimed Hare, then whirled again and snapped someone's arm with a second Snake. Unintelligible Two Hoof yells echoed in the canyon. The cliffs soared, high and black on all sides. A blade went spinning under her and away, like a slice of the moon.

Everyone seemed to be shouting at once, including the centaurs.

"No, Shaiala Two Hoof!" Kamara Silvermane screamed. "Run!"

"Go fetch someone who can kick properly!" shouted Rafiz Longshadow. "Get stallion. Get mares."

"Sneaky Two Hoof spy!" a stocky colt called Marell Storm Temper spat through his cloud of purple mane. "You lead Two Hoofs here. You tell Two Hoofs about herdstones. You betray herd!"

Before Shaiala could protest, more men ran at her. One threw a rope. It tangled in her ankles, fouling her hasty Snake. The ground rushed up and she choked on dust. Their rough hands were on her, tugging her hair, pulling her away from her friends and slamming her against the canyon wall.

A Two Hoof face, his ugly copper-colored skin glistening with sweat, pushed close to hers and snapped out a question. Shaiala shook her head helplessly. After the centaurs' language, his words were harsh and made no sense. Another Two Hoof pointed to her feet and repeated the question. She shook her head again. Her mouth was far too dry to ask him to say it in Herd. The first man gave a disgusted snort and raised his blade above her head. Terror poured into Shaiala's legs, stealing the last of her strength. She couldn't move.

But the blade did not fall. After a moment, she became aware of a faceless Two Hoof silhouette watching from the shadows. The silhouette floated closer, plumes of glowing color fluttering around its head, making her dizzy. Its black face blotted out the canyon, the captive foals, the stars, the raised blade, everything. Through two glittering holes in the night, eyes stared at her, colder than death.

Black lightning flashed.

Shaiala screamed.

The pain that signaled the end of the nightmare exploded in her head.

As always, Shaiala woke with sweat pouring off her, panting as if she really had just run down from a high ledge and fought a herd of Two Hoofs.

She lay still in the darkness while her heartbeat slowed. Then she pushed her hair out of her eyes and tried to stand. Her head hit something hard and she lost her balance as the floor tipped sideways. She sat down again in a hurry. Not the first time she'd done that.

Gripping her knees, she tried to remember where she was. A line of light slid across the floor where she was sitting, turned a sharp corner and rose until it reached the height where she'd hit her head, then turned back until it was above the start of the first line. All three lines swayed from side to side along with the rest of her prison. There were strange noises outside, mingled with the slap and echo of water against wood. Water far deeper and wider than the little streams the herd drank from during their travels across the Plains. Shaiala considered this for a moment then gave a cold shudder.

She must be inside an enchanted Two Hoof building that could move over water. She had seen them sometimes, floating up and down the Two Hoof river with huge cloths billowing above them in the wind. The centaur foals had laughed and said Two Hoofs built them because their legs got tired if they galloped too far. Which reminded her . . . she shifted her feet experimentally, heard the clink of metal, and swallowed a cry of terror.

They'd hobbled her, too.

"Kamara!" she called. "Kamara Silvermane!"

A moment's thought produced another name from her dream. "Rafiz Longshadow!"

Only the creak of the Two Hoof building and the slap of water answered. But centaur hearing was sharper than hers. The horse-ears that pushed through their cloudy manes could swivel to catch the slightest sound. They might be able to hear her even if she couldn't hear them.

She drew a deep breath. "Marell! Marell Storm Temper!" Even the purple colt who never lost an opportunity to tease her about her differences would be welcome company now. At least he couldn't try to blame her anymore for the attack.

Still no answer.

"Anyone!" Shaiala screamed, thumping the wall. "Answer I! Not leave I here with Two Hoofs!"

Footsteps approached and a heavy blow shook the wood that imprisoned her. She held her breath. A black shape, taller than any centaur, blocked the vertical line of light. A rough Two Hoof voice shouted something she didn't understand, then laughed coarsely and went away. The wood creaked, the hiss and slap of water grew louder and the floor tipped in a different direction. She was thrown sideways, the hobbles digging into her ankles.

A sick, cold feeling lodged itself in her belly. Her friends weren't here, and the longer she waited the farther away they'd be.

She studied the lines of light. If the Two Hoof could survive on the other side of them, then so could she. She rose carefully into a crouch. Keeping her head low this time, she leaped at the wall, striking with both heels simultaneously. *Flying Snake.*

She'd forgotten the chain fastened her ankles to the floor. It gave a rusty clatter and snatched her off balance before her toes touched the wood. She landed awkwardly in a twisted heap of hair, metal, and damp straw.

She panicked then, kicking wildly, trying every maneuver she knew — *Snakes, Flying Snakes, Hares, Double Hares, Dragonflies* — desperately attempting to land a blow on the walls of her prison. The only part of it she could kick with any kind of force was the floor, which refused to break. Its strange motion kept knocking her off balance and her feet were getting sore.

"Crack, stupid Two Hoof floor!" she screamed, slamming her bruised heels into the straw again and again. "Crack!"

But it was hopeless. As Marell Storm Temper was so fond of reminding her, you needed four legs to do a successful *Canyon* — the kick that could crack the ground. Shaiala's eyes filled. Her head throbbed terribly. But worst of all was the pain of separation from the herd and her friends. Even in her darkest nightmares, she'd never imagined it would happen like this.

Tears rolled down her cheeks and dripped into her hair.

"Kamara Silvermane?" she whispered. "Rafiz Longshadow? Where you go? How I get here?"

She frowned, trying to remember what had happened after she'd been caught.

Glittering holes in the night. Eyes staring through them, colder and blacker than death.

Her mind shied away. She clutched her head. It hurt when she tried to remember, as if the Two Hoofs had chained her thoughts as well as her ankles.

She relieved herself in a corner as far as the chain would reach, then returned to the middle of her prison and lay down like a centaur, legs folded beneath her, every sense alert. The air was damp and tasted of salt. An eerie, wild song teased the edge of her hearing, only to fade when she tried to understand. An unsettling song, like the wind blowing from a far place.

She shivered, wrapped her arms around the rips in her tunic, and fixed her eyes on those swaying lines of light. Centaurs did not have a word for *door*, but she guessed the Two Hoofs must have put her in here through that part of the wall. Eventually, they'd have to open it again to let her out. When they did, she'd be ready.

This was the hope that kept her courage from failing as the ship sped across the Western Sea to the Isle of Echoes, home of the Singers, where people sent Crazies like Shaiala to be cured by the power of Song.

GLOSSARY:
GUIDE TO THE SILVER SHORE

Isle of Echoes   Island in the Western Sea, about ten days' sail from the Silver Shore. The only place in the world where bluestone is found.

Echorium   Home of the Singers. Constructed entirely of bluestone, this ancient building stands on the highest point of the Isle. There is no glass in the windows because it would be shattered by the power of the Songs.

Pentangle   Heart of the Echorium, where Songs are given for healing, rehabilitation, or punishment. A large bluestone chamber with a five-pointed star (pentangle) engraved into the floor. The recipient sits on a spinning stool in the center. Singers stand on each of the five points. They wear gray silk and dye their hair blue so that bright colors do not interfere with the Song.

Songs of Power   Five wordless songs that have the power to control emotions and memories:

— *Challa*   Dream song. Most common form of healing. Puts people to sleep and helps them forget their troubles.

— *Kashe*   Laughter song. Wakes people up, cures depression.

— *Shi*   Pain song. Forces people to confront their pain, healing through tears.

— *Aushan*   Fear song. Gives life to inner fears. Makes people scream.

— *Yehn*   Death song. Closes doors in the head. In extreme cases, leads to a form of "living death."

Song-potion   Relaxant given to people before they have a Song, ensuring the treatment has maximum effect. The recipe is a closely guarded secret.

Singer   One trained in the proper use of the Songs. A Singer has other, related skills:

— farlistening   *Listening* for vibrations over a distance greater than the normal range of the human ear. It is greatly enhanced by bluestone or water. Skilled Singers can also project their own voice (farspeaking).

   Some young Singers can use this skill to communicate with Half Creatures, but lose this ability as they grow older.

— truth listening   Sorting truth from lies by *listening* carefully to a person's voice and body language.

First Singer   Singer in charge of the Echorium — always remains on the Isle.

Second Singer   Singer in charge of Echorium business abroad — travels a lot.

novice   Child below the age of puberty who is training to be a Singer. Some gifted ones can hear and communicate with half creatures.

orderlies   Men and (more rarely) women who don't become Singers. Employed in the Echorium as guards, cooks, servants, etc. May also act as bodyguards and sailors when Singers leave the Isle.

"Crazy"   Pallet-slang for someone not right in the head who is brought to the Echorium for Song treatment and healing.

pallets   Dormitories where novices sleep.

pallet-whisper   A nearly soundless, controlled whisper for the ears of one person only. Used by novices in the pallets when they don't want their teachers to overhear.

sunstep   An Isle measurement of time. The time it takes the shadow of the Echorium's flagpole to move between two marks on the outer wall (about half an hour).

bluestone   Stone with magical properties. Used by Singers to amplify the Songs and to transmit their voices across great distances.

Birthing House   Ordinary slate house attached to the Echorium, where women who don't become Singers attend Singer-mothers during childbirth and care for the next generation of novices until they're old enough to enter the Echorium.

All Singers are expected to donate at least one child to the Birthing House, but since the mothers return straight to their duties in the Echorium, the children grow up without family attachments.

Five Thousand Steps   World-famous flight of steps, leading from the Isle harbor to the main gates of the Echorium.

Wavesong   Echorium ship, used by Singers when they leave the Isle on official business.

trust gift   Bluestone jewelry, traditionally given to those who agree to let a Singer settle their dispute, and worn as a sign that they are willing to honor the terms of the Echorium treaty.

Karch   Cold, mountainous region of red rock to the northeast of the Silver Shore.

Karchhold   Underground system of tunnels and caves, high in the mountains of the Karch.

Karchholder   Any person who lives in the Karchhold, but normally used to refer to a Karch warrior.

Karchlord   Supreme ruler of the Karch, a hereditary position.

death braids   Worn in the hair of a karchholder to show how many enemies he has slain. Each braid is fastened with the finger bone of a slain enemy.

manhood braid   Karch boy's first braid, to show he has completed his warrior training and is now old enough to fight. Normally fastened with the finger bone of a karchholder who has died but not in battle — often a woman's.

single-braider   Youth who wears only a manhood braid and has yet to make his first kill.

multi-braider   Karchholder with more than one braid. The more braids he wears, the greater warrior he is.

Khiz   Spear of black crystal with similar properties to bluestone. Can be used to sort lies from truth, and to control people's thoughts. A symbol of office and object of worship.

Khizpriest   Chief priest of the Karch. Only person with the power to wield the khiz.

Half Creatures   Ancient creatures, part human, part animal. Limited intelligence and very shy of adult humans, but they sometimes communicate with children. There are many breeds, two of which appear in this book:

— merlee   Part human, part fish. Found in the Western Sea and in the waters around the Isle of Echoes. Their songs have power over the wind and the waves. They have short memories.

— quetzal   Part human, part bird. Found in the dense and unexplored Quetzal Forest, southeast of the Silver Shore. Perfect mimics with excellent memories.